THE WINNERS' CIRCLE

Other Joanne Kilbourn Mysteries
by Gail Bowen

THE WINNERS' CIRCLE

A JOANNE KILBOURN MYSTERY

GAIL
BOWEN

McCLELLAND & STEWART

Copyright © 2017 by Gail Bowen
Paperback edition published 2018

Library and Archives Canada Cataloguing in Publication information
available upon request

ISBN 978-0-7710-2407-8 (paperback)
ISBN 978-0-7710-2408-5 (ebook)

Published simultaneously in the United States of America by
McClelland & Stewart, a division of Random House of Canada Limited,
a Penguin Random House Company

Library of Congress Control Number is available upon request

This is a work of fiction. Names, characters, places, and incidents either
are the products of the author's imagination or are used fictitiously.

Typeset in Trump Mediaeval by M&S, Toronto

Cover design: Leah Springate
Cover image: © Yvette/Getty Images

Printed and bound in the USA

McClelland & Stewart,
a division of Random House of Canada Limited,
a Penguin Random House Company

www.penguinrandomhouse.ca

I   2   3   4   5   22   21   20   19   18

Penguin
Random
House

For Mike Sinclair,
Dean of St. Paul's Cathedral,
with gratitude and great affection

CHAPTER

1

In the dark days after the tragedy that had ripped apart our lives, words lost their meanings. Desperate to find the key to understanding a loss that still seemed unimaginable, I searched for answers, but even sources that had always brought me solace offered nothing. In the end I clung to a remark made by a stranger as we were leaving one of the funerals that, during that bleak month, recurred with the solemn regularity of passing bells.

"Maybe life's greatest gift is that we don't know what's ahead," he said.

The stranger's words were cold comfort but I held them close. They were all I had.

Three weeks earlier, I had no need of comfort. I was blessed, and I knew it. My husband, Zack, our soon-to-be seventeen-year-old daughter, Taylor, and I spent Thanksgiving at the lake with Zack's law partners and their families. Friends since law school, the partners at Falconer Shreve Altieri Wainberg and Hynd owned the cottages on Lawyers' Bay, a horseshoe of waterfront property on one of a quartet of lakes that wound through the Qu'Appelle Valley, forty-five kilometres east of Regina.

Many years before Zack and I were married, his partners had convinced him to build a cottage there. When the construction was completed, he met with a decorator, explained that he was a guy in a wheelchair who lived alone, handed her a blank cheque, and asked her to call him when the cottage was finished. Every time I walked through the bright, uncluttered, spacious rooms of our cottage, I was grateful to that decorator. She had chosen a simple neutral palette that, in the folder of information she left for Zack, she had identified as driftwood grey and creamy latte. With one notable exception, the furnishings were sleek and contemporary. The notable exception had been the decorator's find at a country estate auction: an oak partners' table from a long-defunct law firm. Our dining room overlooked the lake, and the sizeable table and its twenty-four matching chairs made us the hosts of choice when all the partners and their families came together for a meal.

My husband was happiest when every chair at the table was filled. That Thanksgiving Sunday, eighteen of us celebrated the harvest together. Eleven were from our family: Taylor, Zack, and me; our daughter, Mieka, and her young daughters, Madeleine and Lena; our son Peter, his wife, Maisie, and their two-week-old twins; and our younger son, Angus.

Zack's partners and their families made up the rest of the party: Blake Falconer and his eighteen-year-old daughter, Gracie; Kevin Hynd, who had brought Zack and me together; and the firm's managing partner, Delia Wainberg, along with her husband, Noah, their eighteen-year-old daughter, Isobel, and her nephew, the Wainbergs' three-year-old grandson, Jacob.

When our families were together, we ate at five o'clock. If the weather gods were benevolent, an early dinner meant we had time afterwards to go for a paddle in the canoes or just position the lazy lounges so we could watch the sun set over the lake. But Sunday was cold and windy. After we'd eaten dinner and cleaned up, Peter, Maisie, and the twins headed home to their farm; Mieka took the girls back to the city so she could pick up an old high-school friend at the airport; and Angus slipped away to meet the mysterious new woman in his life.

The rest of us took our coffee into the family room. Noah lit a fire, and we played games: *Charades, Pictionary, Heads Up!,* and a game called *How's Yours?* that Taylor said had been a blast when she played it at a party but that fell flat on Thanksgiving. When *How's Yours?* left us yawning, I gave Zack the high sign. He wheeled over to the piano and announced that he was taking requests.

Zack had a good ear and a theatrical flair that buoyed up his performances during the odd musical stumble, so listening to him play was always a pleasure. As we gathered together around the piano, humming along with songs we half-knew, our private concerns faded and we became part of something larger than our individual selves. We were a community.

When Jacob Wainberg requested "Let It Go," Princess Elsa's song from the movie *Frozen,* and began to sing the words in his piping little-boy voice, Taylor, Gracie, and Isobel helped him with the lyrics; then the rest of us joined in. Zack and his friends were all in their early fifties. Too often, their faces were tense and careworn, but the music and the firelight softened the marks of the years, and they seemed young and easy again.

Zack felt the vibe too. He turned to Kevin Hynd. "You're the music man, Kev. What are some songs everybody can sing?"

Kevin shrugged. "Anything by the Beatles," he said. "'Yellow Submarine,' 'Ob-La-Di, Ob-La-Da,' 'Twist and

Shout,' 'Good Day Sunshine.'" As Zack played the first
upbeat chords of "Good Day Sunshine," a smile lit up Delia
Wainberg's face, and it transformed her. For the first time in
the years since I'd met Delia, a tightly wound perfectionist
with an enviable record of wins before the Supreme Court,
she seemed, in my grandmother's phrase, to be "comfortable
in her own skin." As Dee sang along, she was playful and
unguarded. Her exuberance was contagious.

Physically, Isobel Wainberg was uncannily like her
mother: fine-boned and narrow-faced, with a milky-white
complexion and wiry hair. In temperament too, Isobel was
her mother's child, private and seemingly self-contained.
Always particularly tense in her mother's presence, she had
relaxed, leaning in to Delia as they sang. Noah Wainberg, an
affable giant of a man who adored his wife, couldn't take his
eyes off her, even after the last bars ended and the group's
laughter and clapping had subsided.

"Time for my favourite," Taylor said. "Dad, will you play
'Puff, the Magic Dragon'? Jacob will love it."

"Your wish is my command," Zack said, and he began.
The old Peter, Paul, and Mary song did indeed delight Jacob,
but it broke the spell for Delia. As soon as she heard the line
about little boys who, unlike dragons, do not live forever,
Delia stiffened. Before the song was over, she had headed for
the door and left. Noah scooped up Jacob and turned to
Isobel. "Looks like we're taking off," he said.

Taylor was clearly bewildered. "What happened?"

Isobel's sigh was resigned. "My guess is that the song
reminded my mother of Chris."

"Chris has been dead for four years," Taylor said. "And
the song is talking about a boy not a man."

Isobel's voice, like her mother's, was husky and compelling. "It doesn't matter," she said. "These days, it never
takes much to send her over the edge."

Noah moved close to his daughter. "I'm going to take Jacob back to our cottage and check in with your mum. Do you want to come with us?"

Isobel squeezed Noah's arm and kissed Jacob. "You go ahead, Dad," she said. "You know it doesn't matter to her if I'm there or not."

"You're wrong, Izzie," Noah said. "Try to be patient with your mother. She's lost a lot, and Chris's death still troubles her."

"It troubles all of us," Zack said softly. "He was like a brother to Kevin, Blake, and me."

"He was more than that to Delia," Isobel said.

"Your mother believed that Chris led her to the two things that saved her," Noah said. "A love for the law and the people who became her closest friends. But you know the story."

Isobel's eyes were questioning. "Do I? Chris was special – we all felt that way, and I miss him too. But when I try to talk to Delia about him, she always finds a way to end the conversation. What I do know is that when she met him, she was in her first year at the College of Law. Her grades were through the roof, but she was going to drop out because she didn't fit in, then Chris brought her into his study group and everything changed."

"That's pretty well it," Blake said. "After Dee joined our group, she knew she'd found a place where she belonged."

"Practising law." Isobel's smile was small and sad. "She's never needed anything else. The law validates her and gives her a refuge from everything she doesn't want to face."

Zack leaned forward. "Don't give up on her, Izzie. It may be hard to believe, but Dee does need you."

"Then why does she push me aside?" Isobel said. "And she's the same with Jacob. You saw what she just did. Jacob's three years old, but when my mother ran out, she just left him, as if she had no responsibility for him at all."

Kevin touched Isobel's shoulder. "Man stands in his own shadow and wonders why it's dark," he said. "We've talked about that Zen proverb before. Your mother's life is darkened by her own shadow, but for some reason, she's unable to understand that and step away."

Isobel had a kind heart, but her voice was cold. "Well, it's time she moved out of her shadow and realized what she's doing to the people around her. She won't even look at Jacob because he reminds her of Abby, the daughter she lost. And she won't look at me because I know that she gave Abby up for adoption, and that in all the years between Abby's birth and her death, my mother never made a single attempt to discover what had happened to her daughter." Isobel's voice broke.

Kevin's hand remained on Isobel's shoulder. When he spoke, his voice was tender but firm. "Isobel, I know it can't be easy for you. When Abby died, you lost something too. But there are many good reasons why your mother didn't attempt to find the child she put up for adoption. She wasn't much older than you are now, and she still questions herself about what she did."

Isobel closed her eyes and took a deep breath. When she opened them, she looked intently at Kevin. "I understand that, but I'm tired of my mother thinking only about herself. My dad tries to make our family work. So do I, but no matter what we do, it's not enough."

In the way of female friends from time immemorial, Gracie and Taylor offered Isobel the wordless comfort of an embrace. The sense of community that had linked us as we sang together was gone. Once again individuals alone with our private concerns, we carried our coffee cups to the kitchen and said our goodbyes. The party was over.

———

The forecast had called for a weekend of wretched weather, and for once the forecast was accurate. On Monday morning, the lowering sky was dull pewter; the wind whipping off the water was stinging, and the air had a sweet, pungent zing. A storm was brewing, and without discussion, Zack, Taylor, and I agreed to head home.

Leaving Lawyers' Bay was always a wrench for me, and regardless of the weather, I tried to squeeze in one last moment. Zack's all-terrain wheelchair was rugged, so that morning we'd walked our mastiff, Pantera, and our bouvier, Esme, to the tip of the western arm of the bay so we could take in the full brunt of the whitecaps hitting the rocks before we returned to the city.

The four of us were windblown but in high spirits as we wandered back along the shore. The dogs were running ahead of us and when they disappeared into the boathouse shared by the families of Falconer Shreve, we knew we didn't have to whistle for them. Noah Wainberg was a magnet for kids and canines, and Pantera and Esme had sniffed him out. By the time we entered the boathouse, man and dogs were already roughhousing on the concrete floor of the winter storage area.

Spotting us, Noah gave the dogs one last nuzzle and stood up. "Perfect timing," he said. He picked up a large canvas cover and began stretching it over the raft that, until that morning, had been anchored twenty-eight metres from our dock since the May long weekend. "Getting this canvas in place is definitely a three-person job," he said.

Zack steered his wheelchair to the side of the raft opposite Noah, and I found a corner. Securing the snug canvas over the raft was not easy. When we finished, Noah raised his arms in triumph. "Done!" he said. "This raft is cleaned, drained, safe from the elements, and ready for next year."

My gaze drifted to the grey and choppy waters. Noah had attached a yellow vinyl boat bumper to the raft's anchor line, and it bobbed in the spot where the raft had been moored. Come spring, the floating bumper would make finding the anchor point a simple matter. As he always did, Noah was planning ahead.

The rain had started. Zack took one look outside and turned his chair towards the boathouse door. "Noah, if you're sure you don't need a hand with anything else, we'd better make tracks. Rain always makes the path back to the cottage slick as greased owl shit."

"Go for it," Noah said. "I'm almost through here. We're going back to the city early too."

Zack was wheeling towards the door, but he stopped. "How are Dee and the kids today?"

"Dee spent all night preparing for her trial in Saskatoon, and Isobel and Jacob made pancakes this morning."

"So life goes on," Zack said.

"Ob-la-di, Ob-la-da," Noah said, and he gave us a quick wave as we left the boathouse.

As Zack and I climbed towards the cottage, the deteriorating condition of the path demanded our full attention. After Zack gave the hand-rims attached to his wheels a final hard push and we were finally on solid ground, we both heaved a sigh of relief. I glanced back at the lake. Noah had brought a canoe dockside, and as I watched he stepped in and began paddling towards the yellow bumper, checking to make sure the anchor line's knot had been firmly tied.

I adjusted the hood of Zack's windbreaker to protect his face against the rain. "Noah doesn't leave anything to chance, does he?" I said.

"He's the best," Zack agreed. "He keeps Lawyers' Bay running like a Rolex. And he plays an essential role at Falconer Shreve. All law firms have business that needs to be kept under wraps – evidence that can't fall into the wrong hands; clients that need seclusion; confidential meetings – that kind of stuff. Noah takes care of all that and more. He doesn't ask questions, and he knows the law."

"I always forget that Noah's a lawyer."

"Well, he isn't really," Zack said. "He graduated the same year we all did, but he never did his articling year, and he never practised law."

"Do you think he regrets his decision?"

"He and I have talked about it a couple of times. Noah's grateful for the life he's been given." Zack's eyes took in the five handsome cottages that overlooked Lawyers' Bay. "Not many people in our small world can say that."

The screened porch of Kevin Hynd's cottage faced the path to the beach and I saw that, as always after a weekend together, the families had gathered to say goodbye. When Taylor spotted us, she opened the door and hustled the dogs and Zack and me onto the porch of the cottage where she, her brother Angus, and I had spent our first season at Lawyers' Bay.

It was a summer that had changed all our lives. I'd known Kevin for over ten years. He and my friend Jill Oziowy had dated, but her job was in Toronto, and their long-distance relationship was short-lived. After he and Jill parted ways, Kevin remained friendly with my kids and me. When he decided to spend a summer travelling, he asked if my family would be interested in renting his cottage for a loonie. He didn't have to ask twice.

The history of Lawyers' Bay was bittersweet. Kevin's parents had planned on a large family, and his father, Russell, a lawyer, had purchased the half moon of beachfront property around the bay, dreaming that his children would some day build cottages of their own there. The locals, tickled pink with the fact that the big-city lawyer was a regular guy who spent Saturday mornings with them chewing the fat on the stoop of The Point Store, christened his new property "Lawyers' Bay."

The name stuck, but Russell and Harriet Hynd's dream of a big family didn't materialize. Harriet's first pregnancy was difficult, and they had only one child, Kevin.

In his first year at the College of Law in Saskatoon, Kevin met Blake Falconer, Zack Shreve, Chris Altieri, and, after Chris introduced her to them, Delia Wainberg. The story went that, drawn together by their thousand-megahertz minds and unshakeable confidence in themselves and their future, the five students formed what they called "The Winners' Circle." That name stuck too, and as soon as the members of The Winners' Circle finished their articling year, they became law partners. They were young, brilliant, and idealistic, with a lust for justice that potential clients found appealing. From the day Falconer Shreve Altieri Wainberg and Hynd opened its doors, the firm thrived. Within five years, the young partners were all prosperous enough to build summer cottages on Lawyers' Bay.

Seemingly, they had the Midas touch, but as Midas discovered, the ability to turn everything to gold usually comes with a price tag. Blake Falconer became one of the top-ten corporate lawyers in Canada, but his marriage, pocked by his wife's infidelities, ended in tragedy. The first time I saw Blake, he was standing with his daughter on the beach, watching the fireworks at the firm's Canada Day party. We had been at Lawyers' Bay less than a week, so my children and I were still trying to get the lay of the land. Blake's wife, Lily, was standing alone, several metres away. She was clearly angry, and I overheard Gracie ask Blake why her mother couldn't just see how nice everything was.

As I came to know the Falconer family better, Gracie's question haunted me. A member of the Standing Buffalo Dakota First Nation, Lily was a woman with great gifts, not the least of which was her husband's passionate and undying love for her. Gracie, an only child, was a talented athlete and a bright and affectionate girl of whom any parent would be proud. Lily wasn't a lawyer, but she managed Falconer Shreve, and the partners were always quick to explain that, as much as any of them, she was responsible for the success of the firm. She had a loving family, health, professional respect, and financial stability. In short, she appeared to have everything, but she was never able to outrun the demons that had chased her since childhood. Just weeks after the night I saw Lily angry and alone on the beach, a man she had been close to since childhood used the handgun issued to him as a police officer to end her pain and his own.

Blake had never recovered from the loss. Before Lily died, he glowed with the ruddy physicality of a weekend sailor. His red-gold crew cut was carefully barbered; his eyes were clear; and his smile was wide. After Lily's death, his hair turned grey; his gaze became tentative; and his smiles were fleeting. Blake's performance as a corporate lawyer continued to be exemplary, but his personal life was empty. Always devoted to Gracie, he did everything he could to demonstrate his love, but both Blake and his daughter knew he was a shell of the man he had once been. Lily's death had hollowed him out.

The death of Lily Falconer was neither the first nor the only tragedy that summer. Each of the founding partners would be marked forever by the events of a few short weeks. Kevin Hynd had been in India, half a world away, when the first crushing blow came, but by one of those strange accidents of fate that mark our lives, he had unwittingly chosen me to play a key role in Christopher Altieri's last day on earth.

The weather for the Canada Day party had been postcard perfect: clear, sunny, and hot, with just enough of a breeze to flutter a flag. The Falconer Shreve hosts were solicitous, making certain guests were welcomed and familiarized with the array of pleasures awaiting them. By any criterion, it was a great party. But Chris, who had just returned from a trip to Japan, was withdrawn and preoccupied. In the late afternoon, when he and I were matched in a tennis tournament, he suffered a meltdown and walked away mid-game.

Later, Chris sought me out in the gazebo where I'd escaped for a respite from the noise and heat. He apologized for his earlier behaviour and then fell silent. For a few minutes we sat across from each other listening to the small band that had been hired for the dance, watching the bonfire on the beach blaze and admiring the fairyland beauty of the tiny twinkling lights strung through the branches of the willows that dotted the shoreline. When – finally – Chris began to speak, it was clear he was ready to unburden himself. He told me he'd been in touch with Kevin, who had suggested that he talk to me. After that, the words poured out.

He said he felt responsible for the loss of his unborn child because he had committed an act that convinced the woman who had been carrying their child not to go through with the pregnancy. Chris never explained to me what he had done; he simply said he had gone to Japan hoping to find peace. He'd learned that the Japanese have a name for a child who's lost before birth. They call it *mizuko*, "water child," because the unborn fetus is considered a being still flowing into our world. Chris had made a pilgrimage to a Buddhist temple in Tokyo where Jizo, the Bodhisattva protector of children, is worshipped. As was the custom, he left a toy for his *mizuko jizo* and said a prayer, but his suffering had not been assuaged. If anything, his anguish had grown even more intense. He had just begun to tell me why he believed the grace had been withdrawn from his life when Zack appeared. Chris greeted him affectionately and left.

At the fireworks, I saw Chris again briefly. Taylor was with me and Chris taught her a riddle. We all smiled at the riddle's answer and then Chris walked away. It was the last time I saw him alive.

That night, the heat in the cottage was stifling. I'd carried my pillow to the couch on the screened porch where it was cooler, and I drifted off. A streak of light and the sound of tires squealing awakened me. I knew almost immediately that someone must be speeding towards the lake and that whoever was behind the wheel of the car was in trouble.

Calling for Angus, I started running towards the road that led to the boat launch. Chris drove a red MGB. By the time I saw the car hit the boat launch, it had built up enough momentum to lift it to the underwater ledge that separates the swimming area from the sudden drop-off into the deep and treacherous water. The MGB was submerged except for the top of its roof. The bright moon lit up the waves licking the red metal and I thought there might still be time. I ran to the end of the dock, but before I could dive in, the car teetered. There was a sucking sound and then the lake swallowed the car. Angus and I took turns diving in to try to rescue Chris, but he hadn't wanted to be rescued; he'd locked the car doors.

The next morning, the RCMP dragged up Chris's car. He was still in it. What followed was a seemingly endless nightmare of unanswerable questions and grief for all the partners of Falconer Shreve Altieri Wainberg and Hynd.

Soon after Chris's death, Kevin returned to Canada. He came straight to Lawyers' Bay. He was certain there was something he could have done to prevent his friend from committing suicide. After an agonizing night sitting with him on the screened porch repeatedly describing everything I knew about Chris Altieri's last day on earth, I finally persuaded Kevin that nothing he could have said or done would have saved his friend.

The kids and I had been occupying all three of the Hynd cottage's bedrooms. I told Kevin my family could easily double up and make room for him, but he opted to stay with Zack, who lived alone. After Kevin had slept a few hours, he met with his partners and decisions were made.

Falconer Shreve had been planning to open its Calgary office that fall, and Chris had been slated to manage the new space. Accepting without question what he believed was his fate, Kevin agreed to move to Calgary and take Chris's place. It was the second time that Kevin had given up the life he wanted to meet the firm's needs.

When Kevin and I first met, he had owned a Day-Glo–painted patisserie called Twenty Lifetimes. The shop was devoted to designer pastries, cupcakes, a delectable assortment of tarte flambés, and other monuments to hip excess. His profits went to a rehab centre called New Day. The walls of Kevin's bakery were painted the rosy gold of peach butter, and it was impossible to walk through the shop's doors without smiling. Kevin himself had been a happy man. When I found out he'd been a lawyer in his past life, he explained his decision to leave his profession with a wry smile. "The law sharpens the mind by narrowing it. It took me a while, but I finally realized I didn't want my mind sharpened."

It seemed Kevin had made his decision. Then one morning, seemingly out of nowhere, a For Sale sign sprouted among the bed of sunflowers in front of Twenty Lifetimes, and Kevin returned to his corner office at Falconer Shreve. Without explanation or complaint, he did what the firm required of him, until that summer when he went to India. Driving him to the airport, I had sensed that the trip might be the prelude to a permanent break with the firm. Chris's suicide closed off that possibility. Kevin's path had been chosen, but it was not the path that would take him where he wanted to go.

Kevin was not the only one of the group with a past brighter than the future. Since that summer, Delia Wainberg had worked fourteen-hour days, fuelling her sapling-thin body with espresso, Benson & Hedges Whites, and licorice whips. Zack said she was driven by the need to block her memories of Chris and her fear that she had failed him. Isobel's insight that the law offered her mother a safe haven from pain had been right on the money.

Zack alone seemed to have escaped the curse. On the afternoon of the Canada Day party that ended in Chris Altieri's death, Zack offered to open my Coke and our lives changed forever. Despite the forest of warning flags raised by our nearest and dearest, five months to the day after we met, Zack and I were married, and my children, grandchildren, and I became part of the Falconer Shreve family.

CHAPTER

2

On that rainy Thanksgiving Monday, the screened porch smelled pleasantly of woodsmoke, but the rain made the room gloomy, and no one had thought to turn on a lamp. Delia was sitting on the worn, lumpy couch where during that first summer I had spent many nights curled up with a book I wasn't reading, listening to the crickets, watching the moon's path on the lake, and trying to understand all that had happened in the lives of my new neighbours at Lawyers' Bay.

Now, four years later, Blake and Kevin flanked Dee on the couch. Jacob was curled up on a sleeping bag in the corner, with Isobel sitting cross-legged beside him. Zack positioned his chair so that he was beside Blake, and I pulled over a hassock to be next to my husband. Taylor and Gracie stood facing us with their backs towards the screened windows. Outside the rain fell in sheets, creating a dramatic backdrop for the young women. They obviously had an agenda and they'd decided on their approach.

As soon as we were settled, Isobel joined the girls. She wasted no time on preamble. "Taylor is working on a Day of the Dead project for her visual arts class," she said. "We want to talk to you about it."

"I've always loved Frida Kahlo's work," Taylor said. "Some people hate all her images of death, but for me, the presence of death and decay in her work makes everything Kahlo paints more alive."

Taylor was typical of kids her age in every respect but one. She had inherited a prodigious talent in visual art from her birth mother, the artist Sally Love, and her life was driven by her passion for art. That morning as she talked about the famed Mexican painter, Taylor's voice rang with intensity. "Some of Kahlo's most amazing images were inspired by symbols from Día de los Muertos. It's a holiday when Mexicans remember the ones they've lost. When I told Gracie and Isobel that I'd been reading about how Mexican culture has always recognized that dying is part of being human, we decided we wanted to learn more. Since Kevin lived in Mexico, we asked him to tell us everything."

Kevin grinned at Taylor. "You won't make that mistake again," he said. He turned so that he was speaking to the rest of us. "In a nutshell, I explained that Día de los Muertos celebrates the lives of the dead by the living reminiscing and sharing some of the things that brought their loved ones joy when they were alive."

Isobel picked up the thread. "That's when we knew that the Day of the Dead offered something our families needed. We've all lost people we loved or people we wish we'd had the chance to love. Gracie and Taylor's mothers both died. The sister who I never knew existed until three years ago died before I had the chance to meet her."

Gracie stepped forward. Physically, she was very like her father: big-boned, red-haired, and freckled. She had always struck me as a young woman who loped through life with a bounce, a grin, and a great free throw, able to shrug off the slings and arrows without breaking a sweat. That day it seemed that she, too, was suffering.

Public speaking was not Gracie's forte, but she was an athlete, trained to read a situation and react. When her grey-blue eyes took in our faces, she saw our uncertainty. "We know you love us, and you know we love you," she said quickly. "That's not the issue. But we live with you." Gracie directed her attention to Blake. "Dad, I know how sad you are when you think I'm not watching. Last week I overheard you on the phone telling somebody that you dreaded the end of the day because that meant you had to go home and face the emptiness."

Blake winced. "I'm sorry, Gracie. I'd had some frustrating meetings with clients, and I was in a rotten mood. It had nothing to do with you. You're the reason I get up in the morning."

Gracie's voice was gentle. "I know that, but it shouldn't be that way. My mother has been dead for four years. You have a life to live. So do I. Dad, it's time for you and me to talk about Lily, and it's time for all of us to talk about Chris. Everyone loved him, but since he died, you all try to act as if he never existed. It's hurting us, and that's the last thing Chris would want."

The sounds of the rain were everywhere – drumming steadily on the porch roof, splashing from the rainspout to the ground, slapping against the cast-iron birdbath that had been Russell Hynd's gift to his bride decades ago. But Gracie's words had silenced us. When the silence grew awkward, Taylor took a deep breath and squared her shoulders. Sally Love had been a long-limbed blonde with strikingly dramatic features. Taylor was dark-haired and her face was delicately sculpted, but she had inherited her mother's generous and uncommonly expressive mouth. When Sally and I were growing up, I could always read her mood by focusing on her lips. I could do the same with Taylor, and that morning when I looked at the determined curve of our daughter's mouth, I knew she was committed to bringing the lessons of Día de los Muertos to our families.

"It took me a long time to find the right place for Sally in my life," Taylor said. "I was four when she died, but she left not long after I was born, so I never really knew her. When I was young, I ached for her. I remember tracing the lines of a painting she'd made with my fingers so I could feel connected to her. After I started painting seriously, I hated her. I didn't know if the art I was making was any good, but I knew the art she made was brilliant, and I hated her for that. And I hated her for hurting everybody who ever loved her because all she cared about was her work. Most of all I hated her for leaving me."

She gave Zack a quick, private glance. "Dad, I'm still afraid that someone I love will leave me." Her voice until then had been assured and confident, but it grew small with fear, and Zack shot me a questioning look. The moment passed. Taylor shook her head as if to banish dark thoughts and carried on. "Jo and Zack helped me understand why Sally made the choices she made. It took time, but they never gave up, and the day I finally realized Sally had done the best she could with the life she'd been given, I stopped hating her." She smiled. "It was a great feeling."

Isobel gave Taylor a quick hug, then focused once again on us. "Gracie and I are happy for Taylor," she said. "But we want what she has. We want to find a place in our lives for the people we've lost. Taking the time to remember – really *remember them* – will help all of us," Isobel said. Noah came in just as his daughter had begun to speak. "Gracie and I have spent every holiday of our lives at Lawyers' Bay," she said. "Chris died at the beginning of the first summer Taylor and her family were here. Taylor and Joanne never really knew Chris, or what you guys were like before, but Gracie and I remember. We want us all to get together, just to talk and to listen. We thought that, in keeping with the spirit of the Day of the Dead, the evening of October 31st might be a good time to meet."

Noah embraced her. She whispered something in his ear; then he moved to the spot behind Delia and rested his fingers lightly on his wife's thin shoulders. She didn't appear to notice. Beside me, Zack and Blake exchanged smiles. Isobel saw the closeness between the two men and aimed her next words at them. "Every night we fell asleep to the sound of the adults laughing," she said. "Do you remember that?"

"I remember," Zack said, and his voice was rough with emotion.

"So do I," Blake said.

"Good times," Kevin said.

Tears ran unchecked down Delia Wainberg's cheeks. "And then the good times ended," she said. Noah handed his wife a tissue, and she mopped her eyes and blew her nose.

Noah's voice was strong. "I'm in for the evening of the 31st," he said.

The look Zack and I exchanged was quick but it was enough. "Joanne and I are in too," he said.

"So am I," Kevin said. The sweatshirt Kevin was wearing that cool October morning carried a message: "Further Up & Further In." C.S. Lewis's words from *The Last Battle* had driven Kevin's life. Of all the partners, he had aged the least. There was grey in his sandy hair but it was still thick; his smile still reached all the way to his hazel eyes; and his body had never lost its shambling grace. The boundaries of Kevin's world were not fixed.

Only Delia had yet to respond. The attention of everyone in the room focused on her, and for a moment it seemed as though she was shrinking under the weight of a grief I could not understand. Finally, she wiped away the last of her tears, took a deep breath, and straightened her spine. "Let's do it," she said. "Let's bring back the laughter." Her wind-breaker was on her lap. She stood, shrugged into her jacket, pulled up the hood, and, without saying goodbye, walked into the rain.

When a bolt of lightning split the sky, followed almost immediately by an earth-shaking boom of thunder, Kevin laughed. "I believe the dead just cast their vote," he said. "And they approve too. It's unanimous."

And so, on the front porch of the Hynds' quintessentially Canadian cottage, with its squeaky screen door, perma-nently sand-dusted floor, and shelves lined with guest books filled with praise for Harriet's coffee and Russell's hospital-ity, the decision was made. On October 31, the families of the partners of Falconer Shreve Altieri Wainberg and Hynd would gather to remember and honour those we'd lost. Looking into one another's faces, we smiled a little sheep-ishly, bent to sign the guest book for that year, and donned our rain gear. Then, believing our largest concern was what the rain was doing to the gravel road that led to the high-way, we moved towards the door.

I stopped in front of a photograph on the rustic end table that Kevin said had been in the cottage since he was a kid. The legs of the table were birch logs and the photo was framed in birch. Taken during the partners' first summer at Lawyers' Bay, the photo showed the new lawyers, dressed in jeans and T-shirts, in the lake up to their knees in water. Zack was in the middle: on one side of him were Delia and Chris, and on the other, Blake and Kevin. Two-thirds of Zack's chair was submerged. It was a tender photo filled with the light of the sun bouncing off the water and the joy of five young people alive on a summer day with the future shining before them.

Each of the partners had a copy of the photo. Zack's was in a chased silver frame on his dresser. Delia's, in a starkly modern metal frame, perched on the mantel over the Wainbergs' fireplace; Blake's, framed in cherry wood, was on the credenza in his den. Chris's copy had been hung on a wall in the main reception area at Falconer Shreve, and Blake had once given Lily Falconer a copy too. That morning, obeying an impulse I didn't understand, I picked up the photograph, and for a few moments I held it close, trying to imagine what it was like to be one of those five young people on that sparkling July day.

Then, as we had countless times, we ran through the rain to our cars. Hurried and heedless, the Falconer Shreve partners and our families called out our rushed goodbyes and shifted our focus to our workaday lives. It had been a good Thanksgiving.

CHAPTER

3

The ten-minute drive from Lawyers' Bay to the highway was white-knuckle all the way, and I was glad Zack was behind the wheel. Taylor was going back to the city with the Wainbergs. Zack and I were alone, and as soon as we reached the highway I asked the question that I knew was on both our minds. "So, what have we signed up for?"

Zack pinched the bridge of his nose, always a sign that he was troubled. "I honestly don't know," he said. "But the girls are right. Something should be done. When Isobel said that after Chris died the laughter stopped, she zeroed in on something that none of us have acknowledged. The five of us were linked to one another. Chris's suicide broke that link, but instead of facing the truth and forging a new link, we've been flailing.

"Blake's been killing himself working seventeen-hour days. He says the firm needs him, and he's right. Before the energy bubble burst, the Calgary office was a gold mine. Esme could have run the place," he said, signalling to the seat behind me where our bouvier snored contentedly. "But now our Calgary people are scrambling. They have to go cap

23

in hand to companies that were beating down our doors a few months ago. Kevin's doing his best, but we need to snag some very big clients, and, frankly, Kevin's heart isn't in it, so Blake has been stepping in."

"Stepping in and suffering for it," I said. "Meanwhile, Kevin is living a life he doesn't want because, like Blake, he's trying to keep the group together. You're all paying too high a price for something that died with Chris."

Zack didn't respond. I gazed at his profile, trying to read his expression. My husband is a handsome man – strong-featured with deep-set green eyes and a sensual mouth. Years in the courtroom had taught him to present a face that revealed nothing, but I wondered if I'd pressed too hard. "You don't agree with me," I said finally.

He replied slowly. "No," he said. "I do agree with you. And you'll be relieved to learn that I've chosen the perfect person to head the Calgary office and take some of the burden off Kevin and Blake. I should have taken care of this months ago. No excuses, but finding the right candidate was a drawn-out process." He gave me a quick smile. "Anyway, a woman named Katina Posaluko-Chapman is joining the firm's Calgary office. We'll be making the announcement at the beginning of November."

I could feel my gorge rise. Zack had been elected mayor of Regina the year before, and he'd taken a leave of absence from the firm. There were significant changes to be made in the operation of our city, and Zack put in long hours making those changes. I tried to keep my voice even. "Delia is the firm's managing partner," I said. "Why didn't she deal with this problem?"

"Because we knew that if we were going to hire someone to head up the Calgary office, we'd have to offer them an equity partnership, and Delia has always balked at the idea of having anyone outside of the founding partners made an equity partner. It was simpler for me just to handle the situation and present it as a *fait accompli* – which is what I plan to do."

"Good, then let Dee know and let her handle the rest of it," I said. "And the sooner, the better."

"Her court case in Saskatoon starts tomorrow – she'll be gone a week, but as soon as she gets back I'll talk to her." Zack grimaced. "Not a pleasant thought," he said. "Hiring a new equity partner is going to open a can of worms with other lawyers in the firm who've paid their dues and been waiting too long for a promotion."

Watching Zack as he drove, I remembered the pain in Taylor's eyes when she'd spoken of her fear that someone she loved would leave her. My chest was tight. "Zack, you have a demanding job, a family that adores you, and two-week-old twin grandsons who need you to stick around so they can get to know you. You've already taken care of a problem that Delia should have handled herself. If what you've done opens a can of worms, let her deal with it. Just explain what you've done and walk away from the situation."

The wind had picked up, blowing the last leaves from the trees along the highway. The short, dark days were upon us. For the rest of the drive, locked in our private thoughts, my husband and I moved through the grey world in silence. Zack was planning to go to City Hall and work for a couple of hours before supper. When we pulled into his parking space, we unsnapped our seat belts and exchanged a reassuring kiss. "I'll hand it over to Delia," Zack said. "You're right. There's no point in sacrificing the future to something that no longer exists."

I left Zack at City Hall and drove back to the single-storey house overlooking Wascana Creek that, apart from the accessibility ramps, was unexceptional to anyone but our

family. This would be our first winter back in the house
that Zack, Taylor, and I, our dogs, and our cats had moved
into on the day Zack and I were married. We had planned to
live there forever, until someone with a serious grudge
planted explosives in our attached garage. Luckily, when
the bomb was detonated we were at Lawyers' Bay. Our
house on the creek was destroyed, and had we been there
we would have died.

When we had the house rebuilt, we asked the contractor
who had done its original retrofitting to make something
that, in every possible way, was identical to the house we
had all loved. He delivered. But by the time the Wascana
Creek house was habitable again, we had become comfortable in a condo on Halifax Street, in the Warehouse District,
where we moved after disaster struck. By a stroke of good
fortune, more than two years later the house was for sale
again, and we knew the time was right to move back to the
property overlooking the creek. Now, we were finally
unpacked and ready to experience the thrill of reclaiming
our new old house.

That evening the weather had continued to be miserable,
so we turned on the gas fireplace, pulled our table over to
the window, lit candles, and watched the storm from the
warmth of our dining room. Our mood at dinner was lighthearted. Zack had brought good news from City Hall. Since
the day he was elected mayor, Zack had been working to
resuscitate the Saskatchewan Film Production Studios that
had opened fifteen years earlier. For almost a decade the
facility, built on the old University of Regina Campus, had
flourished, producing B movies and TV series. When a new
and conservative provincial government was elected, it
scrapped the tax credit that had drawn the film community
to our province. Seemingly overnight, the production companies decamped and moved to more fiscally hospitable

climes, and the state-of-the-art Saskatchewan Film Production Studios became a white elephant.

That afternoon Zack had received word that Caritas, a
company that had once employed scores of people who
worked in film production, had been given the green light
for a major project and was moving back into its old offices
on the first of December. It was an announcement worthy
of a good bottle of wine, and Zack opened a Napa Valley
Cabernet Sauvignon that was just the ticket. Taylor's boy-
friend, Declan, had sent pictures of his cousin's wedding and
Taylor had them on her iPad. The reception had been held
in a small inn just outside Gatineau, and the images of
young love and Quebec's breathtaking fall foliage provided
the perfect coda to the weekend.

Taylor was too old to be tucked in, but she still liked Zack
and me to come into her room to say goodnight. When Taylor
was younger, her bedroom had been an exuberant bedlam
of clothes, projects "in progress," homework, art books,
cosmetics, hair products, and, during a period when she,
Isobel, and Gracie were creating personal-profile perfumes
for their friends, dozens of tiny bottles of essential oils.

Times had changed. Maturity had brought Taylor an affin-
ity for order, and her bedrooms at the cottage and in the city
were uncluttered and serene. They were also very similar:
Wedgwood lavender blue walls, white wicker furniture,
filmy white curtains, and a crisp pique bedspread, white with
a print of blue allium. At the cottage, a glowing abstract by
Taylor's grandfather, Des Love, hung over her bed; in the
city, the place of honour was given to a Sally Love painting
of two black cats sleeping in a patch of violets.

That night, as she often did, Taylor curled up with her
own cats – Bruce, Benny, and Bob Marley. The scene was
itself worthy of a painting. Taylor has the kind of looks that

always make me think of Audrey Hepburn: clean-cut, boyish yet feminine. She was wearing the sleepwear she currently favoured, a white T-shirt paired with black-silk sports shorts. Her cats – two gingers and a tortoiseshell – had curved their bodies to fit the spaces around her and purred contentedly, but Taylor was in a more contemplative mood. As soon as we came into the room, she moved Bruce, Benny, and Bob Marley to the other side of the bed, sat up, and clasped her knees with her arms. "Declan texted me saying he had a great time," she said. "But he wished I'd been there."

"Do *you* wish you'd been there?" I said.

Taylor glanced at a photo on her iPad. "It would have been fun," she said. "But I'm glad I was at the lake."

I pulled over the wicker bench that nested under the vanity table, and Zack wheeled close to us. "You, Isobel, and Gracie were pretty intense when you talked about the Day of the Dead," he said.

Taylor's eyes, so deeply brown they were almost black, looked to Zack and then to me. "Isobel and Gracie need help," she said. "Neither the Wainbergs or Blake will talk about their problems, and whenever Isobel or Gracie raise the subject, their parents shut down, so the situations just keep getting worse." Taylor picked up Bob Marley and smoothed his ginger coat. "Blake still has pictures of Gracie's mum all over the house, but when Gracie asked if she could put some away, her dad said he wasn't ready."

"Everybody grieves at a different pace," I said, remembering the days and nights that became weeks and months after my first husband, Ian, died. "It can take some people a long time."

My explanation didn't satisfy our daughter. "But what if the way one person is grieving is hurting other people?" she asked. "Blake's grief has already affected Gracie's choices

about what to do with her life. And Delia's inability to face
her problems is having a huge impact on Isobel. Izzie's SAT
scores were amazing. She had letters from universities all
over Canada and the U.S. promising her the moon if she'd
enrol, and it's the same for Gracie. Tons of schools with
great women's basketball programs have offered her athletic
scholarships."

"But both girls stayed here to go to university," I said. "I'd
wondered about that."

"There's nothing to wonder," Taylor said quietly. "Isobel
stayed because she wants to be there for Jacob, and Gracie
stayed because she's afraid of what will happen to her father
if she leaves." Our daughter's gaze took in both Zack and
me. "Isobel and Gracie deserve their own lives," she said.

"Yes," I said. "They do."

Taylor pressed on. "But they won't be able to have their
own lives until their families deal with their problems.
We're hoping that having everybody get together to talk
about Lily and Chris and Abby will help Blake and Delia get
over the past."

Zack frowned. "Delia will never get over Chris," he said,
and his voice was heavy.

Taylor reached out to put a hand over her father's. "I only
met Chris once – that night at the fireworks when he taught
me a riddle. The next day when I heard he'd killed himself,
I kept thinking about that riddle. Do you remember it, Jo?"

"I do," I said. "What three words make you happy when
you're sad, and sad when you're happy?"

"And the answer is 'Nothing lasts forever,'" Taylor said.
"After you told me what happened to Chris, I wondered if
he'd been using that riddle to try to talk himself out of ending
his life." She lowered her eyes. "It's too bad it didn't work."

"It is," Zack said. "Because death is one thing that *does*
last forever."

"I get that," Taylor said. "But isn't that why it's so important to change the things we can change? We only have one life, and Delia's failure to deal with her own issues is wrecking Isobel's life. Why can't Delia move on?"

"Because underneath that terrifyingly capable lawyer the world sees is a wounded soul," Zack said. He hesitated for a moment before going on. "The first time Chris introduced her to us, I wondered what the hell he was thinking. So did Kevin and Blake. We were four rough, cocky guys. And here was this waif of a girl who looked as if a stiff wind or a harsh word could flatten her. None of us had ever seen anyone that broken and vulnerable. It was like she was missing a layer of skin, and every nerve end was exposed."

Taylor cocked her head. "What had happened to her?"

"The year before she started at the College of Law she had suffered a tragedy compounded by a cruelty," Zack said, and I could hear the anger in his voice. "Delia took her kid brother out for ice cream. On their way home, a truck ran a light and T-boned their car. Miraculously, Dee wasn't hurt. But her brother was badly injured. She and her father were in the waiting room at the hospital when the doctor told them that they'd been unable to save the boy. Delia's father went berserk. When she tried to comfort him, her father turned on her. He said, 'The wrong child died.' Those were the last words he ever spoke to her. Until Dee met Kevin, Chris, Blake, and me, her life consisted solely of going to classes and working in the kitchen at her university residence during the day and studying by herself at night. That was it. She was absolutely alone."

Taylor bit her lip. "And you gave her a place to belong."

"We did," Zack said. "According to Delia, our friendship gave her an identity and a life, but Taylor, it was a fair exchange. Once Dee knew she could trust the four of us, she relaxed and we saw the woman she was – brilliant but also warm and funny and considerate." Zack's face softened with the memory of his friend as she had been. "Delia brought us alive in a new way. She strengthened the bonds between us. She made us recognize the possibilities that lay ahead if we stayed together. And she never stopped being grateful to Chris for being the first to see something in her that made her worthy of being accepted."

"But if being part of your lives gave Delia an identity and a life, why is she still unable to deal with her problems?" Taylor said.

"I'm not a shrink," Zack said, "but my guess is that, despite everything she's accomplished, Delia has never believed she measures up. That cruel bastard of a father got through to her in a way no one has been able to since."

"She still believes that the accident took the life of the wrong child?" Taylor said.

Zack sighed. "Something like that. Dee's terrified of failing."

"Because a failure is proof that her father was right," I said. "What a terrible burden to live with."

"It is," Zack said. "And I've seen the toll that burden exacts on her. All lawyers lose cases. You feel like you've been sucker-punched, but you move along. When Delia loses, she's devastated. Sometimes it drives me nuts. Her record of favourable Supreme Court decisions is stellar, but when a decision goes against her, Dee insists that the two of us review every step of the appeal so she knows exactly where she went wrong."

"I understand that," Taylor said. "If a painting isn't working for me, I can't leave my studio until I've figured out the problem and fixed it."

"Seeing your mistakes as part of the learning process is healthy," I said. "But with Delia it goes beyond that. Last year she forgot your dad's birthday. When I came back from my run with the dogs she was waiting on the stoop at the condo. It was five-thirty in the morning. She'd awakened in the night and remembered Zack's birthday, and she'd driven downtown to apologize. She'd been waiting there in the dark for an hour."

Taylor cringed. "Alone, in that neighbourhood? She must have been desperate."

"She was. She needed to apologize to your dad for screwing up. She was shaking with fury at what she called her 'stupidity and self-absorption.' Nothing I said helped. Finally, I just put my arms around her and took her upstairs to our condo. Her body was absolutely rigid, and it was weightless – like a bird's. After she calmed down, she seemed completely defeated, and she said, 'It's not easy being me.'"

"Wow," Taylor said. "That does *not* sound like Izzie's mother. She never lets down her defences."

"I was surprised too," I said. "When she opened up that way, I thought that Delia and I might be on the verge of real friendship. But when I offered to make us tea, she waved me off. She apologized for intruding, took out her phone, began checking her messages, and left."

Taylor was pensive. "That's so sad." She moved closer to Zack. "Does Isobel know what Delia's father said to her?"

Zack shrugged. "I don't know."

"If she doesn't, she should. Delia should tell her what happened. Izzie's a good person, and she wants to do the right thing, but she can't if she doesn't know the whole story."

"I'll try talking to Delia about it," Zack said. He yawned. "Taylor, it's been a long day. Why don't we all hit the sack?"

Taylor peered closely at Zack's face. He didn't look like a man who'd just had a three-day weekend. "Promise you're not going to stay up and work till midnight again."

"I promise," Zack said. "Scout's honour." He gave our daughter a smart salute.

Taylor's smile was mischievous. "You were never a Boy Scout," she said.

Zack drew himself up and squared his shoulders. "Do you want to hear me say the Scout Promise?"

"If Taylor doesn't, I do," I said.

"In that case . . ." Zack had dropped his salute; now he rendered it again. His face was solemn as he began. "On my honour . . ."

Taylor and I fought hard to remain straight-faced as Zack earnestly recited his commitment to God, the Queen, and the tenets of the Scout Law. When he finished with a booming declaration of the Scout Motto "Be Prepared," my daughter and I gave into the inevitable and began to laugh. As she wiped the tears from her eyes Taylor said, "You always make me feel better, Dad." She slid out of bed so that she could embrace Zack with both arms. "I love you so much," she said. "You know that, don't you?"

I could see that Zack was deeply moved. "I do know that, Taylor. And it means everything to me." It was a nice moment, but when I looked into my husband's eyes I saw a sorrow so intense I could hardly breathe, and I turned away.

CHAPTER

4

The next morning when Pantera, Esme, and I got back from our run, the dogs' water bowls were filled, the coffee was made, and Zack was showered and dressed for the day.

I bent to kiss the top of his head. "I like the new cologne," I said.

"I like your scent better," he said.

"It's called sweat."

Zack chuckled. "Way to kill a pickup line."

"You don't need a pickup line. When it comes to you, I'm always available."

"Hold that thought," Zack said. "Because of the holiday, the weekly city council meeting was rescheduled to today at five. It's going to be a long day."

I'd just stepped out of the shower when Margot Hunter called. "I'm in need of adult conversation," she said. "Lexi and Kai are practically perfect in every way, but since they're both under the age of two our banter is pretty basic."

"I'll be there in half an hour," I said. "And I'll bring my copy of *The Portable Dorothy Parker* – time to give those baby tongues a workout."

———

The condo building that we had lived in for the previous two and a half years still had the words "COLD STORAGE" written in two-metre-high block letters on its brick exterior. Margot's then-fiancé, Leland Hunter, a multi-millionaire developer, had owned our unit. The decor was Tuscan and the space had the flawless Old World ambience that only a decorator could create. When we moved in, I thought I would never feel comfortable in that studied elegance, but Margot's family and mine had been through good times and not-so-good times on the fourth floor our condos shared, and that rainy morning as I waited for the security gate to lift so I could drive into the building's underground parking area, I felt the warmth of homecoming.

When I stepped off the elevator, Margot, her almost-two-year-old daughter, Lexi, and her eight-month-old son, Kai, were waiting. I had been in the delivery room when the babies were born, and in my eyes the children were both strikingly attractive. Lexi had wispy white-blond hair, a peaches-and-cream complexion, and cornflower-blue eyes that could cast an unnervingly penetrating gaze when she was thwarted. Kai's biological father, Brock Poitras, was Cree, and Kai had inherited his father's shiny black hair and tawny skin, but he also had Margot's bright blue eyes and full lips. It was a dynamite combination.

As soon as they spotted me, Lexi came running and Kai began struggling in his mother's arms. As I bent to embrace Lexi, Margot's smile was wide. "You've been missed," she said.

I stood to hug Kai and his mother. "So have you," I said. "It's been four whole days since I saw you." I picked up Lexi. She was wearing grey, hooded footie-pyjamas and a gold foil-covered crown with a faux fur circlet. "Hey, you're Max from *Where the Wild Things Are*," I said.

"I *am* Max," she said.

"And that's the only name she responds to," her mother said. "Right, Max?"

Lexi nodded solemnly. "Right."

Margot sighed. "Well, Max, let's go inside and have a snack. I'm sure Jo is itching for one of our special fibre-laden cookies."

Lexi took her cookie and sippy cup to the window seat she favoured, and Margot settled Kai in his high chair and began feeding him puréed sweet potatoes. We adults shared a pot of tea. The plate of fibre-laden cookies was between us. When I reached for one, Margot batted my hand away. "Don't," she whispered. "They taste like recycled cardboard. On the second shelf to the left, above the sink, there's a baking tin filled with sugar cookies that crumble as soon as they touch your tongue." She handed me a napkin. "Sneak over there and hide a few in this. And don't feel guilty. You and I have eaten our share of fibre."

The sugar cookies were indeed guilt-inducing, but I forged ahead. "So what's the deal with 'Max'?" I said.

Margot rolled her eyes. "A rookie mistake," she said. "I took the kids shopping for Halloween costumes prematurely. Lexi put on her Max suit as soon as we got home, and she's been in it ever since. It's starting to get pungent, but I can't get her to take it off."

"Buy her another Max suit so you can switch them," I said.

Margot slapped her forehead with the palm of her hand. "Hard to believe that people pay $650 an hour for my legal advice, isn't it?"

"It's a different skill set," I said. "So how was your Thanksgiving?"

"A lot of fun. I was a tad concerned about how Wadena would react to the kids and me strolling down Main Street with my son's gay, Aboriginal biological father who was a wide receiver for the Saskatchewan Roughriders, but apart from my old piano teacher who chucked Kai under the chin and said, 'Hi there, Little Chief,' people were welcoming, and even Mr. Balmer's chin-chuck was kindly."

"The times they are a-changin'," I said.

"Thank God," Margot said. "But the good things endure. We had an old-fashioned prairie Thanksgiving – turkey, perogies, stuffing, mashed potatoes, gravy, cabbage rolls, vegetables from my siblings' gardens, and five kinds of pies. Everybody ate too much, the arguments about politics and football didn't end in bloodshed, and not a single child cried longer than thirty seconds. A blessedly uncomplicated holiday." Margot replaced Kai's empty sweet potato dish with a bowl of puréed chicken and began spooning. "How was yours?"

"Until yesterday afternoon, pretty much like yours – then it became complicated."

Margot's brow knotted. "Complicated enough that we should wait until the kids go down to talk."

"That might be wise," I said. I sipped my tea. "On a brighter note, Taylor showed us photos of Declan as a groomsman. Very cool."

"My stepson did look handsome in his black tie and tails, didn't he?" Margot said. "But Taylor was wise to defer meeting the Hunter family. They would have taken one look at her, decided she was the next Hunter bride, and swooped in."

"Taylor won't be seventeen till Remembrance Day," I said.

"That wouldn't have stopped them," Margot said. "They believe in training their women young."

"And the Hunters live in this century?"

Margot tilted her head. "I've never been quite sure about that."

The shenanigans of the Hunter family would have provided Dorothy Parker with fodder for a dozen lunches at the Algonquin, and Margot and I were still having fun when we noticed the children's eyes growing heavy. I picked up Lexi and Margot took Kai. It was nap-time.

After Lexi was cleaned up and her crown safely stowed on her night table, I leaned over and kissed her forehead. "You're just playing at being Max, aren't you?" I whispered. "You're still our sweet Lexi."

The hint of a smile touched her little-girl lips. "Yes. I'm Lexi," she said. Then she narrowed her cornflower eyes and lowered her voice to a growl. "But I'm Max too."

When I returned to the living room, Margot was sitting in one of the wing chairs in front of the fireplace. A sewing basket was on the table beside her. Motherhood had revealed a domestic side in Margot that would not have been guessed at by the many men whose tongues lolled as she walked past them during her days as a trial lawyer.

Her signature dagger fingernails were long gone, and she had let her hair return to its natural honey blond. Margot was forty-five years old, but that morning in jeans, a sweatshirt, and sneakers, hair in a loose ponytail and face innocent of makeup, she looked like the young mums I met pushing strollers on the bike path behind our house. In one hand she held a small plush toy, clearly modelled on one of the wild things Max encounters on his adventure; in the other, she held a darning needle. The stuffy was wearing a yellow-and-brown striped shirt and a broad smile. His horns were perky, but his tail was bedraggled and hanging by a thread.

Margot began the repair job. "Okay, fill me in on your complicated Thanksgiving," she said.

Like me, Margot was a pragmatist. I thought she would scoff at the idea of her law partners seeking solutions for their complex problems in something akin to a group therapy session. But the meeting on the Hynds' screen porch had stirred me, and as I talked, I tried to convey the power of the emotional currents that had swirled around us the previous morning.

When I finished, Margot put down her work and rubbed her temples. "So Falconer Shreve's founding partners will be gathering together to memorialize their loved ones for the Day of the Dead," she said dryly. "There's a certain grim irony there."

"Meaning?"

"Meaning that if Falconer Shreve doesn't rethink and restructure before the New Year, the firm just might implode."

"Is it that bad?"

Margot's nod was emphatic. "It's that bad," she said. She picked up the plush monster, eyed its tail critically, and then returned to her sewing. "The best and the brightest are still beating a path to our door. We pay our associates substantially more than most law firms do, and we're a 'quality of life' firm. Associates are allowed to bill fewer hours than they would at most places. They don't have to carry the dreaded FirmPhones that keep them on an electronic umbilical cord twenty-four/seven; they get reasonable vacations; and we're family-friendly. Comparatively speaking, Falconer Shreve is a decent place to work. The problem is morale."

"From what you said, the associates are getting a fair deal."

"A fair deal for *now*, but when these bright young lawyers look at their future with us, they see a logjam. In the normal course of things, associates hang around for seven or eight years. If they're not deemed partnership material by then, they're squeezed out. If they make the cut, they're awarded a partnership."

"That seems straightforward."

"It is, but Delia has always insisted on a two-tiered partnership model: equity partners and partners like your daughter-in-law who are non-equity."

"Maisie's talked to me about her status. She says that for the time being, having less responsibility is better for her. She gets a generous fixed salary, and she doesn't have to worry about the profits and losses of the firm or attend partners' meetings. It's a good arrangement for a young lawyer who's also a young mother."

"True, but the key phrase in there is 'for the time being.' I've known Maisie since she articled with Ireland Leontowich. She's ambitious. When her twins are older, she'll want the prestige and the earning potential of being a full partner with an ownership stake in the firm."

"And that won't happen?"

"In Maisie's case it probably will. She's Zack's daughter-in-law."

"And that makes a difference?"

"It does to Delia. Maisie's marriage links her to the firm's founders."

"You're kidding."

"I wish I were. Falconer Shreve has an enviably deep bench. We have many truly gifted non-equity partners."

"And they want to take the next step."

"Exactly, and that requires the consent of all the equity partners."

"And Delia won't consent," I said.

Margot raised an eyebrow. "You didn't hear that from me."

"Of course not. But, Margot, you made equity partner and you weren't connected to any of them."

"I made it because Zack refused to back down. He really had to duke it out with Delia to get her agreement. The weird thing is Delia likes me. She knew the firm's criminal law division needed shoring up, and she knew I was one of the two best trial lawyers in the province."

"But she still had to be convinced."

"Yes, and I'm the only equity partner in the firm who didn't found it. I used to think the bond between the founding partners was just kind of sweet, but I don't think that any more. The elitism is damaging the firm."

"I had no idea the situation was that dire," I said.

"Well, it is," Margot said. "The non-equity partners know they aren't likely to get the prestige or money they deserve. They're not going to wait forever. And the equity partners can't escape from office business – not even me, and I'm on maternity leave. I'm sure you've noticed that the founding partners are already close to flaming out. Zack included. He keeps getting roped into Falconer Shreve business. With everything he has to deal with as mayor, it's too much."

"Delia must see what's happening," I said.

Margot shook her head. "There are none so blind as those who will not see. I've been thinking about this for weeks. There's only one solution. Delia's partners, including me, have to confront her."

"An intervention?" I said.

"Of sorts. And, Jo, we need Zack onside. He's the only one of us Delia will really listen to."

"He'll support you," I said. "He knows there have to be changes on all fronts."

"Good, because there's something I'd like Zack to look at." She handed me the stuffed toy she'd been darning. "Take care of my friend here. I'll be back in a shake of a cow's tail."

When Margot returned, she was carrying a presentation folder. "Since Leland died and Peyben International landed in my lap, I've had a crash course in corporate management. Falconer Shreve is a mess, but it can be fixed, and I've put together some ideas Zack can use to convince Delia it's time to fix it. Full disclosure – Brock and I worked together on drafting this."

"Where's the firm's human resources department in all this?" I said.

"Having hip replacement surgery."

I flinched. "I've heard that's excruciating. But, Margot, is there really only one person in HR?"

"Only one person who makes the decisions," Margot said, "And she deals primarily with the firm's support staff. Raema Silzer is well liked, and she's good at her job, but frankly there's not a lot for her to do, especially given how few promotions there are among the lawyers. But she has a real gift for choosing executive assistants who are a good match for the partner they're paired with."

"Finding someone for Delia must have been a challenge," I said.

"Apparently Raema was up to it," Margot said. "Delia and Lorne Callow are two peas in a pod: both perfectionists, both absolutely devoted to the firm. Delia wasn't keen on hiring a replacement in HR for the three months Raema's on medical leave, so she added Raema's responsibilities to Lorne's and he's stepped in without complaint." Margot shrugged. "As I said, there isn't much for him to do. Support staff is well paid, their benefits are generous, and we have on-site daycare. Our firm is a regular Sweden."

"But it's not a utopia for the non-equity partners," I said.

"No, it isn't. But if Falconer Shreve restructures, it will be better for them. I've told Brock what I know of the firm's history, and he's come to the conclusion that the trouble started when Lily Falconer died. She was part of every decision the firm made, including the performance assessments of the lawyers. Lily's death was a tragedy on a personal level, but it also left a hole in the management structure of

Falconer Shreve that was never really filled. Blake was in no shape to take on additional responsibilities; Kevin was in Calgary; Zack had just met you and decided to be a family man, so he couldn't give more. Anyway, for a variety of reasons, none of the other partners was in a position to manage the firm, and Delia picked up the baton."

"When she was still reeling from Chris's death," I said.

"Delia got by fine as long as Zack and Norine MacDonald were around," Margot said. Norine was Zack's smart and indefatigable executive assistant. She had been with him since the day Falconer Shreve opened its doors, and she was a pillar of support for him and for the firm.

As she spoke of Norine's contribution, Margot's eyes shone. She had always been a great fan of Zack's EA. "When it came to hiring new lawyers, Norine knew what the firm needed, and she made certain we got it," Margot said. "And, of course, Zack has always been the firm's papa bear. The other partners have always looked to him for the final word about which associates got a partnership offer and which got the boot."

"And then Zack and Norine went to City Hall," I said.

"Yes, at exactly the time Falconer Shreve reached the point where it needed to grow," Margot said. "Lorne Callow has been invaluable, but he's being stretched too far, and he works for Delia. He's not going to tell her that her refusal to accept new equity partners is going to strangle the firm."

"But somebody *is* going to have to make the case," I said. "Zack told me that he's hired a lawyer named Katina Posaluko-Chapman to lead the Calgary office and that she'll be an equity partner."

"We're lucky to get Tina," Margot said. "She's a fine lawyer, and the timing is right. Her appointment will force us to deal with the equity partner issue." Margot tapped the folder she held on her lap. "Jo, Brock has some excellent ideas about how to handle that problem and get the firm on sound footing again."

"And you want Falconer Shreve to hire Brock to implement those ideas," I said.

Margot grinned. "No flies on you," she said.

"You built a solid case," I said. "The firm clearly needs someone to take charge, and Brock is an ideal candidate. But bringing him in while you're dealing with the equity partner issue might be problematic. Delia will already be in a defensive position. She might not be open to an outsider running the firm, especially one who's not a lawyer."

"Ah, but lawyers love precedent," Margot said. "And we have precedent on our side. Falconer Shreve is not the only law firm lacking a partner with management skills and the yen to put them to work. A number of firms are bringing in non-lawyers to handle their business practices. It makes sense. Someone with Delia's legal talent shouldn't be frittering away her time doing work for which she has neither the aptitude nor the interest. As a lawyer Delia can bring in the big bucks, and that's what she should be doing."

"You certainly have logic on your side," I said. "But Delia has a huge emotional investment in the firm the way it is."

"All the more reason for her to realize that Falconer Shreve needs what Brock has to offer. He has an MBA from Queen's and he has experience. When Zack convinced him to spearhead the campaign to get the Racette-Hunter Centre built, Brock was a rising star in an investment management firm that handles more than a billion dollars a year. He's doing a terrific job as director of the R-H Centre and in his work as a city councillor, and he's recognized as an expert on analytical decision-making, change management, organizational behaviour, and strategic leadership. He's conducted seminars for companies all over Western Canada."

"And Brock's interested in making the move?" I said.

"He's always up for a challenge," Margot said. "And God knows streamlining Falconer Shreve will be a challenge. Brock's had conversations with Kerry Benjoe about taking over as director of Racette-Hunter. She's been shadowing Brock for more than a year, and he's confident she could take over now." Margot's pause was pointed. "Of course, all this is contingent upon the partners agreeing to my proposal."

"Delia has a trial in Saskatoon. She'll be away for a week," I said. "That gives you a week to sound out the other partners, but I don't think you'll have any problems there. Both Blake and Kevin have compelling personal reasons for being on board, and Zack's aware of the situation, and he knows how capable Brock is."

"So that just leaves Delia," Margot said. "Wish me luck." She handed me the folder, took the plush toy from me and eyed its tail critically. "I declare this tail Max-proof." After she'd knotted and snipped the thread, Margot looked into the face of the wild thing. "Go in peace, Moishe," she said.

"Lexi calls her stuffy Moishe?" I said.

Margot shrugged. "That's the name he came with. Moishe's comrades in wildness are Sipi, Zippi, and Bernard. They're scary-looking but kind. They want Max to stay forever." Margot's smile was impish. "Maybe restructuring will make Falconer Shreve as welcoming to outsiders as the land of the wild things."

CHAPTER

5

The rainy weather had cleared and it was turning out to be a gorgeous day – not quite the day Keats had in mind when he wrote of the "season of mists and mellow fruitfulness" but close enough. After Thanksgiving in our part of the world, mild, still days are few and far between. Halloween was more than two weeks away, but there had been many times when the kids and I had trick-or-treated in full winter gear, and many more times when I had put up Christmas lights with biting northern winds shaking my ladder. I recognized a window of opportunity when I saw it, so after getting back from Margot's I hauled the boxes of outdoor lights and the ladder out of the garage.

I'd strung about half the lights when Gracie Falconer cycled up on her Trek WSD. She'd been riding hard. Her red-gold braids were coming undone; her freckled face was rosy with exertion; and her smile was a mile wide.

"I can feel the endorphins from here," I said.

"It's a sensational day," she said. "What are you up to?"

I pointed to the house. The east side was ready to sparkle, but a long string of lights hung forlornly from the roof over the porch. "Getting into the Christmas spirit," I said.

"Good for you," she said. "For the past few years I've been putting up our lights and I always leave it too late. Need a hand?"

"I do, and I'll throw in lunch."

Gracie jumped off her bike, walked it into the backyard, and when she returned, she picked up the string of lights. "Let's go," she said. "I've got a lab at two. Takes me half an hour to ride from here to the university. That gives us two hours." She squinted at the house. "Easy-peasy. We'll be done in an hour, plenty of time for lunch."

We finished fifteen minutes early. Gracie flicked on the lights to test them and then took selfies of us with them to send to her dad and to Zack. Mission accomplished, we went inside for tuna sandwiches and iced tea.

Gracie inhaled her sandwiches and made more. "I'm starving," she said. "I went to Standing Buffalo last night and had Thanksgiving dinner with Rose and her family. Rose and I drove in this morning, but breakfast was hours ago."

Rose Lavallee had been Gracie's full-time nanny from the time she was born. At eighteen, Gracie was too old for a nanny, but Rose had been a constant in her life, wheeling her pram through the park twice a day until Gracie was able to toddle along beside her; walking her to kindergarten; baking the cookies for the school bake sales; teaching her to swim; and, perhaps most critically, making certain that Gracie grew up knowing she was part of Standing Buffalo Dakota First Nation.

Standing Buffalo was just across the lake from Lawyers' Bay, so when the Falconers were at the cottage, Gracie spent as much time with Rose on the reserve as she did with her parents. She was fluent in the Dakota language and was an accomplished jingle dancer who always placed in the top three at the powwow jingle dance event.

I refilled Gracie's milk glass. "How was Thanksgiving at Standing Buffalo?" I said.

"Except for the fact that somebody made gluten-free bannock, it was the same as it always is. We ate in the band hall. There were a hundred little kids. My aunties kept rearranging the pies on the dessert table to make sure theirs were in front. And Rose and her sister squabbled over whose wild-rice dressing was the tastiest."

"Sounds like a lot of fun," I said.

"It was." Gracie hesitated before she continued. "I told Rose about our families' plans to gather for our Day of the Dead." Gracie's face clouded.

"Rose didn't approve?"

"No. She doesn't like the idea. She's Catholic. She made sure I was baptized when I was a baby, and we still go to mass together every Sunday. But our people have had first-hand experience with cultural appropriation. It's hurtful when outsiders use stories and ceremonies that have meaning for us without understanding them. And Rose thinks we might be meddling with things we don't really know about in order to bring the spirits close."

"Is that a concern for you?" I said.

Gracie's gaze was steady. "I was raised in both worlds: white culture and Dakota ways. I value them both. If I have something straightforward like a cut that needs stitches, I go to the Medi-Centre. If I have something more complicated, like that rash I broke out in when I was in grade ten, I go to Standing Buffalo and visit Elder Bea." Gracie scowled. "That rash was so gross."

"It was," I said. "Except for your face and hands, it was all over your body. Not a great thing for a fifteen-year-old."

"Dad and I went to every specialist in the city," Gracie said. "He was just about to fly me to the Mayo Clinic when Rose took me out to Standing Buffalo to see Elder Bea. She took us to a ditch where some little white medicine flowers were growing. We picked a bagful and then went back to Bea's house, chewed the flowers until they were paste, then rubbed the paste all over my body. The taste of those flowers was unbelievably disgusting, but the rash was gone the next day."

"That's amazing," I said.

Gracie's voice was matter-of-fact. "Not to me," she said. "I believe in the Catholic saints, but I also believe in the sacred pipe. Elder Bea follows the good path. She has the power to use medicine that heals. But there are people who use their power to do harm. I've seen it."

"I've heard about bad medicine, but I've never heard about anyone actually witnessing it."

"We don't usually talk about it," Gracie said. "But it exists. When I was in high school, a young girl on the reserve was raped. The boy who did it was older, so handsome he'd done TV ads for the local stations. Everybody had been sure he was destined for great things. When the girl told her grandfather what the boy had done, the grandfather, who was a medicine man, paid the boy a visit. The boy said that with his looks he could have any girl he wanted and there was no way he'd screw a runt like the old man's grand-daughter. The next morning the boy woke up with his face twisted like an old Halloween pumpkin."

"Bad medicine?"

"For the boy maybe," Gracie said. "But for the girls who were saved because the boy's face showed them what he was like inside, it was good medicine. Rose says you can't always know ahead of time what powerful medicine will do."

"And Rose is concerned that by taking part in the Día de los Muertos you and your dad might make yourselves vulnerable."

Gracie finished her milk, carried her dishes to the sink, and rinsed them. "There's an old man at Standing Buffalo who hates white people," she said. "His name is Esau Pilger. He loved my grandmother, but she chose to marry someone else. And then her daughter, my mother, married a white man. Even worse, my dad is a white man with a home at Lawyers' Bay. Esau Pilger hates the way our families changed the land around the lake – clearing away the brush, bringing in bulldozers to make roads and construction equipment to build the big houses. He hates the powerboats on the lake and the fact that Lawyers' Bay is a gated community."

Gracie fell silent. She raised her strong, long-fingered hands to her temples and rotated her fingertips in slow circles. "Some people say that when my grandmother married Henry Redman, Esau put a curse on her. If he did, the curse was powerful. A white doctor fell in love with my grandmother, and then went crazy. He killed Henry and then he killed himself. My grandmother and my mother were in the room when he did it." Gracie shuddered at the image. "Some people say that when my parents got married, Esau put a curse on my mother so that she would always do something to destroy her own happiness," she said. "Of course, that's exactly what my mother did. Nothing she accomplished was ever enough. More than anything she wanted people to respect her, and when they finally did she began acting out so she could destroy their respect." Gracie shook her head as if to clear it. "I never understood her." She leaned across the table towards me. "Did you?"

"Lily and I never had an intimate conversation," I said. "I only knew her for a few weeks before she died."

Gracie's shoulders slumped. "That's too bad," she said, and the defeat in her voice saddened me. I racked my brain for something – anything – I could offer that would ease her burden.

Out of nowhere, a talk I'd had with Rose Lavallee came into my mind. Lily Falconer's penchant for casual sexual liaisons had been common knowledge, but believing that Lily's behaviour was her family's concern, I kept my thoughts to myself. My decision to stay on the sidelines ended not long into the short period during which I knew Lily, a day Gracie came to our house in tears. She said that Lily had returned after spending a week with the man who delivered water for the office's water coolers. Lily told her daughter she'd come back because she had nowhere else to go. Gracie's hurt and confusion had touched something deep within me. I was livid. I'd gone to Rose and asked her why Lily was determined to destroy everything she had. Rose often answered a question with a story that contained the answer, so I wasn't surprised when, in response to my concerns, she recounted a Greek myth that she'd studied in school.

That October day, as I looked across the table at Lily's daughter and the lines that pain had etched on her face, I hoped Rose's insight would enlighten Gracie as it had me. "Did Rose ever tell you the story of Penelope?" I said.

The tension drained from Gracie's face. "Rose told me that story a hundred times when I was growing up. It was comforting – like the spice cookies she always made when Lily took off. I still remember it." She smiled wistfully. "Penelope's husband didn't come back from the Trojan Wars. Many men wanted to marry her, but she was determined to remain faithful to her husband. Penelope promised the men that as soon as she finished weaving a shroud, she'd marry one of them. But Penelope believed her fate was to be with her husband, so every night she ripped out her weaving so she wouldn't have to marry another man." Gracie's expression hardened. "I never quite got the connection between faithful Penelope and my mother."

"Rose saw a connection," I said. "Your mother didn't believe that she deserved a good life, so when things were going well for her, she unravelled them by running off with other men."

For a minute or two Gracie was silent, deep in her own thoughts. "My mother, like Penelope, took steps to make sure she got the fate she thought she deserved," Gracie said. She swallowed hard. "I just wish I knew why she believed she didn't deserve a good life."

"Being in the room when the doctor killed her father and then himself must have been traumatic for your mother," I said. "And the suffering continued. Rose told me that Gloria Ryder blamed herself and spent the rest of her life trying to atone for what had happened."

Gracie was clearly exasperated. "But why did my grandmother punish herself for a crime that a seriously disturbed man committed against her family? Rose told me that she was a fine woman, smart and kind and very proud of being a nurse. What happened wasn't her fault. Why did she let it destroy her life? Jo, you might not be convinced of the existence of bad medicine, but sometimes it's hard not to believe in it, especially when I look at my grandmother's life and my mother's."

"So you believe the people who say that Esau Pilger put some kind of curse on them?" I said.

Gracie's eyes were troubled. "They say he has the power."

"What's he like?"

"He's old, shrivelled, and mean – just mean to people, though. He takes in any animal that's hurt or hungry. His hair is white and he wears it long in the traditional way. He's a chain-smoker, and his skin is the colour of tobacco."

I felt a chill. "I saw him last summer in the Lake View Cemetery," I said. "I'd taken some flowers over for your mother's grave and Alex Kequahtooway's. I knelt down to say a prayer, and suddenly I knew I wasn't alone. I turned and saw a man behind me. When I started to stand up, he spat at me."

"What did you do?"

"Nothing. He was an old man, and you and I both know how shamefully the Dakota people were treated by the white settlers."

Gracie was bemused. "So you didn't do anything. You just took one for the team." She shook her head as if to clear away her confusion. "I guess that's what I'm going to have to do for our gathering."

"What do you mean?"

"Rose's concerns really got to me, Jo. But I spoke to Izzie this morning, and she sounded so hopeful. She'd just gotten off the phone with Abby's life partner. Nadine Perrault told Izzie about Abby's favourite music, the books she'd read, and the art she cared about. Isobel is convinced that sharing what she's learned about Abby and talking openly about Chris is going to help her family.

"So there's my dilemma. I'd rather walk on broken glass than make Rose worry, but my best friend needs my support." Gracie shrugged her shoulders in a gesture of helplessness. "So what do I do?"

"Beats me," I said.

Gracie was deadpan. "I knew I could count on you for wise counsel," she said, and we both laughed.

I walked to the backyard with Gracie and we stayed together as she wheeled her Trek WSD to the street. Before she mounted her bike, Gracie looked at me thoughtfully. "Our relationship is different now, isn't it? We're not just Taylor's mum and her BFF."

"We're still that," I said. "But now we're also Gracie and Joanne, two women who are fortunate enough to be friends."

The landline was ringing when I went back inside. It was Head to Toe with a reminder that I had booked a hair appointment and a mani-pedi for 1:30 p.m. and it was now

1:30 p.m. As Chantelle attacked my roots and began talking
about the Latino heartthrob teaching the tango class she
was taking, I felt myself relax. Nothing banished the spec-
tres of imploding law firms and bad medicine like two hours
held in the warm womb of female culture.

When I returned home, Zack was in the kitchen with a
bottle of Corona, an open tin of bean dip, a bag of Fritos, and
Margot's presentation folder on the table in front of him.

"Hey, you're home," I said. "This is a nice surprise."

"I'm rewarding myself," Zack said. "I worked through
lunch, took care of everything that needed taking care of, and
realized I was hungry and I missed you, so here I am." Zack
gave me an approving look. "Incidentally, you look great."

"Thank you. Chantelle worked her magic." I opened a
Corona and pulled up a chair across from Zack. "So I take it
you've read Margot's report," I said.

"I have," he said. "And it's a solid piece of work. Margot's
argument is cogent, persuasive, and absolutely bulletproof.
She enclosed a note telling me that Brock and she had
worked on the proposal together and that if the partners
agree, he'll join Falconer Shreve to manage the firm."

"And you're all right with that?"

"I'm more than all right with it. I called Margot and
told her full steam ahead. She's going to talk to Blake and
Kevin tomorrow, and I'm on deck with Delia as soon as
she gets back from Saskatoon." Before I could say anything, Zack had raised his hand in protest. "I know I
promised I'd let it all go, Jo, but Margot convinced me
that this is the best approach. Dee's proud. It will be easier
for her if the idea comes from me, and I promise, I won't
leave Delia's office until she agrees – at least in substance
– to the changes Margot proposes. When that happens, I'll
back away."

"I'm sure Margot was relieved to hear you'll help."

"She was." Zack took a handful of Fritos and then pushed the chip bag and the bean dip towards me. "By the way, Margot made some recommendations about personnel. Maisie is on the very short list of lawyers Margot has on her slate of potential equity partners."

"Do you think that will happen?"

"Absolutely. Maisie is a terrific trial lawyer. She's smart, and she's combative and tenacious. Watching her tear a witness apart is a joy to behold."

"Sounds like fun for the whole family," I said. "We should take our new grandsons down to watch their mum in action."

"You're mocking me, but as soon as they're old enough, I *will* take Colin and Charlie to see Maisie in court. Never too soon for them to learn that the law is a kickass profession."

"That's what Angus always says. Did he have a place on Margot's list?"

Zack lowered his eyes. "He's a second-year associate, Jo. He's exactly where he should be."

"When it comes time to decide whether to cut him loose or let him make partner, what are you going to do?"

Zack smiled. "He's our son. He won't be cut loose."

"But he's not really good enough to make partner," I said.

"He will be," Zack said. "He and I just have to figure out the right path for him."

"He's always dreamed of trial law."

"Sometimes people have to find different dreams," Zack said. "My dream was to be a major league baseball player. That didn't work out, so I became a lawyer."

I reached across the table and stroked my husband's hand. "And the law's been a good fit for you."

"It has. The moment I wheeled into a courtroom, I knew I was where I belonged. Angus is a good lawyer, but in my opinion he's pursuing the wrong branch of law. He and I have talked about this. I've seen him in court. He doesn't have the temperament to be a trial lawyer."

"Is Angus okay with the idea that he may have to change direction?"

"He is because he knows a change of direction will be no reflection on him. Good trial lawyers will do whatever it takes to get the outcome they want, and when they fail, it's a body blow. There've been times after I lost a case when I barely made it to the men's room before I threw up."

"And Angus doesn't care enough about winning."

"He cares, but he's a nice guy, and nice lawyers lose cases because they get squeamish about delivering the knockout punch. Instead of going in for the kill, they back off. If you want to see what I'm talking about, go watch Maisie. When it's time to nail her case, she never hesitates. She moves in close and pounds away until she's got her opponent on the ropes. That's why Maisie's on Margot's list."

"So what's going to happen with Angus?"

Zack took my hand. "Kevin and Angus and I are going to sit down together during the holidays and figure out how to get our son where he wants to go. Jo, Angus is twenty-five years old. He has all the time in the world."

Most nights before we turned in, Zack and I shared a mutual massage. We had busy lives and we both looked forward to the chance to simply relax and talk. But I had my own reason to press for the nightly ritual. Zack was prickly when he felt that I was overly attentive to his health, but the massage gave me a chance to watch for changes in the skin on the areas of his body that rested against his wheelchair sixteen hours a day. In addition to compromising the workings of the internal organs and the blood's ability to flow without clotting, paraplegia interferes with the skin's ability to heal. Zack was vulnerable to pressure ulcers that, if left unchecked, could be life-threatening. The massage gave me a chance to spot a pressure ulcer at an early stage so Zack could get medical attention before the condition became a problem. That night, there were no reddened areas on his skin, and I was able to exhale.

"Your turn now," Zack said. "Unbutton that pyjama top."

"With pleasure," I said.

Zack and I always tried to pack up our troubles and bring light hearts to the time we spent together before we slipped into bed and turned out the lights. But the body does not lie, and as soon as Zack began massaging my shoulders he felt my tension.

"Your muscles are a little tight," he said. "Problems?"

"Nothing major, but after Gracie and I put up the Christmas lights, she came in for lunch and we had a long talk about the wisdom of getting together on Halloween," I said. "She's torn, Zack. Rose is uneasy about the whole idea. So is Gracie, but Isobel is counting on the evening to bring her family together, and you saw at the lake how worried Gracie is about Blake." I breathed deeply as Zack's fingers began to work down my spine.

"Better?" he said finally.

"Much," I said. "What do you think?"

"Well, something has to be done," he said. "I'm just not certain that this particular get-together is the answer. When we made decisions about Racette-Hunter we consulted every step of the way with Ernest Beauvais and the other elders. You know how adamant Ernest was about us understanding and respecting First Nations customs and traditions before we did anything. I don't know much about Día de los Muertos, but I know it has real spiritual significance for the people who celebrate it."

"That's exactly what Taylor's exploring with her art project," I said. "She's showing how the sugar skulls, marigold garlands, paper skeletons of *Catrinas*, *calaveras*, and all the rest help the living remember their loved ones."

Zack frowned. "But Gracie, Isobel, and Taylor aren't planning to use decorations for our gathering, are they?"

"No, the Day of the Dead decorations are strictly for Taylor's art project. The project was the impetus for the evening the young women are planning, but I think their ideas have evolved. They were drawn to the Day of the Dead celebration because it offered a way of bringing those they had lost back into their lives. It was something Gracie and Isobel needed. Taylor understood that need, and she supported them. Gracie and Isobel have sacrificed a lot to keep their families together. That day at the lake, the idea seemed pretty straightforward. Now there are complications. Rose is worried that meddling with customs and beliefs we don't understand will make us vulnerable. You're concerned that we're cherry-picking what we need from Día de los Muertos without giving serious thought to the belief system behind it. I still think we owe it to the young women to do what we can to help, but I'm concerned about the outcome."

"So am I," Zack said. "Jo, there's so much history, and there's been so much heartache and loss. I wonder if it's possible to resolve all of that in a single night."

"Maybe not, but it will be a beginning." As Zack slid his knuckles down either side of my spine, I exhaled with pleasure.

"Is that helping?" he said.

"It is," I said. "And it's easier to be rational when my muscles are unknotted. Zack, maybe we've been worrying too much about this. The girls aren't expecting any miracles. They just want to open some doors they feel have been closed too long."

CHAPTER

6

On Friday, October 23, I awoke to the first snowfall of the season. Smug about already having our Christmas lights in place, I went to the front door and flicked the switch. The snow was the kind that falls in the romantic movies of the forties – fat, theatrical flakes that float slowly through the air and land on the heroine's long lashes and the hero's broad shoulders. For years, my idea of outdoor holiday lighting had been minimalist: all white bulbs, hung sparingly in select locations. Zack favoured a lavish display of coloured bulbs. I had agreed to his preference reluctantly, but as the lights flashed, pointillist daubs of red, green, blue, and gold against the darkness and the drifting snow, I applauded his choice.

Decades earlier, the city had built levees on both sides of the creek that runs behind our house and planted them with indigenous bushes to protect homeowners from floods during spring runoff. Two days after I put up the Christmas lights, we had had our first hard frost. Since then, the levee's banks had been dun-coloured and soggy with dead leaves. Now a blanket of new snow covered the decaying foliage and revealed the stark beauty of the bushes' bare branches. By March, like everyone else, I would be weary of trudging and shovelling, but on that October morning as I looked out at the fresh, radiant world I felt the familiar thrill that comes with the arrival of the first snow.

Pantera and Esme had joined me at the patio doors. This would be our first snow excursion since we'd moved back to the old house and they were as eager as I was to get going. When it came to running on the snow-covered bike path that hugged the creek, our mastiff was a veteran. He had been abandoned by his very young owners at our son Peter's veterinary clinic because, in their words, Pantera had "stopped being cute and started getting big." For Zack and Pantera it had been love at first sight, and when Zack and I married, Pantera was a sweet part of the package. Esme was a recent addition. We had taken her home with us the previous spring after Lee Crawford, Maisie's twin, died tragically. My own bouvier had died of old age the winter before, so Esme and I needed each other.

That morning the snow and the solitude seemed to calm the dogs. They trotted along without straining at their leashes, freeing my mind to roam and remember. My life, the life of my late husband, Ian, and those of my children had been inextricably linked to Wascana Creek. In every season, the creek was an oasis of peace and beauty. When, as babies, my children were teething or just plain ornery, I had pushed their carriage along the levee to soothe them. Later, when they were toddlers exploding with energy and curiosity, I let them run along the banks with treasure bags collecting whatever caught their eye. Together, my children and I had skated on the creek's ice, snapped photos of visiting pelicans and cormorants, and tobogganed down the creek's banks. When Ian came home after a day of heated debate at the legislature, too filled with frustration and

Scotch to sleep, we had walked along the creek together until his mind was calm and his body could rest. After Ian's death I wandered along the creek for hours trying desperately to block painful memories and unanswerable questions.

As soon as Zack and I had agreed to marry, he scoured the real estate listings to come up with information on the houses he thought Taylor and I might like. When I saw that the first house on Zack's list backed on to the creek, I knew it was kismet. And so our life together as a family began in the neighbourhood where, for the first time in my life, I had found a real home.

Zack and I had a quiet wedding; it was simply part of the normal 10:30 Holy Eucharist at the cathedral. The reception was at our new home, and as a wedding/housewarming gift my old friend Peggy Kreviazuk brought a framed needle-point of Edith Sitwell's words about the comforts of good food, good talk, and good friends in winter. I'd hung the needlepoint next to the bookcase where I kept cookbooks, and when the dogs and I, cold from our run, stepped into the warmth of our kitchen I felt the truth of Sitwell's reflection that winter was the time for home.

Breakfast is Zack's specialty and that morning the coffee was made, the juice was poured, the porridge was bubbling, and the rye bread was in the toaster. Taylor still had an hour to sleep, so after I fed the dogs, Zack and I sat at our kitchen table, eating and looking out at the creek. When he finished his breakfast, Zack stretched lazily. "This is so nice," he said. "I'm tired of playing whack-a-mole, Jo. Just when the city's business is finally humming along, these brushfires break out at the firm."

"But your conversation yesterday morning with Delia went well," I said.

"She was tired from the Saskatoon trial, but she's optimistic about the outcome, so she was in a receptive mood.

I'd asked Norine to incorporate the suggestions Blake, Kevin, and I had into Margot's draft for the restructuring, and Norine merged our lists of possible candidates for equity partnership with Margot's so Dee could get the full picture. She said she'd study it and let me know if she had any questions. Last night after you went to bed, Noah came by with Delia's handwritten comments on the list of candidates."

"Anything major?"

"There was one person who the rest of us felt was worth looking at who didn't meet Delia's approval, and she added the name of a possibility that we hadn't suggested but is certainly fine." Zack smiled. "And you'll be happy to hear that all of us put forth Maisie's name."

"I am happy."

"Good. Anyway, we obviously want this to be kept confidential so Norine's going to draft the letters to the six people, including Katina in Calgary, to whom we're offering equity partnerships. We'll courier the letters next week and we'll make the official announcement on November 2nd."

"There'll be some disgruntled lawyers in the halls of Falconer Shreve," I said.

"This is just round one," Zack said. "According to Margot's plan, if they didn't make it this time, they'll have another chance, but that's all in the future. What's up for you today?"

"It's a teacher in-service at St. Pius X, so Madeleine and Lena don't have school. I'm going to take them to Value Village to scout out Halloween costume possibilities. Then we're going to swing by Margot's to pick up baby clothes that Margot's kids have outgrown. Then we're going to drive out to the farm to drop off the clothes and see Maisie, Peter, and the twins."

"Sounds like a great morning."

"I'll send pictures," I said. "And don't forget, we have the benefit at the Scarth Club tonight."

Zack groaned. "When all I want is a night with you."

"Since you're the guest of honour, I guess we can't duck out early," I said. "But tomorrow's Saturday and you don't leave for Toronto until the afternoon. After I take the dogs for their run, I'll jump back into bed with you. All you have to do is make sure there's a warm place for me."

As always, Value Village did not disappoint. Within ten minutes the girls had their costumes: matching black-and-white striped shirts, black watch caps, and hemp gunnysacks with drawstrings. Perfect getups for cartoon bank robbers, and the price was right: $12.75 for everything. As soon as we were back in the car, the girls pulled out their haul.

"We can print the word LOOT on the sacks in big letters, so people know we're not real robbers," Lena said.

Madeleine rolled her eyes. "We're kids. It's Halloween. People will get that these are costumes."

Lena appealed to me. "Mimi, what do you think? Should we write LOOT on the bags, just to be safe?"

"I don't think you *need* to, but I'll bet if you write LOOT on your bags, people will give you more candy."

"I'm writing LOOT on my bag," Lena said.

"This is a really stupid conversation," Madeleine said, and the discussion ended.

When we pulled up in front of the condo on Halifax Street, I called to tell Margot we were on our way up but wouldn't be staying. She met the girls and me at the elevator with a dolly piled with boxes of baby clothes and four Halloween gift bags on top.

"Where are Lexi and Kai?" Lena asked.

"Having a nap," Margot said. "Brock's with them." She gave the girls a hug and handed them each a bag. "Kai and

Lexi wanted you to have these and give the other ones to your new cousins. You can open the ones with your names on them."

Madeleine and Lena said "thanks" in unison and then dug in. Each bag held a black sequined eye mask and a *Rocky Horror Picture Show* jigsaw puzzle.

"The masks are great for our costumes," Lena said. "Madeleine and I are going trick-or-treating as bank robbers."

"Mum says we're too young for *The Rocky Horror Picture Show* movie," Madeleine said. "But she likes us to do puzzles because they develop our problem-solving ability, so she'll be okay with these."

"That's a relief," Margot said. "Now would you mind vamoosing for a few minutes, so your Mimi and I can talk?"

Margot smiled as she watched the girls sprint towards the couch at the end of the hall. When she turned back to me, her smile had vanished. "Jo, I need to talk to you about the equity partners' decisions. I'm sure Zack told you that the vote for Maisie was unanimous."

"He did, and he also said the partners were all pretty well in accord on the other votes."

"We were, but there's one decision that troubles me. Did Zack mention anything about Emmett Keating?"

"No, Zack's always discreet about anything to do with the firm."

"Well, I'm about to be indiscreet," Margot said. "Emmett was on all our lists but Delia blackballed him. She didn't offer an explanation, just a notation beside his name: 'Not FS equity partner material' and her initials."

"None of the other partners questioned it?"

"No, and I didn't question it either. Delia has been accommodating about the other changes we'd proposed. I guess none of us wanted to rock the boat." Margot frowned. "But there was a whiff of elitism in Delia's comment about Emmett Keating that I found offensive."

"I understand that," I said. "I always find the 'them and us' mentality grating."

"Have you met Emmett?"

"I don't think so."

Margot raised an eyebrow. "I'll take that as a 'no.' If you'd met Emmett, you'd remember. He's a whiz of a tax lawyer but definitely an odd duck. One of those nonstop talkers that makes you feel as if you're being fire-hosed."

I laughed. "I'll try to stay clear of him."

"Very wise," Margot said. "The day I became a Falconer Shreve partner, Emmett cornered me in my office and spent seven solid minutes telling me about myself. I don't know where he got the information – the legal stuff was public, but he had personal details that he'd have had to dig for. It weirded me out, so I told Zack. He said that Emmett is uncomfortable if he doesn't have a head full of facts when he's confronted with a new situation."

"A seven-minute fire-hosing *is* extreme," I said, "but the impulse behind it makes sense. I always like to have at least some background information to bring to a new situation."

Margot nodded. "So do I, but, Jo, Emmett Keating *is* eccentric. That said, he seldom comes into contact with clients, but when he does, all the information he's committed to memory is exactly what they want to know. The restructuring isn't about personalities, though, it's about process. Emmett has put in the time and God knows he's brought in the money. He deserves to be an equity partner. Delia's dismissal of him without citing cause is unfair, and I'm going to challenge her."

"Do it," I said.

Margot flashed me a quick smile. "I knew you'd say that, but I'm going to speak with Zack first. If he thinks opening the Keating decision will make Delia walk away from the restructuring plan, I'll back down. The letters of offer won't be sent out till next week, so we have plenty of time to think this through."

Few sights are lovelier than a farm after the first real snowfall. Pete and Maisie's driveway was ploughed, but the branches of the trees were heavy with snow, and as far as the eye could see the fields were white. Pete and their dog, Rowdy, came out to welcome us. The girls gave Rowdy and Pete a quick greeting and sped towards the house to see the main attraction: their almost-one-month-old cousins, Charlie and Colin. Pete watched them and sighed. "Not long ago Madeleine and Lena thought I was cool."

I reached down to scratch Rowdy between the ears. "We've all been demoted since the twins arrived," I said. "How's it going?"

"I can't stop smiling. The boys seem to like us. Maisie has plenty of milk. She feeds Charlie and Colin at the same time, which absolutely blows me away. The boys don't sleep through the night but they sleep for a few hours at a stretch. Once in a while, the stretches coincide and we all sleep. Truthfully, whether they're awake or asleep, I just love watching them."

"And Maisie's enjoying being a parent?"

"She is, but it's harder for her," Pete said. "Maisie loves the boys as much as I do, but she misses Lee. I always knew Maisie and her sister were close, but I didn't understand how powerful the bond between identical twins is until we had Charlie and Colin. I don't know how to explain it except to say it seems there's never a second when the boys aren't aware of each other. For thirty-three years Lee and Maisie shared that connection, and now Maisie is having all these incredible experiences and Lee's not here to be part of them."

"You're here."

"I'm here, and that part is good for both of us. Maisie and I talk about everything. For me, one of the great things about farming is that we're truly partners, talking things through, making decisions together. This is the life I've always dreamed of."

I looked into my son's eyes – they were the same intense green as my own. I'd always known when Peter was holding something back. "But this wasn't Maisie's dream," I said.

"No. Our decision to carry on Lee's work with the heritage animals and crops felt right to us both at the time, but now I'm wondering if we acted too quickly. Maisie hasn't lived out here since she started university, and she loves the law."

"Has Maisie said she's unhappy?"

"No, but she wouldn't. She's played lacrosse for years, and she believes in playing through pain." Peter shook his head as if to clear away the thought. "I'm probably over-thinking this."

"Pete, give yourselves some time. You'll work this out. You've had an incredibly difficult year, but you're together. You love your boys. You're all healthy. In the meantime, the renovations you've made on the house are beautiful. Maisie's told me many times that her childhood here was idyllic, and this really is a great place to raise a family."

Pete gave me a one-armed hug. "Thanks for the shot of perspective," he said.

"Anytime," I said.

The farmhouse in which the Crawford Kilbourn family now lived had been built shortly before the First World War. It had been maintained meticulously but never altered, so the house Maisie and her twin sister, Lee, grew up in was solid but, in the manner of that earlier time, starchily proper.

The renovations Maisie and Peter made had humanized
the old place. The main floor was now fully accessible and
the kitchen, family room, and bedrooms were spacious
and bright. The walls of Colin and Charlie's nursery were
painted a warm, lemony yellow. Maisie had asked Taylor to
make paintings of the heritage birds that Lee had raised,
and the paintings were hung where Colin and Charlie could
see them from their cribs. The boys would never know their
aunt, but they would come to know the exotic beauty of
the Blue Andalusians, scarlet-combed Langshans, Swedish
Flower hens, Ridley Bronze turkeys, and pink-billed
Aylesbury ducks that she loved.

When Pete and I entered the house, we found Madeleine
and Lena in the nursery, watching wide-eyed as Maisie breast-
fed both babies on a nursing cushion designed for twins. It was
a process that called for quick, sure hands and an impeccable
sense of timing. As a weekend athlete, Maisie was accustomed
to making the right moves, and she and her sons were the
picture of contentment. Maisie's face lit with pleasure when
she saw us. "I was just telling Madeleine and Lena, I'm surrounded by men, and it's nice to have some women around."

I kissed my daughter-in-law and her sons on the forehead
and stood back so I could get a better view of Colin and
Charlie. Like their mother, the twins were long-limbed and
had springy copper curls. Mother and sons were a compelling trio. I caught Maisie's eye. "Pete told me he could watch
the three of you for hours," I said.

Maisie laughed. "I believe that's in the paternal job
description." She glanced at Pete. "And I'm pretty sure the
job description for uncles includes taking nieces for horse-
back rides when they come to visit."

Pete turned to the girls. "Interested?"

Madeleine and Lena were careful to keep their voices low,
but their eyes were pleading. "Mimi?"

"Wear your helmets, and listen to your uncle," I said. The girls were gone before I could add to the list of cautions.

"They love it out here," I said.

"There's a lot to love," Maisie said. "Animals. Freedom. Peace. Quiet." She looked down at the babies in her arms. "Cousins who have fallen asleep."

"I believe that's my cue," I said. I carried first Colin and then Charlie to his crib. The weight of a new baby in my arms was sweet, and I didn't rush. Unencumbered, Maisie stood and stretched her arms above her head. My daughter-in-law was close to six feet tall and her stomach was once again flat as a washboard.

"You're amazing," I said. "No one would ever know you had two babies a month ago."

Maisie grimaced. "I'd know," she said.

"Feeling less great than you look?"

"Physically I'm fine, just a little weepy."

"You're entitled," I said. "There's a lot going on in your life."

"There is," Maisie agreed. "Roiling hormones, aching for Lee, and, as of this morning, another complication." She went to the chest of drawers, picked up an envelope, and handed it to me. It had a Falconer Shreve logo on it, and in it was a photocopied list of names.

Delia's handwriting was distinctive: very small with letters so neatly formed they were almost like print. Beside each name, she had jotted brief notes indicating an acceptance or a rejection, with a note about why and when to reconsider. However, for one name on the list, there would be no reconsideration at a later date. Beside Emmett Keating's name, Delia's curt note was underlined twice: "Not FS equity partner material."

As I read through the list and Delia's comments, my breath caught. "Where did this come from?" I said.

"It was hand-delivered to my mailbox," Maisie said. "As you can see, the sender used a Falconer Shreve envelope, but there's no stamp."

"Do you know of anyone else who received a copy of the list?"

Maisie shook her head. "No. Logic would suggest that it was delivered to some of or all the people whose names appear on it, but I didn't want to exacerbate the situation by calling around."

"That was wise. Whoever gave you this wanted to make trouble. No use helping them. Now, let's not let them ruin our day. I come bearing gifts." I took the brightly wrapped presents Margot had sent for the twins from my tote bag and handed them to Maisie. "My car is filled with boxes of baby clothes that Kai and Lexi have outgrown, but Margot wanted to give you something that was just for your boys."

As she looked at the tiny costumes her sons would wear for their first Halloween, Maisie's expression was wistful. The outfits were practical – footed fleece sleepers with the left side of the sleeper orange and the right side black. There were also matching orange toques with green pompom stems. "Lee and I never dressed alike," Maisie said quietly, "but at Halloween we always wore identical costumes. We had a lot of fun."

In a gesture that seemed to have become characteristic, Maisie squared her shoulders and tried for a smile. "Now if you wouldn't mind keeping an eye on the munchkins, I'm going to check Peter's mac and cheese. He used a Barefoot Contessa recipe, so it should be fantastic."

The macaroni and cheese was indeed fantastic, but when the girls came in, pink-cheeked and beaming from their ride, it was clear they were not going to be picky. "I'm so hungry, I could eat a horse," Lena said.

Madeleine glared at her sister. "Well that was certainly awkward," she said, and we all laughed.

It was a meal with plenty of laughter. The boys woke up just as we finished dessert. After they were fed, we dressed them in their pumpkin suits; sent photos of each of us holding one or both of them to Margot, Zack, Mieka, Angus, and Taylor, and said our goodbyes.

As soon as we had all buckled up to go back to the city, I checked my messages. There were several from Margot. While I was debating whether to wait until we were home to call her, my phone rang. It was Margot, and she sounded harried. "I just got the pictures. Thanks. They're great. Look, I needed to head you off before you mention my ambivalence about the Keating decision to Zack. Delia called me an hour ago. She's withdrawing her veto."

"Did she say why?"

"She just said it was critical that no one outside of the five current partners know about the veto, and that she'd left messages for Blake, Zack, and Kevin saying she was reversing her decision and would join us in putting forward Emmett Keating's name for an equity partnership. She sounded terrible. She's always so forceful, but she seemed frightened. She said she'd had to make a difficult choice and if anyone else saw the list, the results would be dire. Anyway, please just forget I said anything."

"I will," I said. "But, Margot, there's a new development."

After I told her about what had arrived in Maisie's mailbox that morning, Margot uttered her favourite expletive. "Did Maisie know if anybody else received the list?"

"No. She had no idea what was going on, so she thought it was best to do nothing until she did."

"Thank God. I take it you haven't told Zack."

"No, I haven't been in touch with him. The girls and I are still sitting in the driveway at the farm."

"Zack's already texted to say he trusts Delia's new decision," Margot said. I could almost hear her mind clicking. "Do you think I should let them know the list is surfacing outside our little circle?"

"No, Margot, I don't. You shouldn't get more involved," I said. "You're on maternity leave, and Zack has a city to run. You've both gone above and beyond by handling the firm's restructuring. Let Delia, Blake, and Kevin deal with the problem. Running Falconer Shreve is their full-time job."

Margot took a deep breath. Finally, she said, "You're right, Jo. But this is unsettling. We were being very discreet with our discussions. Someone would have to be devious to get their hands on that list." Margot's voice was strong, but she was clearly anxious. "Jo, I have a very bad feeling about this."

"So do I," I said.

Zack came home around four-thirty. The plan was for us to have a drink and relax before we had to dress and steel ourselves for the evening ahead. But, as Robbie Burns famously noted, "the best laid schemes o' mice an' men / Gang aft agley." The phone rang shortly after he rolled through the front door. Zack picked up, turned to face me, and mouthed the name *Blake*. As he listened to his partner, Zack's eyes never left my face.

"Let me guess," I said. "That was about the list."

His brow furrowed. "You knew?" he said.

"Maisie told me this morning," I said. "So how did the news get to Blake?"

"Katina called Kevin this afternoon to tell him that she'd received a copy, and Kevin called Blake."

"Has Blake told Delia about the situation?"

"No. He wants to know the whole story before he brings it to her. So the plan is that Kevin, Blake, and I divvy up the twelve names on that list. We'll call all of them to ask if they received anything in a Falconer Shreve envelope. It's a nasty way to break the news to the ones who aren't receiving an offer, but they'll have to know sooner or later, and if they've received the letter, they already know."

"So what are you going to do if they all got a copy of the list?"

"Ask them to keep it confidential till we have a chance to talk to them tomorrow."

By the time we left the house, we had some answers. Kevin, Blake, and Zack had managed to get in touch with eleven of the twelve people they needed to contact. All had received a copy of the list. There was angst but everyone agreed to keep the information confidential until the next day. Emmett Keating wasn't answering his phone. Given the harsh dismissal Delia had written beside his name, I didn't blame him.

CHAPTER

7

Not long after Chris Altieri's suicide, Patsy Choi, a former client of Chris, approached his partners about her wish to honour his memory by creating a foundation dedicated to funding initiatives that helped young people overcome obstacles in their lives. Falconer Shreve lawyers had done the legal work to set up the foundation, and all the partners had contributed to its upfront funding and made long-term financial pledges, but apart from that, the firm kept its relationship with the foundation arm's-length.

Patsy Choi proved to be a good manager and the foundation, now in its third year of existence, was on solid ground. When Patsy approached Zack and me about a fund-raiser honouring Zack's commitment to helping young people who had lost their way and needed to find a path back, we were hesitant. But Patsy convinced us that the mayor of the city would attract a crowd that could pay a thousand dollars a plate and pointed out that, since a firm other than Falconer Shreve was now handling the Altieri Foundation's legal affairs, there would be no perceived conflict of interest. However, it was Patsy's enthusiasm as she sketched the broad strokes of the event she had been envisioning that finally won us over.

One hundred and fifty invitees would listen to speeches about Zack's individual acts of outreach and learn how the Christopher Altieri Foundation was working to ensure that initiatives like Zack's continued on a larger scale. The event – elite, black tie, and glamorous – would be held in one of the last bastions of elitism and glamour in our city: the Scarth Club. It was exactly the kind of evening I hated, but the cause was worthy, and so on that snowy October evening my husband and younger son, stylish in their tuxedos, and I, in a full-length, sleeveless, black-velvet Vera Wang I'd purchased the year before at an after-Christmas sale, set off for the Scarth Club.

At the entrance a doorman took our car keys, handed them to a valet, and ushered us inside. Built in 1912 and, except for the ghost of a prostitute who had been murdered in one of the upstairs bedrooms eons ago, closed to women for most of its existence, the club was an anachronism. That said, the old codger of a building knew how to party. Antique wall sconces cast a warm and welcoming glow in the foyer, and within seconds a young woman in a white blouse and black skirt, stockings, and oxfords appeared, took our coats, and handed me numbered tags that I tucked in my bag. Her voice was low and friendly. "It's a chilly night and the fireplace in the Portrait Gallery is lit," she said. "Someone will see to your drinks."

We smiled our thanks and sailed into the Portrait Gallery where a male pianist with a pencil-thin moustache and centre-parted hair, smooth and shiny as patent leather, was playing mellow jazz on a baby grand. Men in black tie and women in jewel-toned gowns sipped champagne and looked pleased with themselves.

Zack gave me an approving once-over. "I love that dress," he said.

"So do I," I said. "It's classic and comfortable. I'll be able to wear it forever."

Zack placed his hand on the side of my waist. "Could you turn around for a minute?" When I turned, he sighed with satisfaction. The dress had a very deep V back. For a man in a wheelchair the bottom of the V was at eye level and within easy reach, and Zack reached. "This evening is getting off to a great start," he said.

Angus gave a theatrical cough. "In case you'd forgotten, I'm standing right beside you."

"So you are," Zack said. "And standing right behind you is a server who appears to be waiting for our drink orders."

As soon as we'd ordered, another server appeared with a silver tray of hot appetizers. Zack glanced around the room and smiled. "I could get used to this," he said.

"No you couldn't," I said. "You're the people's mayor."

"'What we desire for ourselves, we wish for all,'" Zack said.

"You have to be the first person who ever quoted J.S. Woodsworth within the walls of the Scarth Club," I said and inhaled deeply. "What is that scent wafting from the kitchen. Prime rib?"

"Whatever it is, it smells great," Zack said. "Another first for the Scarth Club – an edible meal. It's a miracle."

A bourbon-cured bass boomed out behind us. "Not a miracle. Just Annie and me doing something that needed to be done." The voice belonged to Warren Weber, one of our closest friends and the man who, I suspected, was picking up the tab for the party tonight.

As always, his wife, Annie, was beside him. "We gave the club chef the night off and hired Evolution Catering," she said.

The Webers were a striking couple. Warren was eighty, a handsome man with erect bearing, an enviable head of thick snowy hair, an always meticulously trimmed Tom Selleck moustache, and a level, flinty gaze. He was fond of vibrant colours, and that night his black dinner suit was enlivened by a regency-purple tuxedo vest and tie. The Webers were partial to outfits in complementary hues. Annie, a sweet-faced twenty-six-year-old blonde with eyes as steely as her husband's, was wearing a shimmery heliotrope gown and a necklace of purple garnets the exact shade of Warren's vest and tie. Tongues wagged when the Webers married, but the gossips were wrong. Warren and Annie were a love match, and they were one of the happiest couples we knew.

Annie looked fondly at her husband. "Patsy Choi convinced us that we couldn't ask people to shell out a thousand bucks a plate and serve them shoe leather," she said.

Zack guffawed. "Aren't you afraid the club's chef will wreak his revenge on you, Warren?"

Warren shrugged. "I've been eating here for over fifty years. He's already done his worst."

"Maybe, but you're still my hero," I said.

Warren's bow was courtly. "Thank you, Joanne, but the person who performed the real magic is coming our way."

I'd been present at three of the planning meetings for the dinner, and Patsy had always worn business clothing – simple, corporate, and chic. That night she was stunning in a poppy-red cheongsam dress that clung to her slender figure and set off her translucent ivory skin and dark eyes.

In my dealings with her, I'd been impressed by Patsy's quick intelligence and openness to ideas other than her own. Her passion for creating a foundation that provided funding to help young adults was not surprising. Salvaging a damaged life was a cause about which Patsy had reason to feel passionate.

At fourteen Patsy Choi was already a violin prodigy in her native China. A wealthy uncle brought Patsy to Canada, gave her a home, arranged for tutors to educate her and for the finest of violin teachers to give her private lessons. When she turned seventeen, Patsy rebelled, saying she was tired of living a life of isolation. She wanted to be a girl like other girls and she was moving out of her uncle's house. Patsy's uncle happened to be tenderizing a piece of round steak with a wooden mallet when she declared her independence. Enraged, he grabbed Patsy, forced her hand down on the chopping block, and after systematically smashing the fingers on her left hand, grabbed her right hand and began pounding.

The case against the uncle was a civil case, tort of assault; the charge, in the archaic language of the law, was "wrongful touching." As plaintiff, Patsy had to prove her damages. The uncle's defence team was convincing, arguing that the uncle was a philanthropist, a loving relative who had done everything in his power to nurture his niece and her talent. The trial was long, drawn-out, and expensive, but ultimately Patsy was awarded a seven-figure judgment and she set about rebuilding her life. She appeared to be doing a fine job.

Patsy's speaking voice was very soft and her manners impeccable. She welcomed us all and then gestured to the rapidly filling Portrait Gallery. "Joanne and Zack, many people are eager to speak with you. Please allow me to take you around to greet your guests."

"Annie and I can handle that," Warren said. "Patsy, you've worked hard pulling this evening together, and I know you have a long night ahead. Why don't you and Angus find a quiet place and have a glass of champagne together," he said, winking at the two young people.

Angus and Patsy shared a glance. "I think that's a lovely idea," she said. "Thank you, Warren." When she and our son left in search of a place where they could be alone, they were both beaming.

Zack waited until he was sure they were out of earshot. "I think that, thanks to Warren, we've just discovered the identity of Angus's mystery woman," he said.

"Fingers crossed you're right," I said. "Patsy's a keeper."

"She is indeed," Warren said. "Now, I've promised that Annie and I will squire you two around, so we'd best get started."

The Scarth Club's Portrait Gallery always made me smile. The walls were filled with paintings of all the men who had served as the club's president. Throughout the years, trends in men's clothing and tonsorial preferences came and went, but overweening pride was always in fashion and, to a man, the faces of the club's president glowed with the sheen of self-regard. The words carved into the mantel above the fireplace said it all: "They builded better than they knew."

By nature gregarious, my husband was always quick to join the party. After Warren and Annie had finished taking us around to greet our guests, Zack smiled at me. "Time to mix and mingle," he said. "Are you ready?"

"I think I'll linger with the portraits for a while," I said. Zack moved closer and ran his hand up my arm. "I really do love that dress," he said. As he wheeled towards the door to the reception area, my husband was still smiling.

I was admiring the mutton chops of James MacLennan, club president from 1916 to 1920, when I smelled the aftershave, heavy with the scent of musk, that proclaimed Darryl Colby was in the room. Tall, heavy-set, raven-haired, and always deeply tanned, Darryl, like his cologne, did not respect personal space, and when he reached me he positioned himself so close that the toes of our shoes touched. Zack's relationship with most of the trial lawyers in town was cordial, but Darryl got under his skin. In my husband's opinion, Darryl was a junkyard lawyer who, somewhere along the line, had misplaced his conscience and who, even when he was winning, relished the chance to take a chunk out of opposing counsel. He was not a person with whom I wished to touch toes, and I stepped back.

"This is a surprise," I said.

"And not a pleasant one," Darryl said. His bass was big and rumbling. A nearby couple turned towards us.

I lowered my own voice, hoping Darryl would take the hint. "The Christopher Altieri Foundation is doing important work," I said. "It's good of you to support it."

"A friend gave me a ticket."

"Generous friend," I said. "Anyone I know?"

His laugh was jeering. "An admirer of Falconer Shreve," he said. "But aren't we all?" And with that, he walked away.

I was trying to regain my equilibrium through deep breathing and a closer examination of James MacLennan's mutton chops when I was ambushed again. My new acquaintance had a disproportionately large head – bald and egg-shaped, like Humpty Dumpty. He was disinfecting his tiny hands with a sanitizing wipe, and he was thorough. "Just about done," he said.

When finished, he dropped the wipe into the brass pot of a weeping fig and introduced himself. "I'm Emmett Keating," he said. I glanced around to see if one of the partners was close enough to flag if the situation with Keating became awkward. I was out of luck, so I focused on the man standing in front of me. He didn't extend his sanitized hand, and I didn't offer mine.

"Joanne Shreve," I said.

"I recognized you," he said. "And it's time we met. Falconer Shreve is a family firm, and I'm happy to say I'm about to become part of the family."

The prudent course of action would have been to offer a vague pleasantry and move along, but it was already too late for that. Emmett had begun his monologue, and the fire-hose of his speech that Margot had warned about was aimed directly at me. There was nothing to do but listen. His voice was pleasant – low-pitched and well-modulated – a story-teller's voice, and Emmett Keating had a story to tell.

I didn't need a timepiece to measure how long it took him to weave together the many strands of Falconer Shreve's history. When it came to oral narrative, Emmett was an adherent of the leisurely pace. He started with the meeting of Zack and his colleagues during their first year at law school and moved through their academic triumphs into their articling year: Delia at the Supreme Court; Blake in Toronto; Kevin in Calgary; Chris in Vancouver; and Zack in Regina with Fred L. Harney, a brilliant lawyer and a drunk prone to blackouts who needed a smart young law graduate to supply replays of exactly what had happened in court when he sobered up. Emmett Keating described Falconer Shreve's firsts in meticulous detail: the firm's first law office in a building they shared with a company that made dentures; Delia's first appearance before the Supreme Court; the first of Zack's wins that garnered national attention; Chris's first million-dollar settlement; Blake's first Top 100–ranked corporate client; Kevin's first defection to Tibet in search of answers he wasn't finding in law practice. Listening to Emmett Keating's glowing recitation of the firm's growth was mesmerizing, and when Blake, Kevin, and a woman with a confident stride and edgy, silver-grey cropped hair approached, I had to shake myself to rejoin the real world.

Blake and Kevin were smooth, but it was clear their desire to socialize with Emmett was less than fervent. They greeted him civilly, embraced me, and then Kevin introduced his companion. "This is Katina Posaluko-Chapman from Calgary," he said. "Tina, meet Joanne Shreve and Emmett Keating."

The woman who would soon head the Calgary office had a firm handshake; the faint dusting of freckles across her pert nose was appealing and her smile was unforced. I liked her on sight. "So you're visiting Regina and have to spend the evening listening to speeches praising Zack," I said. "I hope Kevin is at least paying for dinner."

Katina's deep-set hazel eyes showed amusement. "I made sure of that. I'm here on business, but I've already booked a spa day at the Hotel Saskatchewan."

"Very wise," I said. "I've heard the Honey Detox and Chocolate Truffle Body Wrap is decadent."

"A Chocolate Truffle Body Wrap is a definite step-up from the Lifebuoy soap of my youth," Katina said and, grateful for an end to the awkwardness that Emmett Keating's presence had brought, I smiled.

Blake looked towards the door. "It appears dinner is about to be served." He offered me his arm. "Jo, Zack asked me to tell you he'll meet you inside. Shall we . . . ?" Kevin held his arm out to Katina and turned to Emmett. "Have a pleasant evening," he said.

Emmett Keating raised his hand in a halt sign. "Not so fast," he said. "I haven't congratulated Ms. Posaluko-Chapman on being hired by Falconer Shreve, and as an equity partner no less."

Tina was clearly surprised at Emmett's breach of etiquette, but she was gracious. "Thanks for the good wishes," she said and offered her hand.

Emmett ignored it and pressed on. "Now it's your turn, Ms. Posaluko-Chapman," he said. "This is where *you* congratulate *me* on being named an equity partner." He pronounced each word slowly and precisely. My grandmother would have said his articulation was that of a man teaching a cow to speak.

It was Blake who responded. "Perhaps it's best to defer the congratulations until the news is official," he said.

Emmett's small mouth curled in a smirk. "No need," he said. "Delia Wainberg and I have settled my offer to our mutual satisfaction." He turned to join the crowd that was moving towards the dining room.

Tina spoke first. "I'll bite," she said. "So Mr. Keating will be promoted as one of the new equity partners after all?"

Kevin shook his head in disbelief. "I'm not going to bull-shit you, Tina. We *have* decided to promote Keating. We assumed he would keep his lips zipped, but I guess he couldn't wait to trumpet the happy news. I'm sorry you were put in an awkward spot."

"No harm done," Tina said, and then she rolled her eyes. "But Holy Crudmore, you guys in the Regina office really know how to screw up big-time."

Katina's pithy comment didn't require follow-up, so without further discussion the four of us trooped in to dinner.

Patsy Choi had arranged the seating, and I was happy to see that Kevin and Tina were at our table. Kevin and I had demanding lives and we lived in cities 760 kilometres apart, but our friendship was a comfortable shoe that, even after weeks without seeing each other, we were able to slip into effortlessly. The Falconer Shreve partners had always enjoyed that same ease in one another's company, but tensions at the firm had frayed Zack and Kevin's relationship, and I knew they would welcome another chance to re-establish the old closeness.

Tina had won me with her eye roll and snappy assessment of the Regina office's handling of the equity partnership list. She was right. They had blundered badly, and I looked forward to hearing more of her straight talk at dinner.

Warren and Annie Weber were always good company, and I was pleased to see their names on the placecards at our table. Patsy Choi and Angus were seated with us as well, and as we all took our places, I caught her eye and mouthed the words *thank you*.

The dinner was excellent. Airy, golden Yorkshire pudding accompanied succulent prime rib, the vegetables had not spent a millisecond on a steam table, the wine was plentiful, and the talk at our table was serious without being stolid. Not surprisingly, much of the discussion focused on the life and times of Chris Altieri. His photograph was on the front of the program. It was a photo taken in summer, and Chris was deeply tanned. His dark hair, obviously wet from a swim, curled at the nape of his neck. His eyes were piercingly blue, and his smile was shy but winning. This was the man whom Chris's friends had remembered at his wake. I turned to Zack. "How old was Chris in this picture?"

Zack's face grew soft. "Maybe in his late thirties," he said, taking my hand in his. We were both still focused on the photo. "Hard to imagine that man committing suicide, isn't it?" Zack said. I had no words of comfort, so I simply squeezed his hand.

There was laughter across the table. During exams at the end of their first year at the College of Law, Kevin and Chris had discovered that practical jokes offered surefire relief from pressure. Later, as the stresses of establishing and growing a new law firm mounted, the two men found respite in dreaming up increasingly elaborate but always lighthearted pranks. As Zack listened to Kevin recount some of Chris's successful if sophomoric practical jokes, I could feel his spirits lift and mine lifted too.

I was still laughing at the tales of office hijinks when I spotted Darryl Colby in what appeared to be a heated conversation with Emmett Keating at a table across the room. I drew Zack's attention to the pair. "Darryl made his presence known to me earlier. He didn't mention that he'd be sitting at a table with Emmett Keating," I said. "What do you make of that?"

Zack shook his head. "Maybe just a case of birds of a feather flocking together," he said.

"Do you really think Emmett belongs in the same category as Darryl Colby?"

"I wouldn't have said so before," Zack said. "But I'm uneasy about Delia's sudden reversal on Emmett's candidacy for equity partner. Dee's a stickler for precise wording, and the four words she wrote beside Keating's name left no room for interpretation."

"'Not Falconer Shreve material,'" I said. "That certainly is definitive."

"And yet Dee overturned her own ruling. That's not like her," Zack said. He looked again across the room. Darryl Colby and Emmett still appeared to be going head to head. "I wish I knew what those two were talking about," he said.

"Do you really wish you knew?" I said.

Zack's laugh was short. "No. Whatever it is, it will wait. My old mentor Fred L. Harney always said, 'Never trouble trouble till trouble troubles you.' Of course, trouble often troubled Fred L., but it's still good advice."

Before she introduced the first speaker, Patsy Choi gave a graceful, brief welcome to the guests. After thanking everyone for coming, she touched upon the role Chris Altieri had played in her own life, saying that at a time when she believed there was nothing good ahead, Chris had worked tirelessly to get her justice and to give her a future. She explained that the mandate of the Christopher Altieri Foundation was to give young people like her a second chance. Tonight's speakers would, she said, show how the experience of rebuilding his own life had given Zack the determination and the skills to help others rehabilitate themselves. Patsy turned so she was focused on Zack. "I should tell you that when the news that you were being honoured tonight spread, my phone never stopped ringing. Many people are grateful to you, Zack, and tonight's presenters will be speaking on behalf of others as well as themselves."

The first to come to the podium was Debbie Haczkewicz, Regina's chief of police, and as she adjusted the microphone, handsome in her off-white trouser suit, Debbie was clearly relishing the chance to talk about Zack. She began by saying that, like the orca and the great white shark, police officers and trial lawyers are natural enemies, and that until her teenaged son, Leo, was in a life-threatening motorcycle accident, the relationship between Zack and her had been one of mutual distrust. When the doctors told Leo he would never walk again, he was determined to die. He lashed out at everyone who offered to help him. Finally, exhausted and desperate, Debbie asked Zack to intervene.

Debbie didn't sugarcoat her account of the battle that raged between Zack in his wheelchair and her newly paraplegic son. Leo attacked Zack verbally, and when that didn't work he used his fists and, in a moment of inspiration, detached his catheter and aimed the hose at Zack. Every day for a month, Zack showed up and Leo went into full battle mode. Finally, beaten down, Leo began to listen.

He agreed to attend rehab, and when he was ready to handle life in a wheelchair he enrolled at the university, majoring in English with a specialization in teaching English as a second language. When he graduated, he went to Japan to teach, and met and married Myoshi, a faculty colleague. Leo and Myoshi now had a little boy named Nikko and were expecting their second child at the end of December.

Debbie's concluding sentence made my husband grin. "Zack will always be a great white shark and I will always be an orca, but we've learned to cherish the times when we're able to swim side by side."

The story ended happily, but I knew there would be no happy ending for the next speaker. Morgan Dafoe was twenty-seven and completing his residency in pediatrics. Slightly built and fine-featured, Morgan seemed boyish at first glance. But guilt freighted him down, and his young face was knifed with sorrow.

When Morgan was fourteen, one of the guests at a week-end party at his family's cottage decided it would be amusing to get him drunk. Morgan was young and he was willing. After he and the woman had consumed most of a bottle of tequila, she asked him to drive her around the lake in the family's speedboat. He obliged. When he attempted to bring the boat to shore, he ploughed into the dock and killed two children who'd been watching. It had been thirteen years since the nightmare, but Morgan's voice broke as he explained how Zack had talked him out of suicide by telling him that we are all better than the worst thing we do and that we must all live larger than the pain we cause or the pain we're suffering.

There were four other speakers. All told stories about lives interrupted by tragedies but resumed because Zack had intervened. Each speech had been brief but emotional, and as Margot and Brock strode towards the microphone to introduce Zack, the mood in the room lightened noticeably. Margot and Brock had opted to introduce Zack together, in part to speed the evening along, but largely because, as impressive as each was individually, together they were riveting.

Brock was a big man who knew how to wear a tuxedo. Red was a great colour for Margot, and that night in a shoulder-baring pomegranate satin dress she was a knock-out. Brock adjusted the mic; she smiled her thanks and then spoke directly to Zack. "Before you start polishing your halo, I'm going to give everyone a peek into your less saintly side." Margot's expression was puckish. "Just a peek," she said. "There isn't world enough and time to tell all." She pivoted to address the audience. "Zack and I have always locked horns. Since female members of the deer-elk-moose family don't have antlers, I use strap-ons."

The audience took a few seconds to react, but when it came, the laughter Margot's ribald comment evoked was full-throated. After the room quieted, she continued. "Once, after we had a real knock-down-drag-out in court, I marched into Zack's tastefully appointed office, dumped a box of tacks onto his hardwood, told him I hoped the tacks would shred the tires on his wheelchair, and stormed out. The next morning a courier delivered three-dozen American Beauty roses to my office with an invoice for the course in anger management that Mr. Charm had enrolled me in. I passed," she said wryly. "Top of my class." The laughter that rang through the room after Margot's anecdote was tonic.

When the laughter died down, Brock began. He focused on how, from the inception of the Racette-Hunter Community Centre, Zack had insisted that the centre determine and meet the needs of those seeking a second chance. Brock ran through the statistics of the number of students who, having completed courses that prepared them for employment, had found jobs and continued to be employed. The figures were not overwhelmingly positive, but Brock pointed out that behind each number was a life that was no longer being wasted and a citizen who had become a contributing community member.

Margot talked about Zack's extensive legal work on behalf of young offenders. She said that lawyers at Zack's level usually steered clear of *pro bono* projects, regarding them as a training ground for novice litigators, but that Zack understood the full meaning of the phrase *pro bono publico*. He believed that young clients facing a court appearance are at a crossroads. With guidance, they can turn their lives around and, when that occurs, a lawyer's work has truly been done for the public good. Margot pointed to the number of what she characterized as "meaningful talks" Zack had in his office with at-risk youth. She noted that Zack's billable rate was as high or higher than that of any lawyer in Western Canada but that when Zack was talking to a troubled adolescent, he was never on the clock.

Margot ended her speech on a personal note. "This afternoon I talked to my stepson, Declan Hunter. He asked me to send him a copy of my remarks for tonight. Having read them, he insisted that I include one more case where Zack made the difference.

"Declan himself was one of the youths that Zack helped to put his life back on track. On Declan's sixteenth birthday, Zack took Declan to The Broken Rack to shoot pool and talk about his future – a future that, in Zack's opinion, almost certainly would include jail time. Their talk that night was the first of many. Somewhere along the way, Declan got the message. He stopped indulging in risky behaviours. He buckled down at school, and he had the good sense to become friends with Zack and Joanne's daughter Taylor. Today, Declan's in his second year at the University of Toronto. He's a great support to me and a terrific stepbrother to my son and daughter, and he and Taylor are a romance." Margot twinkled at Zack. "Just think – we could be looking at a lifetime of family dinners together." Zack harrumphed, but he was clearly pleased.

I wrote all of Zack's political speeches and most of his policy speeches. That night, he spoke off the cuff. I'd

forgotten how skilled he was at winging it, and it was a
pleasure to sit back, relax, and watch him in action. His
reminiscences of Chris were tender but on point. A client
had given Chris a framed motto that said, in Hebrew and
English, "In places where there are no good people, be a good
person." Zack told the audience that Chris had been
Falconer Shreve's good person, and he had made everyone at
the firm better by his presence. The Christopher Altieri
Foundation now made it possible for Chris's goodness to
change the lives of people he would never meet. It was a
wrap-up line and I leaned forward, prepared to join in the
applause, but Zack wasn't finished.

When he continued, his voice was low and intimate.
"Since Chris died, his friends have struggled with the question of what we could have done to wrest him from the
depression that led him to take his own life." He paused.
"None of us has come up with an answer. Margot Hunter's
late husband, Leland, used to say there can be no phoenix
without the ashes.

"I don't have to look far to see that a new life started for
me on the day Chris died. I met the woman who would
become my wife, and a life more fulfilling than anything I
could have asked for or imagined began for me."

Zack was a loving husband who made me feel cherished
in a hundred different ways, but a public expression of affection was unlike him, and, surprised and touched by his
words, I found myself blushing.

Pleased at my obvious pleasure, Zack gave me a quick
smile and carried on. "There are times when we're all faced
with the ashes of what we'd hoped for. People will tell you
to be grateful for what you have left, but when all you can
see is ashes, gratitude isn't an emotion that comes easily. So
I'm not saying be grateful. I'm just saying, 'Don't walk away.
Wait. See what happens next.'"

The stream of guests coming over to our table to congratulate Zack after his speech was steady, and our dinner companions drifted off to make room for the newcomers and do their own visiting. When the last well-wisher left, Zack turned to me. "Time to say our farewells and pack it in?"

"Yes, but it was a nice evening, wasn't it?"

Zack brushed my shoulder with his lips. "The evening's still young."

"I've wanted us to be alone together since you said how much our marriage meant to you." I touched his cheek. "I'll find our driver."

"I'm guessing Angus will be where Patsy is," Zack said.

"And Patsy will be overseeing the lines of people signing cheques in the Portrait Gallery," I said.

We started towards the Portrait Gallery but detoured when we saw that Delia, Noah, Margot, and Brock were still sitting at their table and that the Webers had stopped by to visit.

Margot stood and held out her arms when she saw Zack. "Hey, it's the man of the hour," she said. "Great speech, but what was that last part about? Have you been watching *Oprah* reruns again?"

"No. That was a pre-emptive strike. Before the speeches started, I ran into Emmett Keating in the men's room. I said, 'How's it going?' and he told me to go fuck myself. I didn't have a clue what was going on, but when I spotted Keating in the audience, the story of the phoenix and the ashes came to mind and I thought I'd give it a shot." Zack wheeled closer to Delia. "You're going to have to help me out here. After I got your text reversing your veto, I assumed the situation was in hand. So what changed, Dee?"

Delia shook her head. Her face registered genuine confusion, not an expression I had seen on her face in the years I'd known her. "I don't know," she said.

Brock had stood when we joined them. He was positioned with a view of the tables to our right and something had captured his attention. "We may be about to find out," he said. "Emmett Keating is coming our way."

I turned just as Emmett stopped, removed a disinfecting cloth from his seemingly inexhaustible store, and began cleaning his hands. When he finished he dropped the cloth on a nearby table and strode towards us. He homed in on Delia.

"You lying bitch," he said. "You broke our deal, and now I'm going to break you. All the firm's dirty secrets will be revealed, and everyone will know the truth about the sainted Christopher Altieri and the rest of the partners at Falconer Shreve."

Delia had gone dead white. Noah was out of his chair. His eyes were blazing. He was a physically powerful man, and I knew he could do real damage to Keating. Brock obviously shared my concern. He was moving towards Noah when events took an unexpected turn. Annie Weber had been standing next to Keating. Her eyes were steely, and so were her biceps. In a quick, graceful move Annie took hold of Keating's arms and pinned them behind his back. "Time to go," she said with a voice that rang with the authority of a woman who, until she married, had managed a biker bar. Without a single unnecessary move, she frogmarched Emmett Keating across the room and through the door that led to the foyer.

The rest of us were clearly shaken, but Warren was calm. "Annie will handle the situation," he said, "but I'll check the foyer to make certain there's no unpleasantness. We'll come back to say goodnight."

CHAPTER

8

Delia was shaking. Noah took off his jacket and draped it around his wife's slender shoulders.

"Okay," Margot said. "Can anybody tell me what just happened?"

Delia's silence lasted so long that I wondered if she was in shock. Finally, ignoring Margot's question, she looked straight at Zack. "After the list was circulated, Emmett came to me. He'd seen what I'd written beside his name and he was so angry he was barely coherent. He told me he had devastating information about Chris Altieri and unless he was promoted, he'd make what Chris did public and destroy Falconer Shreve."

Zack's shoulders tensed visibly. "Did he say what the information was?"

Delia's lips barely moved as she uttered her reply. "No. But, Zack, we both know there are things that happened in the past that have to stay in the past."

"And that's why you reversed your decision."

"Yes, and I thought the problem was solved," Delia said.

"It was," I said. "Blake, Kevin, Tina, and I were talking to Emmett Keating before dinner. He told us you and he had settled his offer of an equity partnership to your mutual satisfaction."

"We had," Delia said. "Something must have happened tonight during dinner."

Zack and I exchanged a look that was quick but intense enough to let me know we shared the same thought: Darryl Colby. He turned to the others. "We have to move quickly. I'll text Blake and Kevin."

"I'm assuming that, as an equity partner, I'll be included in the meeting," Margot said, and her tone was icy.

Zack leaned forward and splayed his hands on his knees. "You should have been included in this long ago," he said. "For what it's worth, I'm sorry."

"Sorry is not going to cut it," she said. "You need to tell me what the hell is going on."

I looked around. Guests still in the dining room were watching our table with interest. "We need to get out of here," I said.

"Our condo is five minutes away," Brock said. "Okay with you, Margot? We told the sitter we'd be home by now. I'll take care of the kids. It'll be easier for you to handle this privately."

Margot picked up her evening bag, shot Zack a poisonous glance, stood, and slid her arm through Brock's. "Thanks," she said. "It's reassuring to know that there's someone who's looking out for me. Let's get out of here."

Annie and Warren returned looking fresh as the proverbial daisies. "The doorman was going to call a taxi for Mr. Keating," Warren said. "But someone from Falconer Shreve stepped in. He said he had his car here and if Mr. Keating was amenable he'd drive him home."

"And Mr. Keating was amenable?" Zack said.

"According to the doorman, Mr. Keating was past caring, but he didn't object. The doorman waited with them while the valet brought the Good Samaritan's car around and they left without incident." Warren handed Zack a business card. "The Falconer Shreve employee left this for you, Zack, in case you had questions."

Zack glanced at the card and turned to Delia. "Lorne Callow," he said. "I didn't know he was here tonight. Anyway, I'll call to thank him tomorrow morning."

In her husband's tux jacket, Delia looked like a child playing dress up, but her voice was firm. "I'll call Lorne. This is my mess."

Zack shook his head. "He left the card for me, Dee. I'll take care of it. Let's just get through tonight."

Delia stood. "I'll meet you all at Margot's."

Warren was quick to read the situation. "This is obviously Falconer Shreve business," he said. "Zack, text our driver when your meeting is finished and he'll drive you and Joanne home."

Zack turned his chair towards the Webers. "You're a good friend, Warren. And thanks, Annie, for stepping in. I'll call and let you know where matters stand before I leave for the airport tomorrow."

Blake was on his way home, and Kevin had just dropped Tina at her hotel when they received Zack's texts. Both men agreed to meet us at the condo on Halifax Street. I found Angus, told him something had come up and that Warren's driver was on call.

When I explained the change in plans, my son gave me the thumbs-up sign. "Great. Patsy and I will go back to my place, have a beer, and see if the Blue Jays are still in the World Series."

"Zack checked the final score on his phone," I said. "Do you want me to tell you?"

Angus clapped his hands over his ears. "Patsy would kill me. We've watched all the games together and I PVRed this one for us."

"Sounds like you two are having a lot of fun."

"We are, and it just keeps getting better and better. We're both really happy about the way things are going."

I felt a frisson of unease. Patsy idolized Chris Altieri. If she learned he had feet of clay it would be a blow to her. Angus waited for my reaction and when none came, he frowned. "I thought you'd be pleased, Mum."

"I am pleased," I said. "Patsy's terrific. It'll be great getting to know her better."

Angus heaved a mock sigh of relief. "Good. For a moment there, I thought there might be a problem."

"No problem at all," I said. "We're going to the lake for Taylor's birthday dinner. Why don't you ask Patsy to join us?"

Angus gave me a quick hug. "This has been the best night," he said. "And it's not over."

I inhaled deeply. "No," I said. "It's not over."

Kevin and Blake arrived at the condo around the same time we did, so we went up in the elevator together. When we exited at the fourth floor, we all followed Margot into her condo. After a brief whispered conversation, Brock said goodnight and headed upstairs to the children's rooms and we took off our coats and filed into the dining room.

Margot sat at the head of the oval mahogany table and the rest of us filled the places closest to her. "I'll tell Brock what he needs to know later," she said. "He deserves to have an accurate picture of the firm he's being asked to manage."

Delia was clearly still shaken, but her spirit was fiery. Even her wiry salt-and-pepper hair seemed to have regained its electrical charge. She was herself again, and she waded right in.

"I thought about this in the car coming over. I'm sure Emmett's weapon is the Patsy Choi case. A few weeks ago, Lorne told me that Keating had been going through old files. I didn't think anything of it at the time. Lots of us go through old files searching for precedents, but if Emmett was looking closely at the movement of capital, which we know he would do, a few educated guesses could have led him to surmise that something was off."

For the first time, Delia looked directly at Margot. "To understand this, you'll need context," she said. "So I'll start at the beginning.

"People always said Chris was the conscience of Falconer Shreve, and he was. But life is filled with moral ambiguities – times when it's necessary to do wrong in order to do right. Patsy Choi's case was one of those times. I assume you're familiar with the facts of Patsy's story, Margot."

When Margot nodded, Dee continued. "Then you know that Patsy's uncle crushed her fingers when Patsy asserted her independence. In retrospect, it's easy to apportion blame. A grown man attacks a young woman with a weapon that causes her grievous bodily harm and changes her life forever. But Patty Choi was the plaintiff. The onus was on her to prove her damages, and her uncle had deep pockets. He was able to hire some very skilled lawyers, and they put together a compelling case."

Zack shifted his weight in his chair, an unconscious gesture to protect his skin against pressure ulcers. "I can take it from here, Dee," he said. "It was Chris's case, but he and I talked about it every day. Chris knew the defence was sandbagging him. They painted Patsy as an ungrateful child who had been given everything and threw her benefactor's largesse in his face. Chris and I agreed that if he was going to win his case, the firm had to hire a shitload of plaintiff-friendly professional experts.

"We hired the best, and they did their jobs. They proved that the physical and psychological damage Patsy's uncle had inflicted on her was irreparable. They painted a new picture for the jury: one in which a seventeen-year-old girl had a moment of adolescent rebellion and her uncle responded by ruining her life. I was sitting in court when Chris did his summation. It was brilliant. The uncle was sobbing, but if his remorse was genuine it was too late. He was found guilty of 'wrongful touching' and Patsy got a large settlement. Justice was done," Zack said. "But as we all know, the wheels of justice grind exceeding slow."

I had been watching Margot's face to gauge if she was buying Zack's explanation. Until that moment, her face had been a mask, but as she sensed that Zack had reached the point that was the fulcrum of his argument, the mask dropped, and I saw how fervently she wanted to believe that whatever her old friend said next would make everything right again. Zack looked at me and shook his head. The gesture was almost imperceptible, but it conveyed as clearly as words that he knew what he had to offer was not enough to change anything.

He took a breath and carried on. "There were appeals," he said. "And meanwhile there were bills to be paid. Experts don't come cheap, and the firm's larder was seriously depleted. We'd opened an office in Vancouver two years earlier. The decision to expand had been rushed, and the office was a disaster from the beginning. When we decided to cut our losses and close shop, we had to face another problem. We'd made some commercial real estate investments that we knew would ultimately turn out to be profitable, but it was 2008, the stock market had tanked, and we couldn't unload the properties without losing a bundle. All of us had personally taken a hit with our investments. So we were up against the wall."

Margot had been listening intently. Now she tensed. "You're not going to tell me you dipped into clients' trust funds." Her eyes were fixed firmly on Zack. "I'd heard that Falconer Shreve had money problems a while back, but *defalcation*. You could have been disbarred. You *should* have been disbarred." Her voice wavered. "Zack, I believed in you, and I looked up to you."

Zack looked down and didn't speak. For a painfully long time, no one did. Margot's anguish had silenced us all.

After what seemed like an eternity, Delia said, "Zack wasn't responsible, Margot. It was Chris. Zack didn't find out about the defalcation until after Chris died. None of the partners knew."

Margot balled her hands into fists. "How could they not know?"

When Blake spoke, it seemed the words were being pulled from him against his will. "Lily – my late wife – kept the firm's ledgers. We had always trusted her judgment. We had no reason not to. We were all aware that the firm was going through a rough time financially, but we knew the real estate was a gold mine. Lily said it was just a question of keeping the cash flow steady and moving the money around until the market righted itself."

"But Chris knew," Margot said.

"Yes," Blake said. "But not until it was over. When every account had been balanced to the penny, Lily told him. No client had been hurt. Patsy Choi had received a fair settle-ment. Justice had been done. As far as Lily was concerned, the matter was closed."

"But now Emmett Keating has opened it again," Margot said. "And he's used what he knows to force you to reverse your decision about promoting him. But, Delia, there's something I'm still not clear on. Why was your initial assess-ment of Keating so harsh? I went through his performance reviews – they were excellent. He's brought many lucrative clients into the firm, and they're loyal to him. I didn't see anything in the reviews that would have made you suddenly decide that, in your words, Emmett Keating was 'Not Falconer Shreve material.'"

The air in Margot's condo was cool. When Delia shivered, Noah crossed the room, picked up a Dora the Explorer blanket that had been left on one of the chairs, and handed it to his wife. Dee pulled the blanket tight around her shoulders.

"The decision wasn't sudden," Delia said. "I voted against offering Emmett Keating an equity partnership for the same reason I voted against hiring him the first time he applied for a position with the firm."

Zack's eyes widened. "Keating applied to Falconer Shreve before?" he said. "Where was I?"

Delia's lip curled. "Racking up wins in the courtroom; playing poker with the boys; romping with the ladies. You were living life large, Zack. The internal affairs of the firm were not a priority for you."

"Okay," Zack said. "*Mea culpa.* Let's stay focused. Why didn't you want to hire Keating?"

"Because Emmett Keating had articled with Darryl Colby, and stayed on at Colby's firm for several years after that. Colby's a snake. I didn't think his ethics were something we wanted to bring into the firm. I was in Ottawa when Keating applied the second time; by the time I got back, he'd been hired."

Kevin was sitting across the table from Delia with his hands folded in front of him. He looked around the table. "And I approved the hire. None of you were available to consult, and Raema Silzer in HR recommended Keating highly, as she had every reason to. He had solid credentials in an area the firm needed to bolster. Raema did her job, but

I didn't do mine. I should have dug more deeply." Kevin reached across the table to his partner. "I'm sorry, Dee."

Delia's smile was weary. "Kev, we all make mistakes. Firing him then would have meant firing him without cause."

"And now Keating has proved he's as slimy as Colby, and the firm's reputation is on the line." Margot said. She turned to Zack. "When you approached me about becoming a partner, you had a duty to make me aware of any potential problems areas," she said. "A defalcation is certainly a potential problem. Why didn't you tell me about it?"

Zack's misery was palpable. "Because it was in the past," he said. "No one had been hurt. I honestly didn't see the relevance."

"Then you were lying to yourself," Margot said. "A first-year law student would have known that a reputable firm can't sweep something as serious as defalcation under the carpet and pretend it never happened. Lily and Chris are both dead. So there won't be legal repercussions, but when Emmett Keating makes this little nugget public, Falconer Shreve's status will take a hit and that affects me."

"You can resign," Zack said quietly.

Margot's voice was cutting. "I'm seriously considering that possibility. You'll have my decision by noon tomorrow." She stood. "We're finished here." She walked to the front door of her condo, held the door open, and watched as we shrugged into our coats. Her partners all attempted to reach out to her, but she shook them off. When I passed her, she said, "Did you know about this?"

I nodded.

Margot's laugh was short and bitter. "So you drank the Kool-Aid too," she said and shut the door hard behind me.

CHAPTER

9

It had been close to one-thirty in the morning when Zack and I settled into bed, but the misery of the evening hung like a pall over us, and neither of us slept well. When I awakened, the sun was up and, eager for our morning walk, Pantera and Esme were pacing restlessly. Zack's side of the bed was empty, so I checked my phone and saw a text suggesting the day ahead might contain some rays of sunshine. *Having breakfast with Warren – possible solution to the Keating problem. Will try to make peace with Margot. Love you, Z.*

I texted back wishing him luck, poured myself a glass of juice, and pulled on my running clothes. The forecast was for blue skies and unseasonably balmy temperatures. We were in for a fast melt. Since the first hard frost I'd been keeping pots of marigolds in the mudroom, hoping for a break in the weather. That morning it seemed the break had come, and after I brought the dogs their post-run water, I began carrying the marigolds outside. The pots were heavy and I was struggling with the last one when Lorne Callow walked up our front path. "May I help you with that?" he said.

I groaned. "My back will thank you," I said.

Lorne picked up the pot and followed as I led him to the spot where I wanted the marigolds placed. Before he put down the pot, he lifted the flowers to his nose and breathed deeply. "I've always loved the scent of marigolds," he said.

"So have I," I said. "It brings back memories of my daughter Mieka's first day of school. She made a bouquet for her teacher – no stems, just flowers. She carried them off in a yogurt container."

When Lorne grinned, he had the roguish charm of the actor Michael J. Fox. "Marigolds always remind me of the two old mansions on College Avenue where Falconer Shreve had their offices before they moved into the glass tower," he said.

"I remember those marigolds," I said. "They were in big brass pots at the entrances."

"When the stress level at the office was reaching a danger point, I'd step outside and smell the marigolds," Lorne said. "It always did the trick." He bent and moved the pot so it was closer to the others. "Too bad we don't have marigolds in the glass tower. These days we could use them."

"As last night proved," I said. "Zack had an early meeting, but he's planning to call and thank you for extricating Emmett Keating from what was a painful situation for everyone."

"No need for him to call," Lorne said. "Your husband's a busy man."

"I'm glad you were there," I said. "Lorne, how did Emmett seem on the drive home?"

"Angry," he said. "Emmett didn't say a word. I was in your neighbourhood this morning, and I thought I'd see if I could catch Zack. I'd like to get his advice. Our regular HR person is on medical leave, and until she returns, I'm in charge. Emmett needs help, but, Joanne, I'll be frank. I have no idea what to do because I don't understand what has happened. There have been no indications that Emmett was unhappy with Falconer Shreve, but last night he caused a scene that may cost him his job."

The concern in Lorne's eyes almost compelled me to set discretion aside and tell him what I knew, but if the partners hadn't informed their acting head of HR about their plans or the debacle of the list, it wasn't up to me. I shook my head and told him the only version of the truth I could. "I don't understand what happened either," I said. "But, Lorne, there is something I wondered about. I noticed that Emmett and Darryl Colby had a very intense conversation during dinner. Darryl makes no secret of his antipathy to Falconer Shreve. I've been wondering if he told Emmett something that disturbed him."

"That does sound odd," Lorne said. "I'm planning on speaking to Emmett, and when I do I'll ask him about his talk with Colby," Lorne said. "If I get any answers, I'll give you a call."

"I'd appreciate that," I said. "What you're doing goes beyond the duties listed in your job description. Not many people would spend their Saturday following up on a troubled colleague."

"I don't know how this situation can be salvaged, but I owe it to Delia to do what I can to keep it from getting worse." He paused and then gave me an endearingly boyish smile. "And you know, there are times when we really are our brother's keeper," he said. "I guess this is one of them."

When I came back inside, Taylor was standing over the kitchen sink, still in the T-shirt and sports shorts she slept in, enjoying her favourite Saturday breakfast – crumpets dripping with butter.

"Everything okay here?" I said.

Taylor gave me a buttery grin. "Perfect. I slept in till nine and this is my third crumpet. There are two crumpets left.

Come join me." My daughter and I were still standing over the sink in the midst of our goof and gossip session, laughing, when Zack came through the door.

He reached for his phone. "I need a picture of this."

"No way," Taylor said. "My hair's weird, and I'm covered in butter."

"And I'm sweaty," I said. "You'll have to hold this moment in your heart."

Zack wheeled towards us and opened his arms. "Consider the moment held," he said.

Taylor kissed her father on the head. "I'm going to shower and then go out to my studio to work," she said. "Don't leave for the airport without saying goodbye."

"Wouldn't dream of it," Zack said.

Taylor floated off, and I turned to Zack.

"So how did you make out with Margot and Warren?"

"Margot's still a question mark," he said. "I sent her a peace offering, but I haven't heard back."

"Give her time," I said. "She feels betrayed, and she has every right to. I'm going to drive over to her place after I drop you at the airport." The shadows under Zack's eyes were dark. I took his hand. "It'll be all right, Zack. We love Margot, and she loves us."

"I hope to God you're right," he said. "On a brighter note, Warren's offered Emmett a job as house counsel in his Halifax office, and Emmett is thinking it over."

"And the offer is conditional on Emmett forgetting his threat to Delia and moving away."

Zack shrugged. "It's a *quid pro quo* world, Jo."

"I know, but what's Warren getting out of this? Does he really want to hire a lawyer who tried to blackmail his previous employer?"

"Warren's a businessman," Zack said. "Last night, I got up and reviewed Emmett's performance reports. Jo, he's great at his job. Tax law is boring as hell, but he has a gift. There've been no problems like this before. Emmett's eccentric, but he's always been ethical. Warren is willing to overlook last night's episode based on my recommendation and on what I told him about Emmett's ability to bring in significant clients."

"Zack, Emmett cornered me last night and talked to me about Falconer Shreve," I said. "He knew everything about the firm. He seemed to believe that being part of the Falconer Shreve family would be like finding the Holy Grail."

"A lifetime of happiness and eternal youth," Zack said, and his tone was plaintive.

"I can't believe the man I talked to last night is going to give up on his dream."

"It's his only option, Jo. Keating has no future at Falconer Shreve. Last night he was publicly humiliated in front of half the lawyers in Regina. Warren is offering him a graceful exit – a significant position in a beautiful city with unlimited opportunities and a chance to start over."

"Did Emmett seem as if he was open to Warren's proposal."

Zack's smile was self-mocking. "I wouldn't know. Emmett insisted the meeting be held at his apartment. When Warren and I arrived, Emmett buzzed Warren in, but he said I wasn't welcome."

"So what did you do?"

"I went back to Warren's car and spent half an hour arguing with Warren's driver over whether Peyton Manning was a better quarterback than Tom Brady. When Warren came out, he said he'd given Keating twenty-four hours to decide about the job, but he seemed optimistic."

"That's promising news," I said. "Hey, I almost forgot. Lorne Callow stopped by about an hour ago – officially in his capacity as acting head of the firm's HR."

"Is he worried about Keating?"

"He is, and he's confused because he has no idea what's going on. Lorne's planning to talk to Emmett. I just hope one of the partners tells him about the restructuring and the list before he hears it from Emmett. Lorne is trying to do what's best for everyone. The last thing you need is for him to feel alienated."

"I'll try to reach Delia before I go," Zack said. "Callow's a good guy."

"He seems like it," I said. "When I thanked him for handling the situation last night and attempting to connect with Emmett today, he said there are times when we really are our brother's keeper."

Zack was thoughtful. "Why is it always a shock when someone does something out of sheer decency?" He glanced at his watch. "No time for pondering the imponderables. I have to finish packing and make tracks to the airport."

"This is the first time we've been apart since we were married," I said.

"I'm no happier about this than you are, but I'll be back next Saturday morning, and the meetings Norine has lined up for me – especially the ones with the production companies – will be terrific for the city."

"Thinking about your legacy?"

Zack shrugged. "When I was sworn in as mayor, we said we'd be satisfied if we left the city in better shape than it was when I started. Bringing the film industry back here is just one step, but it could be a big one."

"I'll keep that in mind when I spend the next seven nights trying not to stare at the place where you should be in our bed."

Zack is no fonder of goodbyes than I am. As soon as he checked his bags, we embraced. Then, he went into the departures area and I headed for Margot's. She buzzed me up and was waiting at the elevator with her jacket and boots on when I arrived.

For a beat we just stood apart, arms stiffly at our sides. "I didn't call ahead because I thought you might not want to see me," I said finally.

"I was on my way to your place," Margot said. "I didn't call ahead either – same reason. The kids are already across the hall at Brock's." She put her arm around my shoulder. "Let's go inside and sort this out."

Margot made tea and we took it to the armchairs by the window that overlooked the terrace. On the low table between our chairs was a huge bouquet of American Beauty roses in a crystal vase. A box of tacks was on the table beside the roses and Zack's business card was propped against the box. I picked up the card and read the message Zack had written in his large, loping hand: *Name your time and place.*

"Are you going to take him up on it?" I said.

Margot chuckled. "I've never been able to stay mad at Zack. What he did was wrong, but I've made my share of mistakes. That said, Jo, I really do need some answers."

"Whatever answers you find will be connected to the bond between the original partners of Falconer Shreve," I said. "In the years since Zack and I married, I've been struck time and time again by how fiercely they defend one another. Margot, Chris took his life because the woman who was carrying their child discovered Chris's role in mishandling the firm's trust funds, and as a result she had an abortion. After Chris's suicide, Zack and the others made protecting his reputation their first priority."

Margot was a compassionate person, and as I told her about my meeting with Chris on the day he died and about my attempts with Angus to save Chris on the night of his death, her eyes filled. "God, what a tragedy," she said. "For everyone. And Chris believed the mother of his child decided she couldn't go through with the pregnancy because of what he'd done."

I nodded. "So much suffering," I said. "Not long after the facts about the trust funds money came to light, Lily Falconer died. Under normal circumstances, even I would have realized how serious the implications of the defalcation were, but there was nothing normal about that summer. Everyone was torn apart. All that mattered was finding a respite from the pain."

"And Zack found that respite with you."

"He did, but he still finds it difficult to talk about the circumstances surrounding Chris's death. I do too."

"So the subject is closed?"

"Yes, and Margot, except for the day he found out about the defalcation, Zack and I have never discussed it. It simply never occurred to me to tell you about it. I hope you believe that."

"I do," Margot said. "But Zack's another matter."

"That's a conversation the two of you will have to have," I said. "He'd be devastated if you left Falconer Shreve."

"I'm not going to," Margot said. "I care about the firm too. And I care about the people who work there. If Keating throws mud at us, we'll just have to find a way to prove that we're a firm with integrity and carry on."

My phone vibrated. I checked. "It's Zack," I said. "Do you want to talk to him?"

"Sure," she said.

I picked up. "Where are you?"

"At the gate. Just about to board."

"I'm at Margot's. She'd like to talk to you." I handed her the phone.

"I'm giving you another chance, big man, but no more of that 'some partners are more equal than other partners' shit.

We're all on equal footing, and that includes the new equity partners." Margot listened and purred, "God, I love it when you're abject." Her lips twitched towards a smile, but whatever Zack said next wiped the smile away. "What's going on?" I said.

Her forehead creased. "Zack's texting us a video. He wants us to watch it and call him back."

We stood side by side to watch the video on my phone screen. When it ended, we turned to each other, perplexed. The video was of Annie Weber frogmarching Emmett Keating out of the dining room and into the foyer. Whoever took it had been standing close enough to capture the fury on Emmett's face and the determination on Annie's. The person with the camera had followed them to the front door, where Annie handed Emmett off to the doorman.

I called Zack back. "Who sent it?"

"Amicuscuriae@hotmail.com" he said. "Latin for 'friend of the court,' so probably a lawyer, and lawyers were not in short supply at the Scarth Club last night. If I were a betting man, which, of course, I am, I'd bet this little vignette is making the rounds in the legal community. Dee and Maisie and a few lawyer colleagues have already texted to say they received it."

"So the video is being sent to people outside Falconer Shreve," I said. "Who would want to humiliate Emmett like this?"

"Someone who wants to keep the pot boiling," Zack said. "Darryl?"

"It's possible. But I don't see what's in it for him. When you were talking to him last night, did he say why he was at the dinner?"

"Just that a friend gave him the ticket."

Zack chuckled. "Those tickets were a thousand dollars a pop – generous friend."

"That was my response too," I said. "When I asked Darryl if the friend was someone I knew, he said the ticket was from 'an admirer of Falconer Shreve,' and then he gave me his Snidely Whiplash smile and said, 'But aren't we all?'"

"Good old Darryl. Never passes up a chance to stick in the shiv," Zack said. "Gotta go. Boarding time. I love you."

"I love you too," I said. "Call me when you get to Pearson."

I looked at Margot. "Dee and Maisie already texted Zack to say they'd received the video."

Margot walked across the room, picked up her phone, and checked. "I got it too." For a moment, she stared at her phone screen. "*Amicus curiae*," she said. "Very lawyer-like. So I guess we start with every lawyer's favourite question, *Cui bono*? Who profits?"

"Whoever took the video," I said. "And there were a lot of people at the Scarth Club last night."

Margot stood. "Yet again, more questions than answers," she said. "Time to tackle something where we're guaranteed a happy outcome. Let's go across the hall and tell Brock we've made up. He was worried."

Brock had taken over our old condo after we left. It seemed strange to walk into a space as familiar to me as the back of my hand and see unmistakable evidence that someone else now lived there. The condo had been completely furnished when we moved in. All we had brought was our own art. At first, Brock had filled the empty spaces where our art had hung with framed black-and-white photos of football greats. Now the sports photographs had been replaced by two monumental pieces from Wally Dion's *Red Worker* series. Margot and I had attended Dion's first solo show at the MacKenzie Gallery together, and we had both been impressed by his huge portraits depicting First Nations peoples in their workplaces.

"Two Wally Dions," I said. "*Pipe Carrier* and *Nurse Tracy* – did you win the lottery?"

Brock was on the floor playing trucks with Lexi, still in her Max suit, and stacking cups with Kai. "Margot thought the kids should be proud of their community," he said.

"Plus," Margot drawled, "I always wanted a Wally Dion, but I ran out of wall space."

"I have wall space," I said.

Brock grinned at us. "I take it you two have worked everything out."

"Not quite everything," Margot said. "But there are trucks to be driven and cups to be stacked. If Lexi and Kai will let us join you, we'll fill you in."

Margot and I knelt on the floor with Brock and the kids, and between zooming trucks and arranging cups Margot showed Brock the video of Annie escorting Emmett from the Scarth Club. She also filled him in on Warren's job offer.

"Has Keating responded?" Brock said.

"Not as far as I know," I said. "And, Brock, at this point I don't imagine Emmett Keating will be interested in talking to any of the partners. This morning, Zack stopped by with Warren to discuss the offer. Emmett wouldn't even let Zack in his apartment – and that was before the video surfaced."

"Do you think Emmett would talk to me?" Brock said. "I was there when he made that scene with Delia, but I don't have any official connection with the firm yet. If I explained that I had just come as a messenger to tell Emmett that everyone at Falconer Shreve felt sick about how the evening ended, he might feel less alone."

Margot covered Brock's hand with her own. "You can be very persuasive," she said. "Why don't you give it a shot?"

"Norine will have his contact information," I said.

Emmett's phone number was unlisted, but Norine quickly produced it and Brock called. When Emmett didn't pick up,

Brock was sanguine. "I'll keep trying," he said. "And I'll let you know if I get through."

"Okay," I said. "I should go home and see what Taylor has planned for the day." After I'd kissed Margot, Lexi, and Kai goodbye, Brock walked me to the elevator. "I miss our morning runs," I said. "But living across the hall from one another seems like a perfect arrangement for you, Margot, and the kids."

"It's great for all of us. The kids have two parents, and Margot and I have each other, and we're free to have other relationships – at least in theory."

"But not in practice?" I said.

"We've both gone out with other people, but there are never any sparks. Margot and I have more fun together with the kids than we do dating people we're not interested in, so except for work we stick pretty close to home."

"Like an old married couple," I said.

Brock smile was surprisingly bashful. "There are worse things to be."

CHAPTER

10

The scene I walked into when I got home was a familiar one. Over the years, Gracie, Isobel, and Taylor had undertaken many projects. Seeing the three of them sitting together at our kitchen table plotting and planning brought a rush of memories: the summer they positioned inuksuit around the half moon of Lawyers' Bay so that a traveller who had somehow wandered into our gated community could always find his or her way; the autumn I drove them around the countryside on a pumpkin-seeking mission for the rustic/elegant Halloween party they were planning; the December they mixed essential oils to create personality signature scents as gifts for friends, parents, and each other. Now Gracie and Izzie had joined Taylor to mull over how she could best use traditional Día de los Muertos decorations in her art project exploring the function of death images in the work of Frida Kahlo. The young women had come a long way from personality signature scents.

"FedEx just brought all this," Taylor said when she saw me. She gestured to the table. It was a fiesta of brilliantly coloured, elaborately dressed skeletons made of papier mâché, cardboard, foil, or wood and of skulls made of sugar, glass, plastic, and who knew what else.

"*Calacas* and *calaveras* everywhere," Gracie said. "Do you think you might have over-ordered?"

"I think that's a possibility," Taylor said ruefully.

Isobel pulled a skeleton dressed in early twentieth-century finery from a box, straightened the skeleton's large and elaborate picture hat, and looked at the facial bones of the skull below it. Isobel's expression was intent. "Who were you?" she said, and there was no whimsy in her question. She had always been a girl who needed answers.

Taylor was happy to comply. "Catrina Calavera, the Skelton Dame," she said. "She fascinated me too, so I did the research. A graphic artist named José Guadalupe Posada made the first image of her to mock the Mexican elite."

"To show them that death takes us all – rich or poor," I said.

"I guess," Taylor said.

Gracie reached into the box in which Catrina had been packed and pulled out another skeletal female figure, this one with her face framed in delicate paper flowers and her body draped in a gold lamé cape. The figure was small, no more than twenty centimetres high, and her arms were raised in benediction. The Catrina Calavera had been striking but was cheaply made. This was the work of a true artist.

"That's Santa Muerte," Taylor said. "Sometimes she's just called Bony Lady. Her followers – and online it says that there are millions of them – believe she's a saint who will protect them in their lifetime and, when death comes, deliver them safely and lovingly to the afterlife."

Gracie's face was grave. "It would nice to believe in Bony Lady," she said.

Isobel and Taylor had already started repacking the decorations. Gracie had spoken softly and they hadn't heard her, but I had.

I caught Gracie's eye. "It *would* be nice to believe in her," I said.

Gracie touched my hand and then said to the other girls. "Taylor, is it okay if I keep Bony Lady for a while?"

Taylor didn't hesitate. "Keep her forever," she said. "There are probably at least six more Santa Muertes in these boxes."

"Thanks. I'll take good care of her." Gracie looked thoughtfully at the doll she was holding. "Looks like you and I are joining forces, Santa Muerte."

Our house was on a double lot, and when we'd moved in the first time, we'd had a studio built for Taylor on the second lot. The arrangement worked for us all. Taylor had a spacious place with a north window where she could make art, and Zack and I knew she was safe and doing what she loved. Laden with FedEx boxes, the girls headed for Taylor's studio. When I closed the door behind them, it occurred to me I'd skipped lunch. I found a bowl of chili in the fridge, stuck it in the microwave, picked up an old *New Yorker*, and thumbed through it until I found an article about Julianne Moore I'd started months earlier. By the time Isobel and Gracie returned, I'd finished both the chili and the article, and I'd made a list of the Julianne Moore movies Zack and I could curl up and watch when he got back from Toronto.

"Taylor's working on that portrait of the three of you she's giving you and Zack for Christmas," Isobel said.

"Have you seen it?" Gracie asked.

"No," I said. "It's top secret."

"It's also really good. Have you ever noticed that your hands and Taylor's are exactly the same," Isobel said. "Graceful, but with the same long, powerful fingers."

"I know our feet are the same," I said. "Because Taylor's always borrowing my shoes."

Gracie laughed, but Isobel was determined to drive home

her point. She cocked her head. "And there's something about your mouth," she said. "I'd never noticed it before, but the similarity is definitely there."

"There's a theory that people who've been married for a long time grow to look alike," I said. "There's no blood relationship between Taylor and me, but she was four when I adopted her. We've been together more than ten years."

"Genetic osmosis," Isobel said thoughtfully. "I wonder if such a thing is possible. I'll go online and check it out. But right now, I'd better motor. I've got some shopping to do."

"Getting a jump on the holidays?" I said.

Isobel shrugged into her jacket. "Nadine Perrault sent me a list of my sister's favourites – the books Abby loved, the music, the flowers, and some other random things. A lot of Abby's favourites are mine too." Her forehead furrowed. "It's difficult to think that I share traits with someone I never knew and never will know."

Gracie moved closer to her friend. "I'm worried that you're counting too much on our evening."

Isobel's smile was small and tentative. "I know," she said, "but it's hard not to hope."

After Isobel left, Gracie opened her backpack and slid Santa Muerte carefully into it. "I'd better hit the road too," she said. "Today is Rose's sister Betty's birthday, and I'm going out to Standing Buffalo for supper." Gracie was sociable by nature and she loved Rose and Betty, but as she started towards the door she was clearly troubled.

"Not so fast," I said. "Gracie, is this whole Día de los Muertos thing still getting to you?"

Gracie made a face of mock dismay. "Am I that transparent?"

"Only because you shared your concern with me."

Gracie placed her backpack on the table and pulled up a chair. "Yes, it's still getting to me – it's getting to me big-time. I'm trying to deal with my feelings rationally. Taylor's right. The art that's grown out of Día de los Muertos is brilliant, and it's inspired us to find a way for our families to heal." Gracie reached into her backpack and withdrew Bony Lady. "But I don't know. Take my friend here," she said. "All those followers of Santa Muerte that Taylor mentioned – they believe she has the power to protect them when they're alive and ease their passage into the afterlife. For us she's just a curiosity." Gracie touched the doll's face gently with one finger. "Maybe that's the real problem I'm having with all this, Jo. I wish I truly did believe that invoking my mother would help my father move on from her. I wish I *could* believe there was a saint who could protect the dead – and one who could keep the living safe from bad medicine."

"You're still thinking of that old man at Standing Buffalo," I said.

"Esau Pilger," Gracie said. "I can't get him out of my mind."

"Neither can I," I said.

"But you're not afraid of him," Gracie said.

"No, I'm not afraid. Esau Pilger has every right to hate what people like me did to his people, but spitting was just a way of showing his contempt. It wasn't bad medicine. Don't give him power over your life, Gracie. Your grand-mother was at the centre of a tragedy involving two men who loved her. Unfortunately, that happens. Your mother had her own demons, but Esau Pilger didn't put them there."

"Her childhood did," Gracie said. "At least that's what Rose believes. Rose says all of our people have sorrows that just keep repeating themselves."

"Because of bad medicine?" I said. "Or because of wounds that haven't been given an airing so they can heal? Gracie, that day at the lake, the arguments you and Isobel and Taylor raised for coming together to understand and accept the past made a lot of sense. But see the gathering for what it is – a therapy that, as you pointed out to Izzie, may or may not work."

"In psych class, we learned that to test a hypothesis, you have to identify the effect of the independent variables," Gracie said.

"Those that affect the way the other variables respond in a controlled environment," I said.

Gracie chuckled. "I see I'm not the only one to have taken Psych 100," she said. "Well, in this case, my mother's life is the dependent variable and the independent variable is bad medicine. If I can keep my courage up, tonight after Betty's birthday dinner I'm going to ride my bike over to Old Man Pilger's and ask him whether there was a curse on my grandmother and my mother." She held her hand out. "Look at that," she said. "Even the thought makes me tremble."

"Would you feel braver if I was standing beside you?"

"Are you serious?"

"Very. Taylor's got a pizza and movie night with her art class. Do you think Rose would mind having an extra guest at her party for Betty?"

"She'd love it."

"Okay then. But I'd like to bring Betty a gift," I said. "Any suggestions?"

"Elizabeth Taylor's White Diamonds. Betty worshipped Elizabeth Taylor, and Shoppers sells her perfume, so we can stop there for you to pick up a bottle on our way out of town."

Gracie had been uncharacteristically withdrawn as we drove out of the city, and I wondered if she was revisiting her decision to confront Esau Pilger. But, in fact, a choice about her future was on Gracie's mind.

"Penny for your thoughts," I said.

"Canada doesn't have pennies any more, so you're going to have raise the ante," Gracie said, and her tone was playful.

"Okay, a nickel for your thoughts," I said. "But I want the full story."

"I got the first recruiting letter of the season today," Gracie said. "It was from my dream college: Notre Dame."

Touted as the best shooting guard in a decade on the university's women's basketball team, Gracie had been scouted the year before by American colleges with heavily funded athletic programs. Now it seemed the pursuit had begun again. "Notre Dame's a terrific university," I said. "They have a solid academic reputation, and from what Zack tells me, they're conscientious about preparing student-athletes for life after graduation."

"It was tough turning them down last year," Gracie said. "It's going to be even tougher doing it this year."

"Blake wouldn't want you to turn them down again," I said. "You know that."

"I do," Gracie said, "But every time I think about Dad rattling around in that great big house alone, I know I don't have an option."

"Gracie, you don't have to make a decision today. Things change. The gathering on Halloween might be just the push your dad needs."

"Dream on," Gracie said. And for the next half-hour, we did just that – we talked about all the possibilities that lay ahead for both Blake and Gracie. The topic was absorbing, and we were both surprised at how quickly we arrived at the turnoff to the reserve. Standing Buffalo Dakota First Nation was on a physically stunning setting overlooking the Qu'Appelle Valley. Once, a mighty and seemingly never-ending river of buffalo had been driven over the reserve's hills. Over time, white hunters decimated the herds; the river of buffalo slowed to a trickle and then dried up completely.

When the Falconer family was at the lake, Rose Lavallee lived in the house next door to her sister Betty's. The sisters were close, but they were as different as two sisters could be. Everything about Rose announced that she was a no-nonsense woman: her body was small and wiry; her skin care regime was simple: sunscreen during the day and Vaseline at night; her grey hair was styled in a tight perm; and her wardrobe was strictly wash-and-wear. At seventy, Betty was still a looker, with a plump, curvy body and hair as black as a raven's wing. She prided herself on the fact that no one, including her three late husbands, had ever seen her without full, perfectly applied makeup.

That night both sisters greeted us at the front door. Gracie and I brought in the gifts and Betty *oohed* and *aahed* as she unwrapped them while Rose got supper on the table. Gracie had informed me that Betty preferred the White Diamonds eau de toilette to the perfume, and the information was spot on. As soon as Betty saw her gift, she opened the box and spritzed herself and Gracie and me. "Rose will give me Hail Columbia for doing this," Betty said happily, "but it's my birthday and I want everybody to feel like a movie star."

Zack called just after Rose had stopped giving Betty Hail Columbia and had brought in the bannock. My husband was in a good mood. "Hey, I have primo accommodations – corner room overlooking Lake Ontario. Great big bed, but I'm looking at your spot and it's empty. God, I wish you were here."

"I wish I was there too, but I guarantee whatever you have for dinner won't be as good as what I'm about to have. Gracie and I are out at Standing Buffalo celebrating Betty's birthday. Rose is serving moose chili."

"You win," Zack said. "Tell Betty happy birthday from the mayor."

"I will," I said. "But we're just about to eat, so I'll call you later.

As she placed my bowl in front of me, Rose gave me a conspiratorial wink. "I know you like moose chili, Joanne," she said, "so I gave you a double portion."

I was still comfortably full from my late lunch of chili, but I'm a gamer, so I happily dug in. Supper was a lot of fun. Rose put on a CD of mellow love songs by Betty's favourite artist, Lionel Richie, the chili and bannock were excellent, and, safe in the warmth of her second family, Gracie relaxed. After Betty had blown out the candles and we'd had our cake and tea, Gracie caught my eye. "I'm going to take a spin on my bike and burn off a few calories. Want to join me, Jo?"

I stood. "Sure. Rose, promise me you'll leave the dishes. We'll get them when we come back."

"I never make a promise I won't keep," Rose said. "But you're our guest, and lately Gracie's been looking like she could use a little fun. You can take my bike, Joanne. It's in the shed with Gracie's. Don't forget your helmets."

The mountain bike the Falconers had given Rose the previous Christmas was the duplicate of Gracie's – a Trek – and as soon as I jumped on, I knew it would be a joy to ride. "Just follow me," Gracie said, and I did.

Rose believed early dinners gave a person the chance to digest her food properly before bed, so it was a quarter past five when Gracie and I started out. The sun was just beginning to set, and we were enjoying the ride when Gracie stopped and pointed to a house at the top of a side road that wound up the hill.

"That's his place," she said. She turned to face me. "Jo, this might not be such a good idea. Esau's old, and people say he suffers from dementia. He really is obsessed with what happened to my grandmother, and that was close to fifty years ago. I'm not sure how he'll handle confrontation."

"We're not here to confront him," I said. "We're here so that you and I can clear the air with Esau Pilger and assure ourselves that there's nothing to fear from him. Let's get it over with."

We pushed our bikes the rest of the way up the road. When I turned to take in the view, I was surprised at how visible our property at Lawyers' Bay was from the top of the hill. I always referred to our place at the lake as a cottage, but the truth was that, like the other four dwellings on the horseshoe of land, ours was a large and beautifully designed summer home. As the sun descended towards the horizon, the houses on Lawyers' Bay were bathed in golden light. Years ago, landscapers had planted Amur maples around the property, and their foliage glowed in the vibrant colours of autumn: orange, scarlet, and burgundy. For me, the beauty of the scene was breathtaking, but for Esau Pilger it could have served as a constant reminder of what had been lost.

Rose and Betty were house-proud, and their bungalows were neat as two pins. Esau Pilger's was a shambles. The area around the house was a graveyard of rusting farm machinery, old tires, husks of abandoned cars, and – incongruously – a bathtub, a sink, and a toilet. Even in the dying light of dusk I could see that the roof was missing shingles and that the wood on the front steps sagged.

A quartet of barking dogs approached. My kids mocked me for always carrying dog treats in my jacket pocket, but that night the treats came in handy. I took out the baggie and scattered some desiccated liver on the ground. The dogs wolfed it, and when I held out more on the palm of my hand, they approached, took the liver, and sniffed at me. I apparently passed muster. They calmed enough to let me pat them.

Gracie had been watching. "Jo, the dog whisperer," she said, and she knocked on the door. When there was no answer, she knocked again and waited. "He's not here," she said, and I could hear the relief in her voice. Just then, the old man opened the door. The stench of rot, feces, and cat pee from the air inside hit us like a wall.

The old man was shrunken with age, and Gracie dwarfed him, but he had a powerful voice. "Get away, white girl," he said.

"I'm not a white girl," Gracie said. "I'm Gloria Ryder's granddaughter."

Esau scowled. "I know who you are," he said. "If Gloria had married me, she wouldn't have had no white grand-daughter. She threw away her life, and that daughter of hers – your mother – married white and threw away her life. They deserved what they got and you'll deserve what you get." He stepped back inside, slamming the door behind him.

Gracie pivoted to face me. Her eyes were wide, and her voice was urgent. "Not one of my better ideas," Gracie said. "Let's get out of here."

We rushed to our bikes and started down the hill. Just as we began to pick up speed, Gracie hit a rock that, in the growing darkness, seemed to come out of nowhere. The impact threw her from her bicycle.

"Are you okay?" I said.

Gracie started to push herself into standing position, and then she groaned. "Better call 911," she said. "I've done something to my knee."

I pulled out my phone. "That won't work here," Gracie said. "You'll need to use a landline."

I looked around the dark valley. The closest house was at least a fifteen-minute ride away. "I'm going to go back to Esau Pilger's and ask to use his phone," I said.

"Don't," Gracie said. "He might hurt you."

"He's frail. I bet he weighs less than a hundred pounds," I said. "I'll take my chances."

The words were brave, but as I walked up the hill my pulse was racing. I knocked, and when there was no answer, I opened the door. The stench was stomach-turning. Esau was sitting on a kitchen chair under a naked light bulb with a tray-sized board balanced on his knees. On the board was a whetstone, and Esau was rhythmically stroking the blade of what appeared to be a hunting knife against the stone. The play of light and shadows on the old man's face made him seem otherworldly; so did the cats that prowled around him, mewing.

"There's been an accident," I said. "Where's your phone?"

Esau turned the knife over and began stroking the other side of the blade against the stone. He was ignoring me. As the rasp of the blade continued, my nerves tightened. "Gloria Ryder's granddaughter is lying by the side of the path to your house and she's hurt," I said. "I need your phone."

He kept his eyes on me, but he jerked his thumb over his shoulder, indicating the wall behind him. Getting to the phone was tough – the floor was covered in newspapers spongy with animal urine and feces, and I had to pass closely by Esau. When I dialled 911, I realized I had no idea where I was. I turned to the old man.

"They need directions," I said.

"Tell them Esau Pilger's place – they'll know," he said. I gave the operator our location and broke the connection.

As I made my way to the front door, I looked around. Two of the walls were covered in old newspaper clippings and photographs yellowed and curling with age. Hanging next to the door were two framed photographs: one was of a striking young woman. At first I thought it was Lily Falconer, but of course it was her mother – Gloria Ryder, the woman Esau

Pilger had loved. The second was the photo of The Winners' Circle up to their knees in the lake their first summer at Lawyers' Bay. I went cold. It was a personal photo, and how it had come into Esau's hands was a mystery, but Gracie was in pain and waiting. "Thanks for letting me use your phone," I said.

The hunting knife was still in his hands. "What's happened to the girl?"

"Her bike hit a rock and she fell," I said. "She'll be fine. It's just her knee," I said. As soon as the words left my mouth, I realized how foolish they were. Gracie's life was basketball and for that she needed both legs.

By way of answer, he put down the knife and placed his hands on the table on either side of it. I opened the door and left. Outside, I zipped my jacket and made my way as quickly as possible back to Gracie. "How are you doing?"

"I've been better," she said.

"The ambulance is on its way," I said.

I bent to look at her leg by the light of my phone. "Some scrapes. Not much blood, but your knee *is* swelling," I said.

"I'm pretty sure I've torn my ACL," Gracie said. "I heard a pop when I went down."

"That doesn't sound good," I said.

"It's not," she said. "But no use complaining. Coach always says, 'The game honours toughness.'"

By the time the ambulance arrived, Gracie and I had agreed on what to do next. She wasn't in pain, but she'd moved her knee gingerly a few times, and she was convinced that her diagnosis of a torn anterior cruciate ligament was correct. Gracie had been playing basketball seriously since she was ten, so she was knowledgeable about the protocol for injuries related to her sport. At the hospital, the orthopedic surgeon on call would examine her. There would be tests, including an MRI, and the surgeon would decide on treatment.

Gracie was in complete control. She said that there was nothing I could do at the hospital, so once she was safely stowed in the ambulance, I should ride Rose's bike back to her place and tell her what had happened. Blake was in Calgary, and she asked me to call from Rose's to tell him the situation, and then she wanted Rose and me to drive back to the city in Gracie's car. Rose would stay at the hospital with Gracie and I'd go home, fill Taylor in on the night, and get some sleep. Neither of us mentioned Old Man Pilger's curse or the rock that had appeared seemingly out of nowhere in front of Gracie's bike when we sped down the hill.

I followed Gracie's instructions to a T. When I got home, I told Taylor what had happened and reassured her that Gracie would be fine. Then I took a long shower in an effort to scrub away every trace of Esau Pilger and the fetid air of his house. But no amount of scalding water could banish the memory of that shadowy room with its walls filled with yellowing newspaper clippings and the old man at the table, sharpening his knife. I brushed my teeth, put on my pyjamas, and started for bed, but my mind was racing. "Monkey mind," Buddha had called it, filled with thoughts that jump around, screeching, chattering, carrying on endlessly, and clambering for attention. I stood at the French doors that opened from our bedroom onto the creek, hoping the chill night air and ribbon of light the moon drew on the water would calm me. By the time I slipped into bed I thought I was ready to sleep, but one monkey had not been tamed – the strongest one. Fear.

When I closed my eyes, two images appeared so real and dimensional I could have reached out and touched them. The first was the framed portrait of Gloria Ryder, the woman Esau loved and had lost. The second was the photograph of Zack and his friends, who, if Gracie was correct, had become the focal point of Esau's hatred. I had been skeptical of the idea that the old man might have cursed Gracie with bad medicine, but remembering how, just minutes after Esau told Gracie she would get what she deserved, she suffered a serious accident, I was no longer certain of anything.

CHAPTER

11

At eleven the next day, Blake Falconer and I were having an early lunch at the very crowded Robin's Donuts on the main floor of Pasqua Hospital. Blake had caught the 8:25 flight from Calgary. I'd picked him up at the airport and we'd come straight to the hospital. Six of Gracie's teammates from the university had just gathered en masse in her room when we arrived, so Blake and Gracie hugged each other hard and then, having reassured himself that his daughter was fine and enjoying the camaraderie of her friends, Blake promised Gracie he'd be back in twenty minutes and we went downstairs to eat.

When I met Blake my first summer at Lawyers' Bay, his red-gold hair, like Gracie's, seemed to draw the light to his face. He'd joined me on the raft where Rose and I were watching the girls swim. His grey eyes and ruddy complexion glowed with the vitality of a man eager to embrace life's pleasures. He'd settled in so close on my towel that I could smell the sharp citrus of his aftershave and watch his chest rise and fall as he breathed. It was too much intimacy with a stranger and I'd moved away.

The man sitting opposite me now was no longer a stranger. Over the years, I'd come to know Blake and to respect him for managing to bridge the immense gulf between his career and his private life. In the last weeks of his marriage to Lily Falconer, his life was a shambles. After her death, Blake's existence was the stuff of tragedy, but he was always a committed and loving father to Gracie, a consummate professional with his clients, and a loyal friend to his law partners and their families. That morning at the hospital, it was clear Blake was running on empty – a man pushing himself to get through whatever lay ahead.

"Did you sleep at all after I called last night?" I said.

Blake shrugged. "Probably not. I played Dr. Internet and went online to read about the treatment of ACL injuries."

"Always a mistake," I said. "Our grandmothers were right. 'A little knowledge is a dangerous thing.'"

"Agreed. But in this case I was glad I had enough superficial knowledge to understand what Gracie's orthopedic surgeon was saying when she returned my call this morning."

"An orthopedic surgeon actually *called* you," I said. "I'm impressed."

"Astrid and I went out for a while this summer," Blake said. His brow furrowed. "For the life of me I can't remember why it ended. She's a terrific woman. Anyway, Astrid waited to call until she'd seen the MRI. Gracie's anterior cruciate ligament is so badly torn it will have to be replaced – probably with a ligament from a cadaver."

"Wow. A cadaver. That's an amazing thought," I said. "I'm leaving my body to science. I always figured I'd end up at some medical school, but I like the idea of my ligament being part of a player as skilled as Gracie."

Blake narrowed his eyes. "Are you really that cool about what happens to your body after you die?"

"No, but none of the options is appealing. That one makes the most sense for me."

"I should probably look into it," Blake said.

"Don't tell me you don't already have it in your will."

He tried a smile. "Okay, I won't tell you. Anyway, back to the immediate concern. Gracie has a long slog ahead of her, Jo. There are non-surgical options, but because Gracie's an athlete who wants to return to her pre-injury level of competition, she'll need surgery."

"How soon can they do it?"

"Not until Gracie's through with what Astrid called 'pre-habilitation' – exercises to strengthen the muscles that surround the knee. That can take up to five months. After the surgery there's serious rehab, and that's another six to nine months."

"So a year without basketball," I said.

"It will be a blow, but Gracie's strong." Blake lowered his eyes. "I guess she's had to be," he said.

"She's a remarkable young woman," I said.

"She's a miracle," Blake said. "Now why don't you tell me exactly what happened?"

"I will, but eat something first. The soup's actually pretty good."

Like many virtues, stoicism is a two-edged sword. Given her turbulent family life and her passion for sports, Gracie's physical and emotional toughness had served her well. But her unwillingness to discuss her feelings often made it difficult for those close to her to gauge her true state of mind. I was certain Gracie hadn't told her father that she had become deeply ambivalent about the gathering on the Day of the Dead, so my account of the previous day's events was detailed. When I explained Gracie's uncertainties, Blake was surprised.

He ran his hand through his crew cut. "Maybe this Day of the Dead thing is too much," he said. "When the girls talked about it at the lake, it seemed innocent enough. In fact, it seemed like a good idea. There've been too many deaths, and we haven't dealt with them well. But if this is taking Gracie to a dark place, perhaps we should just deep six the whole idea."

"It's not that simple," I said. "The girls were right that our families all have wounds that need healing. Noah and Izzie want to make remembering Abby a part of her son Jacob's life and their own. And you heard Dee that morning at the lake. She believes embracing Chris's spirit will bring back the laughter and reignite the fire the firm once had." I leaned across the table. "And, Blake, Gracie believes you need this too, because it's time you let Lily go."

Suddenly, Blake seemed ineffably weary. "Easier said than done." He cleared his throat. "So how does Esau Pilger figure in all this? You said Gracie's accident happened on the path to his house on the reserve. What were you two doing out there?"

"Gracie was looking for answers, and I didn't want her to go alone," I said. "Blake, did Lily ever talk to you about the Ryder family's history?"

"Outside the office, Lily and I didn't talk about much of anything," he said. "Lily certainly didn't talk much about her past. She was determined to leave everything behind."

"Yet she was fine with Gracie spending all that time on Standing Buffalo with Rose?"

"We never talked about it. To be honest, I was afraid to. I was grateful that Rose was helping Gracie understand what it meant to be part of the Dakota Nation, but I didn't know how Lily felt about it, and I didn't want to risk alienating her by asking."

"Why would talking about how to raise your daughter be a problem for Lily?"

He shrugged. "It might not have been, but I never knew how Lily was going to respond to things. Whenever I pressed Lily about a decision she'd made, she'd shut me out or, worse, she'd take off. It was better for both of us if I just stayed silent."

Blake was watching my face. "You look shocked."

"I'm sorry," I said. "Every marriage is different."

"Jo, I don't expect you to understand this, but right up until the end, there were times when Lily opened herself completely to me, and the two of us would be filled with such joy that all we could do was grin like kids and shake our heads at the wonder of it all. I couldn't risk losing that."

Blake's naked display of emotion overwhelmed me. Lily had never hidden her serial infidelities, her disappearances, and her indifference to the needs of her husband and daughter, and I had wondered, as everyone did, why Blake stayed with her. Now I knew.

"Lily was my life," he said softly. "She's been dead four years now, but even the memory of how good it could be between us brings me to my knees with gratitude." He laughed. "Maybe the curse extended to me," he said.

My nerves twanged. "There really was a curse?"

"Before we married, Lily told me about her mother's history with Esau Pilger and how people said Esau used bad medicine to put some sort of curse on Gloria for not marrying him." Blake's eyes flashed with realization. "Gracie went over to Old Man Pilger's house because she wanted to ask him about that curse."

"Blake, I believe that traditional medicines can heal, but Gracie and I were both uneasy about the possibility of medicine being used to harm. We went to see Esau Pilger to prove to ourselves that the tragedies that happened in the Ryder family weren't caused by bad medicine, just by human beings making decisions that turned out badly."

"And when Gracie went to find proof that bad medicine doesn't exist, she had an accident that will take her out of basketball for an entire year." Blake's face was troubled. "So what do you think, Jo?"

"I don't know. I keep telling myself that what happened to Gracie was just an accident, but there's part of me that wonders . . ."

"There's part of me that wonders too," Blake said. He glanced at his watch, his half-eaten soup, and his still-wrapped sandwich. "Time to go," he said.

The hospital staff had done their best to brighten the public areas with Halloween decorations. But plastic jack-o'-lanterns, cardboard cut-outs of snaggle-toothed witches, and foil garlands of black cats were no match for the painfully slow promenade of the walking wounded as they dragged their IV stands down the corridor on the way to the hospital's front doors and the opportunity to grab a smoke. The sight of Gracie, her face lit with gladness, sitting on the bed, dressed and clearly ready to blow the joint, was just the tonic Blake and I needed to lift the gloom of the past half-hour.

"You look great," I said.

"Feeling great," she said. "They're fitting me with a Donjoy Drytex knee brace in four days, but until then I'm on crutches. I can live with that."

"You're getting out today?"

"As soon as Dr. Abramsen signs my release."

Rose was sitting in the corner knitting. "Gracie wants to go to the university and watch her team practise."

"If that's what Gracie wants . . ." Blake said.

Gracie smiled at her father. "That's what Gracie wants."

"I'll drive you," Blake said.

I said goodbye to Blake and Rose and kissed Gracie on the forehead. "I'll call later and see how everybody's doing," I said.

"Everybody will be doing just fine," Rose said crisply, and the set of her mouth was the only guarantee I needed.

It was eight o'clock our time and ten Toronto time when Zack and I finally connected. We'd missed each other, left messages, called again, and missed again. Zack was triumphant when he heard my unrecorded voice. "Hey – finally," he said. "First things first. I love you and I wish you were here."

"Ditto," I said. "But I'm glad I was here for Blake and Gracie."

"How's she doing?"

After I delivered my précis of the medical news, Zack sighed. "I guess it could be worse," he said. "Gracie will hate being on the bench for the rest of the season."

"She's handling it well," I said. "As soon as she was released from the hospital, Blake drove her to the university to watch her team practise."

"And Blake's hanging in?"

"Barely," I said. "I picked him up at the airport and he and I had lunch together at the hospital. He talked about his love for Lily. Every time I think about Blake's grief when he remembered her, my throat closes."

"Lily grieved too," Zack said. "She loved Blake, Jo."

"You and she were close, weren't you," I said. "I remember watching you drive the boat for her when she was waterskiing. She took so many chances, but every time you did a shoulder check she just indicated you should go faster."

"And I did. Lily and I understood each other's demons. But that's a topic for another day. Jo, I have news too, but I honestly don't know what to make of it. Warren Weber gave Emmett Keating twenty-four hours to give him an answer on the job offer, but by ten o'clock this morning Warren still hadn't heard from him. Warren tried calling and texting, but no response, so late this afternoon Warren sent someone

over to Emmett's apartment building to check out the situation. When Warren's guy buzzed Emmett's apartment, no
one answered, so he had a little chat with the super of the
building, and the super took him up to Emmett's apartment
and let him in."

"Just like that," I said. "That's a little unusual, isn't it?"

"Maybe, but it worked out. The super picked up a couple
of hundred bucks and the guy Warren sent found something
interesting. Here's where it gets weird. You know that photo
of Chris, Dee, Blake, Kevin, and me in the lake the summer
after we opened the firm."

"Of course. Delia says it's 'iconic,'" I said. I swallowed
hard. The sight of the photograph hanging in Esau Pilger's
house still lingered in my memory, but there was no point
troubling Zack about it while he was away.

"Apparently Emmett couldn't resist being part of the
icon," Zack said. "He photoshopped himself into the picture, and the result is framed and sitting on his desk."

"That's bizarre," I said.

"It is that," Zack said. "I'm sending the picture now."

When I saw the photo, I felt a chill. Emmett was not as
young as the Falconer Shreve partners had been when the
picture was taken, but he was in their age range. He'd placed
himself beside Chris and, like the other freshly minted lawyers, he was wearing blue jeans, a T-shirt, and the confident
smile of a person who knows the future is dazzling. I couldn't
take my eyes off Emmett's comb-over and his hope-filled
face. "That is so sad," I said.

"Agreed," Zack said. "It's also frightening. What do you
think was going through Emmett's head when he sat at his
computer inserting his younger self into a photo that was
taken thirty years ago?"

"I don't know, and I don't want to know," I said. "Zack,
Emmett's not going to accept Warren's offer. This is his

dream. He's not done with Falconer Shreve. He wants to rewrite its history. He wants to be a part of the firm from the very beginning."

"And all we can do is wait for his next move," Zack said.

"No other option," I said. The words were measured, but even I could hear the tremor in my voice.

CHAPTER

12

The dogs and I had just come back from our run when Kevin Hynd phoned. "You free for breakfast?" he said.

"In Calgary?" I said.

"Nope, right here in Pile O' Bones. I flew in last night. Gracie's my goddaughter, and I had to make certain all was well. She really is amazing, Jo. Losing the rest of her season has to be a blow, but she's rolling with it. And that's more than Emmett Keating seems to be doing."

"Zack sent you the photo?"

"He did, and it freaked me out."

"Us too," I said. "Why don't we have breakfast here? You and I can talk without worrying about being overheard, and you can say hi to Taylor and the dogs."

"I'm not screwing up your plans?"

"I have no plans. I'm giving myself a morning off."

"A morning off from what?"

"From everything," I said.

When Taylor, late for choir practice, blew through the kitchen on her way to school, the dogs were flattened on the rug under the table. I was making waffle batter and Kevin was pouring juice. Kevin and I were both wearing blue jeans, flannel shirts, and walking boots. Taylor took one look at us and grinned. "You guys are so cute." She cupped her ear with her hand. "Is that the seventies I hear calling?"

Kevin passed Taylor a glass of juice. "You are now officially out of my will, missy. No Led Zeppelin, no Pink Floyd, no Janis Joplin for you. I'll have to take that trunk full of vinyl classics with me when I go."

Taylor brushed his cheek with a kiss. "You'll forgive me, Kev. You always do. Besides, I think you and Jo look really nice – folksy, like you're off to chop wood or churn butter or something."

"Now you're out of *my* will," I said.

Taylor picked up an apple from the bowl on the table. "Love you, Jo. Love you, Kev." And with that, she was gone.

I poured batter into the waffle iron.

"Want to listen to 'Stairway to Heaven'?" Kevin said. "It's on my playlist."

"Best offer I've had all day."

Kevin and I listened to Led Zeppelin's rock classic, and then we read the paper while we ate our waffles. After Kevin cleared away the dishes, I poured us each a second cup of coffee. "This is nice," Kevin said. "We should do it more often."

"I'd like that," I said. "But since you live in Calgary . . ."

"I won't be living in Calgary any more," he said. "Katina and I have taken a hard look at the Calgary office and we've made some decisions about restructuring." He leaned towards me. "Jo, Katina's the only person I've talked to about this, but she's taking over. I'm through being a lawyer." He touched the sleeve of his flannel shirt. "I'm through with three-piece suits and weekend meetings and business lunches. I'm through with the whole thing."

GGG

"Finally," I said. "Congratulations."

"I've given the law my best shot," he said. "You know that. I went to law school because that's what my mum and dad wanted, and I loved them. I would have bailed after first year, but by that time, I had met Zack and the others and we'd become close. Except for a hiatus here and there, I've stayed with the firm for almost thirty years."

"Because that's what your partners wanted. But now it's your turn."

Kevin's face lit up. "Yes, now it's my turn. I'm fifty-three years old, and for the first time in a long time, I'm looking forward to what's ahead. There is so much I want to see and learn and experience. I'm going to start by going back to the Jokhang Temple in Lhasa."

"A place of peace and power," I said. "I still use the post-card you sent me from Lhasa as a bookmark. I like to keep you close." Kevin reached over and took my hand. It was a moment of perfect connection broken when the landline rang.

Delia sounded tense. "Jo, I need to talk to Zack."

"He's in Toronto," I said. "And he's in meetings all morning."

"His phone is going straight to voicemail," Delia said, and her own voice was tight with frustration.

"He turns it off during meetings," I said. "You know that, Dee. Is there something I can do?"

"Exterminate that rat Emmett Keating," she said. "Have you checked your mail today?"

"Our mail doesn't come till the afternoon."

"This will have been hand-delivered. Emmett made a copy of that photo of the five of us at the lake that first summer and defiled it. How could he do that to us?"

The whine of privilege set my teeth on edge. "Dee, I'm not following you. Zack texted me that picture. What Emmett did is pathetic, and it's creepy, but I don't understand why you're so upset. The only person that photo hurts is Emmett."

"You're not making any sense." Delia was clearly exasperated. "How does it hurt that little toad? We're the ones whose faces were covered in excrement."

"Dee, you've lost me."

"Just check your mailbox," she said.

I tamped down my anger. "I'll be right back," I said. "Stay on the line."

Kevin was looking at me questioningly. "Delia," I said. "Apparently there's a problem."

I brought the padded mailing envelope inside, and heeding Delia's words about what the envelope contained, I took the trash can out from under the sink and opened the envelope over it. Kevin was standing beside me. As the picture slid out, he whistled.

I picked up the phone. "Okay, Dee," I said. "Obviously we were talking about two different versions of the same picture. Warren Weber had an investigator go to Emmett's apartment yesterday morning. The investigator found a doctored picture on Emmett's desk." When I described the photo, Delia was outraged afresh. "That photo is iconic. Keating had no right to steal it or tamper with it, and he had no right to defile it with excrement."

"I agree that was an ugly thing to do," I said, "but none of you was harmed. It was just a photo."

"You can't understand how it felt to open that envelope and see us like that."

Delia's comment struck a nerve, and I made no effort to warm the chill in my voice. "Dee, people around you are dealing with far worse things than seeing poop smeared on an old picture. Maybe it's time you thought about them."

She hung up. Usually after I lost my temper, I was sick with remorse. That day I didn't feel a scintilla of guilt.

Kevin sipped his coffee. "Dee certainly raised your hackles."

"I don't like being treated like Aaron Slick from Pumpkin Crick."

Kevin chuckled. "No one who saw you in that black gown you wore to the dinner at the Scarth Club would have mistaken you for Aaron Slick."

I smiled. "You're a good friend. Anyway, we have real problem to deal with." After I told him that no one had seen or heard from Emmett since Warren made his offer, Kevin raised his eyebrows. "So we've got Emmett, the Missing Person, and Emmett, creator of the Emmett-as-Zelig photo. And we've got Emmett, the Poop Smear-er. Doesn't add up, does it?"

"No," I said. "Emmett was obsessed with being a Falconer Shreve partner. He was so devastated about Delia's summary rejection of him that he tried to blackmail her into promoting him. When the video that showed him being hustled out of the fund-raiser became public yesterday morning, it was too much, so he decided to take off. But before he left, he took the time to distribute a poop-smeared copy of the same picture he photoshopped himself into, and he still doesn't seem to have made good on his blackmail threat."

"It *was* the weekend," Kevin said. "Emmett could show up at Warren Weber's office this morning, explain that he needed some time to think and accept Warren's offer. Or he could follow through on his blackmail threat."

"Do you really believe he will?"

Kevin shook his head. "I don't know. But whether or not he accepts Warren's offer, I do think Emmett will turn up. Right now, he has no reason to believe anyone has seen his strange, sad alteration of our picture. The idea that anyone at Falconer Shreve could find out how desperately he wanted to be part of the firm will bring Emmett back – at least to clear out his apartment."

"And then what? More photos smeared with excrement? Kevin, Emmett has done some terrible things, but no matter what Delia believes, he didn't do that. There's no way a man who can't get through an hour without sanitizing his hands would dig into a pile of excrement just for the sheer pleasure of wiping it on the faces of Falconer Shreve's founding partners."

Kevin frowned. "You're right, of course. Delia has always had this laser focus, but lately she's just not thinking clearly."

"And that has to end," I said. "Kevin, I like Delia, and I understand that she's going through a bad period in her life. She's a perfectionist and nothing's working for her. But, sympathetic as we all are, Delia's doing real damage. If Zack and Margot hadn't stepped in, Delia's mismanagement of the firm would have pushed Falconer Shreve over the edge.

"And that's just the beginning. This whole mess with Emmett Keating started with Delia, and God knows where that's going to lead now. The firm can't afford to have Delia going around accusing Keating of defacing the photo. He still has the information about the defalcation in his back pocket, and if he's feeling cornered, he'll use it."

Kevin pushed his chair back. "Was Dee at work when she called?"

"She'd just found the envelope, so she was probably still at home."

"I'll track her down and try to talk her off the edge." Kevin gave me a quick hug. "Thanks for breakfast. I wish we'd managed to do it more often."

"Me too," I said.

After Kevin left, I put on a pair of disposable latex gloves, slid the photo back into its envelope, and put it on a shelf in the mudroom. If there were any further developments, the police would be interested, but at the moment, I was simply hoping the old adage "out of sight, out of mind" would be proven true.

It wasn't.

Nagging as a toothache, a vision of Esau Pilger's living room pushed itself into my consciousness. I closed my eyes and I saw that foul room and the two framed photographs on the wall: the one of Gloria Ryder, who broke Esau's heart, and that of the five young lawyers whose presence across the bay was a constant reminder of the land and life Esau's people had lost. Logic had eliminated Emmett Keating as the person who dropped the envelopes into Delia's mailbox and ours, but someone had done the deed, and Esau Pilger seemed a likely suspect. I took out my phone and called the Falconers. When Rose Lavallee answered, I told her about the photo and said I'd stay on the line until she'd checked the family's mailbox.

When she picked up again, Rose's voice was taut. "Who do you think did this?" she said.

"I don't know," I said. "But I think we have to consider Esau Pilger."

Long pauses in conversations never troubled Rose. If she didn't have anything to say, she didn't say anything. So when she was silent, I didn't assume our talk was over. I waited.

"I've been with Gracie since the day she was born," she said. "Last night I called Esau. I asked him flat out if he'd used bad medicine against Gracie and her family. He flew off the handle. He said white people were the ones that used bad medicine – they took what our people had and all they gave us was sickness and death. Esau said other things but none of them bears repeating. When I told him I'd had enough – that unless he calmed down and started making sense, I was going to hang up – he beat me to the punch and hung up on me."

"Do you think he was angry enough to deface the photos? He has a copy. I saw it in his house."

"Hard to credit that a person you know would do something as nasty as that."

When Rose lapsed into silence again, I pressed her. "We should talk about this face to face," I said.

"Face to face is always better," Rose said. "Could you come here? The heating people are scheduled to give the furnace its fall checkup and I don't want to miss them."

"I'll be there in ten minutes," I said.

The Falconers lived in a mock-Tudor house on Leopold Crescent, in a historic and affluent neighbourhood known as the Crescents. Rose met me at the door and ushered me into a pretty sitting room that overlooked the street. Two upholstered club chairs faced each other across a small table upon which rested a tray set for tea with a plate of Rose's homemade ginger cookies, a Brown Betty in a knit tea cozy, and two delicate cups and saucers.

Rose gestured for me to sit. "We'll give the tea a few minutes to steep," Rose said. "I know you like your tea to have a good colour."

"I do," I said.

"Might as well get down to business then," Rose said. "This morning after I drove Gracie to school, I went out to the reserve to talk to Esau. He wasn't there and neither was that old truck of his. He never leaves Standing Buffalo. He could have been anywhere."

Rose picked up the teapot, poured a little in my cup, and looked at me questioningly. The tea had good colour. I nodded, and Rose filled my cup and then her own.

"Possibly delivering those pictures," I said.

"It's possible," Rose said. "The band office has a scanner, and they've given up locking the building, so Esau could have just walked in and used the machine. There are office supplies there too." The sentence trailed off.

"So he could have taken what he needed," I said.

Rose sighed. "Yes, but I don't believe he did. Esau's been around my whole life," she said. "He's over twenty years older than me. In most places, that would mean different worlds, but there's only one world on Standing Buffalo. People said he was a sweet, friendly boy, but he went off to residential school and that changed him the way it changed so many – some for better, some for worse."

"And with Esau, it was for worse?" I said.

"He was afraid of people. He withdrew. When his mother and brothers moved into the city, Esau wouldn't go with them. He stayed in that house by himself. He hired out as a farmhand and when winter came, he did odd jobs in town. He earned enough to keep body and soul together and – here's the sad part – he earned enough to buy an engagement ring for Gloria Ryder."

"Gracie's grandmother," I said.

"And the woman Esau fell in love with," Rose said. "The way I hear it, Esau and Gloria had never even been alone together. He loved her from afar. By the time he got up the courage to give her the ring, she was already set to marry Henry Redman. When Esau asked her to marry him, Gloria fainted dead away. When she came to, she told him about Henry Redman, and people say when that happened, Esau went a little crazy."

"So crazy that he cursed her?"

"Some say that. Some don't. But the fact is Esau never got over her turning him down. He was one person before Gloria told him she couldn't marry him. After that, he was another person."

"Gloria must have been extraordinary to inspire that kind of love."

"There's something about the Ryder women," Rose said. "I can't put my finger on it, but it's there. I've seen pictures of Gloria, and she wasn't a beauty. Neither was Lily. Not like my sister. Betty was a looker from the day she was born. Men have always been drawn to her like moths to a flame, but here's the difference. When Betty said no to a man, he just flew on and found another flame. But once a man fell in love with one of the Ryder women, he never flew on. He just stayed where he was, staring at the flame and hoping."

A landline in the next room rang and Rose sprang up to answer. When she returned, she was frowning. "That was Gracie. Her class was cancelled, so she's ready to come home." Rose glanced at her watch. "The furnace people were supposed to be here by now."

"And if you leave, they'll arrive just as you pull away," I said. "I'll be happy to pick up Gracie. If she's in the mood, we might go to Magpie. Gracie loves their cinnamon buns."

On our way to the front door, Rose and I both stopped to look at the portrait of Lily that was hung over the fireplace. Rose was right about Lily's appearance. She was not conventionally pretty. Her features were too sharp, and her obsidian eyes too sorrowful. But her body was lovely – full-breasted, slim-hipped, and long-legged. She had chosen a strapless silk dress the colour of a new leaf for the portrait, and she'd allowed her hair to fall loose to her shoulders, brush strokes of jet against the glowing bronze of her skin. She was mesmerizing.

"Blake will never get over her," I said. "The other day at the hospital when he talked about Lily, I wanted to weep."

Rose nodded. "There were many, many nights when I did just that," she said.

———

Rose had arranged to pick Gracie up at College West. During all the years I taught at the university my parking spot was in the faculty lot close to the building, and it seemed odd not to pull into my old space, grab my briefcase, and head for my office. When Gracie got into the car, she kissed my cheek, thanked me for pinch-hitting, then slid into silence.

As I turned off Wascana Parkway to take the route home, Gracie touched my arm. "Jo, could we drive around for a while. My class wasn't really cancelled. I just didn't feel like going."

"Think you might have rushed your re-entry into the world a little?" I said.

"No, I'm fine – at least physically. No pain, and the meds aren't affecting my energy level. I'm bummed about losing my season, but I'll get over it. I just need some time to think."

"I know just the place," I said. I chose a parking spot overlooking an area on the shore of Wascana Lake, which because of its shallowness often attracted water birds. The path around the lake was busy. Retirees in sensible walking shoes and young mums with babies in jogging strollers had replaced the super-fit young joggers whom I often saw on my morning run. When offices closed for the day, the second wave of super-fit young joggers would appear. After their run, they'd meet friends for coffee or drinks. Later, in the gloaming, lovers and lonely people who had nowhere else to go would take their place.

For perhaps five minutes, Gracie and I sat in companionable silence. "You were smiling," Gracie said finally. "What were you thinking about?"

"I was remembering something significant that happened here," I said. "Zack and I hadn't been married very long. On my run that morning I'd seen a pair of American avocets."

"Those shore birds with the slender legs and the long thin beaks," Gracie said. "This spot is on my running route too. Avocets are lovely, but we don't see them often in the city."

"That's why I told Zack about them. He was going to be in court all day, but we agreed to come here when he was finished. As it turned out, we had a fight – a serious one, and we weren't speaking. Finally, Zack said, 'If an actuary were here, do you know what she'd say? She'd say, Count up the years you two have left to be together, and then go and see the fucking avocets.'"

"And did you?"

"We did."

Gracie's laugh was rueful. "Why can't everybody be like you and Zack?"

"Has something happened?"

"Isn't there always something?" Gracie said. Her voice wavered between anger and despair. "Isobel wasn't in our ten o'clock class, so after it let out I called her. There was a big blowup at their house this morning. Izzie's mother said she'd changed her mind about the dinner on Halloween. Izzie tried to convince her not to back out, but Delia was adamant. She said she was already under a great deal of stress and she pleaded with Isobel to accept that she couldn't be part of the evening."

"Dee's had a difficult morning. She might come around," I said.

"Isobel told her mother the evening would go ahead without her, and Noah supported Isobel. That, of course, was a seismic shock to everybody. Delia lost her temper and stormed out. She said she'd send her assistant to pack her clothes and she'd be at the Hotel Saskatchewan until the Day of the Dead nonsense was over. Isobel's absolutely miserable. She believed that if Delia could see how much Abby meant to their family, she'd start to be more open about her so that Noah, Isobel, and Jacob would feel they could be too. Now the gathering that was supposed to bring everyone together is driving Izzie's family further apart."

"The distance has been there for a long time, Gracie. You know that."

"Do you think we should forget about the evening?"

"It's a tough call," I said. "It's right for Izzie, Jacob, and Noah. You think it will help your dad, and I agree. Zack and Kevin need to acknowledge how much Chris meant to them. But Delia won't do it, and you'd rather not."

"I have to admit getting hurt out at Esau's has made me more nervous about our plans."

"That's understandable," I said. "And, Gracie, there's a new development in the Esau Pilger saga."

When I told Gracie about the photographs that had been hand-delivered to our mailboxes that morning, she made a moue of disgust. "Gross, but I don't believe it was Esau. He's been nursing a grudge for over fifty years, and he hasn't acted out like that."

"Rose doesn't believe Esau defaced the pictures either, but there's something puzzling. Rose was upset about your accident and she called him last night to ask him directly if he'd used bad medicine on you. Apparently, he lost it. He said some ugly things and hung up. This morning after she dropped you off, she drove to Standing Buffalo to straighten out the situation. Esau wasn't there. Neither was his truck."

Gracie frowned. "He's always there," she said.

"Not this morning," I said. "And it's a troubling coincidence. I don't think Rose believes Esau used bad medicine on the Ryder women. She pointed out that the men who fell in love with Gloria and Lily suffered as much as Gloria and Lily did, and these men were never able to move on."

"That's true of my dad. He's an intelligent person, but his obsession with my mother has ruined his life." Gracie looked resolutely out at the lake. "My dad deserves what you and Zack have," she said. "He deserves to move on."

CHAPTER

13

During the last week of October, the weather continued to be unseasonably mild. High-school boys wearing shorts and high-school girls wearing far too little sipped slushies as they meandered home from school. People raked leaves, and when little kids jumped in the leaf piles, they smiled and raked again. Outdoor cafés were crowded. Pansies and marigolds continued to thrive. Every night at dinnertime, the piquant smoke of barbecues drifted through our neighbourhood. The snow we'd awakened to on the day of the dinner honouring Zack was only a memory. Our lives seemed suspended in the pleasant haze of an endless late summer, but I was on edge. I knew the succession of perfect days would end. I just didn't know when.

Zack once said that it's the loose ends of our lives that hang us, and there were many loose ends. Emmett Keating had not reappeared. The police were looking into his whereabouts, but so far their investigation had yielded nothing. Keating's credit and bank cards hadn't been used, and it seemed his cellphone was off. Outside of a few acquaintances at Falconer Shreve, Emmett Keating apparently did

not have personal connections. The police were being dili-
gent in following every lead, but nothing had panned out.
Debbie Haczkewicz and I both speculated that Emmett
Keating had committed suicide, and it would be only a
matter of time before his body was discovered, but as the
minutes ticked by and nothing happened, tempers frayed.

On the Saturday morning that he was to return, Zack
called to say his plane had been delayed and he'd be arriv-
ing at around three that afternoon. Mieka was having a
Halloween party at April's Place, her café and play centre
that was UpSlideDown's twin in the city's core. Taylor had
volunteered to help out, but I had begged off, anticipating
a romantic reunion with my husband. Suddenly, I was free.
I looked dolefully at the black silk nightgown I'd draped
across our freshly made bed and hit speed-dial on my phone.
Mieka picked up on the first ring.

"Synchronicity," Mieka said. "I was just about to call
you."

"You'll be able to see me in about twenty minutes," I said.
"Zack's plane was delayed so I can help with the party."

"Great. Two of my right-hand women are down with
the flu and the joint will be jumping. Taylor suggested I
call Angus to see if he could give me an hour or two of his
time, and he and Patsy are coming to help. Maisie has a
meeting with an old friend, so Pete's bringing the twins. A
Kilbourn family reunion – it'll be terrific. And, Mum, if
you have a Halloween costume hanging around, the kids
would love it."

The Archie Goodwin suit I'd worn when Zack and I went
to a costume party as Nero Wolfe and Archie a few Halloweens
ago was at the back of my closet. As I zipped the fly of my
slick vintage suit and adjusted the angle of my fedora, I took
a last look at the black silk nightgown lying forlornly on
the bed. An afternoon with a group of sugared-up kids wasn't

quite the diversion I'd had in mind, but a kids' party was always an adventure, and I was smiling as I headed for the play centre.

Even before I opened the door to April's Place, I knew that, as Mieka had promised, the joint was jumping. My daughter believed in old-fashioned games, and from the squeals and laughter it was clear that pin the tail on the donkey and bobbing for apples hadn't lost their appeal. Zack always loved seeing our kids and grandkids together, so I took plenty of pictures. Mieka had dressed as a Keystone Kop with an oversized plastic nightstick, a zany complement to her daughters' old-time bank robbers' outfits. Angus and Patsy wore the uniforms of the now-defeated but still-defiant Toronto Blue Jays, and Peter came as the exhausted but delighted father of twins. Charlie and Colin were dressed in the outfits Margot had given them, and they were two very lovable pumpkins. It was a happy afternoon, and when I finally checked my watch, I realized I'd lost track of the time and wouldn't be able to get home to change before I picked Zack up at the airport.

As soon as he spotted me in my fedora and suit, Zack beamed. "Archie Goodwin," he said, "it's been a long time, but I still remember our night together." The line was smooth, but it was interrupted by a hacking cough.

By the time we got home, I knew that Zack was headed for a serious cold. "I'm calling the Wainbergs to tell them we can't make it tonight," I said.

Zack was adamant. "We have to be there, Jo. Delia's not going. If we don't show up, that just leaves Kevin, Blake, Noah, and the girls. I can't let them down. I promise I'll stay in bed all day tomorrow."

There was no point arguing. I showered, checked our supply of juice, chicken broth, and ASA, replaced the silk sheets on our bed with flannelette, and plugged in the humidifier. Then I dressed for an evening out and hoped for the best.

The Wainbergs, like the Falconers, lived in the Crescents. But in that neighbourhood of elegant old homes, the Wainberg house, with its stark asymmetrical lines, large expanses of glass, and open-concept floor plan, was an anomaly. The house had been designed by an architect as a gift for the man with whom he planned to spend the rest of his life. On the eve of the men's commitment ceremony, the architect's beloved found another beloved. The house was on the market the next day.

The Wainbergs, a star-crossed couple themselves, purchased the property for a song. It was a house designed for entertaining, not family life, but from the first, Noah was determined to make the house a home, and he had succeeded. He painted walls in earth colours, arranged deep couches and welcoming chairs in clusters that encouraged intimate conversation, and filled the walls with folk art. Noah was a talented woodcarver, and his life-sized carvings of animals – sometimes beautiful, sometimes whimsical, always awe-inspiring – warmed the rooms in which they appeared like gifts from a fairy-tale kingdom.

From the first time I visited the Wainbergs' house, I'd been taken with the three oak bears, astonishingly realistic, grouped on the lawn beside the path leading to the entrance. The bear in front was a large male. Initially, he had been flanked by a smaller female bear and a cub. When Isobel grew to young womanhood, Noah replaced the cub with a young female bear. After Noah Wainberg learned that Abby, the daughter he didn't know existed, had left instructions for Delia and him to raise her infant son, he carved two more oak bears: another adult female and a cub. The young cub had joined the group on the lawn, but Dee had refused to let Noah place the bear that represented their long-lost daughter with the others.

When we started up the walk, I drew Zack's attention to the carvings. The third female bear had joined the family. The cub was beside her. "Abby," Zack said. "Noah's given her a place in the family."

I rubbed his shoulder. "A good beginning?" I said.

"Either that or a full-blown declaration of war," Zack said. "I guess we'll have to wait and see."

Isobel had arranged my planters of marigolds on either side of the front door. When she'd picked up the flowers, Izzie told me that she, Gracie, and Taylor had decided that when it came to the evening's decorations, the byword would be "less is more." There would be no shrines with Día de los Muertos *calacas* and *calaveras* in the house. According to legend, the vibrant blooms of marigolds at the entrance to a dwelling would let the spirits of the dead know they were welcome. For tonight, the flowers would be enough.

Zack and I were the last to arrive. Noah and Jacob met us at the door. Zack and his wheelchair fascinated Jacob, and as soon as he heard Zack's voice, he ran to him. Most often, Jacob would climb on Zack's lap and Zack would give him a ride, but when I saw Jacob headed for the wheelchair, I scooped him up and gave him a hug. "No rides today," I said. "Uncle Zack has a cold."

Jacob's small face pinched with concern. "I'm sorry you're sick."

"So am I," Zack said "But next time I come, I'll bring my all-terrain wheelchair and we'll go on the bike path."

I put Jacob down and Noah took his hand. "Why don't you two head for the fireplace and let Jacob and me bring you some refreshments. Zack, I have a pitcher of martinis in the refrigerator waiting for you."

"Your martinis are stellar," Zack said. "But they'll have to wait. I'm feeling lousy and I have too much respect for Bombay Sapphire to waste it."

"Noah, why don't I come with you to the kitchen and make Zack some tea?"

"Good idea. Jake, I think it's just about time for *Bear in the Big Blue House*. You know your big pal, Ryan, doesn't like watching that show without you."

Jacob nodded solemnly. "I don't like watching it without him either."

"Then why don't you go upstairs and ask Ryan to please turn on the TV. I'll be up with your supper before your show's over." *Bear in the Big Blue House* was apparently as much a hit with Jacob as it had been with Madeleine and Lena. He was gone in a flash. Noah grinned. "Note my grandson's speed. Watching TV while he eats a meal is a treat."

Noah and I were often together with the girls, so the Wainberg kitchen was familiar territory. I picked up the kettle and filled it. "You seem to have lucked out with Jacob's new 'big pal, Ryan,'" I said.

"The 'big pal' designation was Jacob's idea," Noah said. "He clouded up when we referred to Ryan as his babysitter. But by any name Ryan is a godsend. He's terrific with Jacob, and he and I have arranged our schedules so Ryan can get to the university for his classes and when he's back here, I can take care of whatever needs attention at Falconer Shreve."

"The evening seems to be off to a good start," I said. "Any word from Delia?"

"No, and I wasn't expecting any. I'm certain that when Delia said she wouldn't be part of the evening, she believed that would be the end of it, but Izzie stood her ground, and I supported her. I love Dee, but I love my daughter too, and she needs this evening. I've tried to heal the breach. I've called Dee. I've left messages saying her place tonight is here with us. She hasn't responded."

"You've done your part," I said. "How's Isobel?"

"Honestly? Better than she's been in a long time. This afternoon I brought out the bear that represents our older daughter. While we chose a place on the lawn for the carving, we had a good talk. Jacob calls the new piece 'the Abby bear.'"

"Finding a place for the Abby bear was the right thing to do, Noah."

"It felt right," he said. "And Isobel's put together a few thoughts about her sister for tonight."

"That feels right too," I said.

"Agreed. Now I'd better get back to our guests." Noah slapped his forehead with his palm. "Jo, I'm sorry. I totally forgot about getting you a drink."

"I'll share Zack's tea," I said. I touched his arm. "Noah, this is going to work out."

The girls had planned the evening carefully. Concerned that we would be disturbed by trick-or-treaters, Isobel had placed jack-o'-lanterns along the front path, and shortly after we arrived, she, Gracie, and Taylor ran outside to light them and to position a washtub full of candy bars with a sign: *Please leave something for the next person.* As we sipped our drinks in front of the fireplace, we could watch the shadowy figures of kids in costumes dart up the front walk, stop, choose their treats, and take off for the next house, but we were undisturbed.

Eight of us sat down to dinner in the dining room. Supper was a simple meal – homemade chicken soup, crusty bread, a platter of crudités with aioli, and a crisp, dry Chablis. The conversation was inconsequential and easy. We were people who knew each other well and were comfortable in one another's company. Zack was tired from the trip and his incipient cold was taking its toll, but he was enjoying himself and he asked for a second helping of soup.

The girls had just cleared away the dishes when Delia walked into the dining room. The effect was electric. As soon as he saw his wife, Noah sprang to his feet. Whatever the season, Dee always wore some combination of black, white, and grey. That night, she was wearing a closely fitted, lightweight grey coat, a black cloche, and black fashion boots. She was carrying a bottle of wine in a gift bag.

"We've been through so much together," she said. "I wanted to be here."

Noah enfolded her in his arms. "And we wanted you here," he said.

I glanced at Isobel. She had been radiant but, as was so often the case when her mother was around, Izzie's features grew tense.

Noah took his wife's coat and carried a chair to the table for her. "There's still soup and bread, Dee."

Delia had taken off her cloche. She ran her hands through her wiry salt-and-pepper hair and gave her husband a quick smile. "Thanks, I'll just have coffee when it's ready."

Delia's arrival put an end to our gathering's easy bonhomie. Kevin, ever the peacemaker, quickly made an effort to restore it. He excused himself and came back to the table with an old cassette player. "I was waiting for the right time to play this, and I believe the time has come," he said.

Kevin turned on the cassette player and the room was filled with the sounds of a bar – laughter, loud voices, and a lively band comprised of drums, an accordion, a flute, a fiddle, and what sounded like a large number of banjoes and guitars. The band was playing "Whiskey in the Jar" and the audience was singing along. When the music ended, I heard Zack's voice, authoritative as always, but with the careful enunciation of a man determined not to sound drunk. "And now for some real music," he said. Beside me, my husband shook his head when he heard his young self. He leaned towards me. "It was St. Patrick's Day, and the beer was green and free." Across from us, Dee, Kevin, and Blake were all smiling.

On the tape, Zack continued to control the microphone. "My friend Kevin and I are about to sing you one of the saddest songs ever written. All Irish songs are sad – a lot of them are about rum, sodomy, and the lash; not much to laugh about there – but this song is not about that. This song is about a proud ship named *The Irish Rover*, which set sail from Cork to New York on July the 4th, 1806. Kevin and I will be assisted by our band, The Winners' Circle. Delia Margolies on drums, Chris Altieri on flute, and Blake Falconer on guitar. He only knows three chords, but that's all he needs."

Zack always managed to rise to the occasion, and on that long ago St. Patrick's night, accompanied by drums, flute, guitar, and Kevin's baritone, Zack's sonorous bass cut through the fog of green beer and bar noise to bring real emotion to the tragic tale of the death of a noble ship that sailed the seas for seven years, till measles decimated the crew, a collision with a rock destroyed the ship and drowned the ship's dog, and the only soul left was the sailor singing the song. By the time Zack's voice rang out the final verse, he, Delia, Blake, and Kevin were wiping tears from their eyes. It was hard to tell whether they were tears of mirth or heartbreak. It didn't seem to matter. Delia had picked up a table napkin to mop her eyes.

Delia was ordinarily a woman of sharpness and angles, but in that moment, her expression grew tender and her features softened. "We did have fun, didn't we?" she said. "So many bad things have happened. When Chris died, I lost a piece of myself. I thought it was irretrievable, but hearing his voice – hearing *all* our voices – reminds me of what it was like to feel hopeful." She laughed sadly. "It was a good feeling."

Isobel seized the opening. "And we can hold on to that feeling, if we let the people we've lost come into our lives. Everybody in this room needs what Chris can give us, and our family needs what Abby can give us. Let me help you get to know how incredible she was."

Delia covered her eyes with a pale hand, pushed her chair away from the table, and stood. "I'm sorry. I'm not ready to do this," she said.

Isobel went to her mother, and in a moment as perfectly contained as a teardrop, the two women faced each other, their profiles as identical as their need for each other. "You don't have to do it alone," Isobel said. "You have us. Please give us a chance."

When Delia didn't respond, Noah joined his wife and daughter and draped an arm around the shoulder of each of the women. "Why don't we all move into the living room," he said. "I'm sure Gracie and Taylor will help me bring around the coffee and dessert."

We arranged the chairs in a circle around a table I had long admired. Noah had found the top of an old oak dining table at an estate sale, refinished it, and built an oak foundation for it. The table was large enough for people to gather round it for coffee and desserts in the Scandinavian tradition. That night the dessert was honey cake.

When Isobel chose to sit beside her mother, Delia moved her chair closer and took her daughter's hand. After the coffee and dessert dishes were cleared away, Isobel left the room and came back with a cloth tote bag, which she placed in front of her on the table. She glanced around the circle. "I've known and loved most of you for my entire life," she said. "Joanne and Taylor came later, but I can't imagine my life without them either." She reached into the tote bag and pulled out a framed photograph of a girl who could well have been Isobel herself: the same curly jet hair, the same pale skin, the same wary, intelligent eyes. "This is my sister, Abby, when she was eighteen," Izzie said. "My age. She'd just finished her second year studying political science and economics at the University of Toronto.

"By the time she was twenty-five, Abby had earned a doctorate in political science. I read her dissertation. I'm a science nerd, so it was pretty heavy going for me, but knowing that Abby had written it made me feel close to her. And that's important, because I never knew her. I met her for perhaps thirty seconds when she came into our high-school Christmas concert and handed me Jacob. Since that night, I've been hungry to learn everything I can about her.

"She and her life partner, Nadine Perrault, met in grade five. The first time I called Nadine, we talked for almost two hours." Isobel's eyes danced at the memory. "At first, Nadine and I were awkward with each other, but then we relaxed and talked about things that may seem trivial but aren't when they involve someone you love or want to love. For example, I learned that Abby's favourite candy was licorice whips." Isobel gave her mother a tentative smile. "Same as you," she said. "Abby liked being alone. She was happiest when Nadine and she were in the cabin they shared near a creek on her parents' property. Abby was a reader, of anything and everything, but especially the poems of Elizabeth Bishop.

"Elizabeth Bishop wrote a poem called 'The Fish' that I'm going to read to you sometime, Dad. You too, Zack and Kev. It's about a battered old fish the woman in the poem caught. His body was scarred and there were pieces of fish lines and a wire leader hanging from his lower lip. The woman knew how nobly the old fish had fought to live and so she let him go." Isobel's lips twitched into a smile that was both affectionate and mischievous. "I wonder why that poem made me think of the three of you."

Noah glanced quickly at Zack and Kevin. They were both clearly moved. "Old guys like us don't often get compliments," Noah said. "Thanks, Izzie."

"You're welcome," she said. She took a breath. "Another thing about Abby. She loved string quartets, especially Ravel's *String Quartet in F*. He wrote it when he was twenty-eight. The same age Abby was when she died. She was very precise – like me, and like you, Mum. Anyway, Abby liked the Ravel because she could feel the way he paid attention to every note. Her favourite recording of the piece was by the Hagen Quartet. She felt they were as careful with the notes on the score as Ravel himself was. Three members of the group are siblings. Abby was fascinated by the way they seemed to be able to read each other's minds when they played." Isobel's eyes sought her mother's. "Abby always wanted a sister," she said. "So did I." She walked across the room and plugged her phone into a speaker.

"Here's the Ravel," she said. When Isobel hit Play, the room was filled with the quivering restraint of the quartet's first movement. As the controlled emotion of the first movement gave way to the lyrical freedom of the second, Noah crossed the room to stand behind his daughter. By the time it ended, Delia had joined them. It was a family photo none of us thought we'd ever see, and it clearly struck a chord with Blake.

"Now you know why I wanted to talk about Lily," he said, and then he faltered, unsure of where to go next.

When the Wainbergs came back to resume their places at the coffee table, Noah gave Blake an encouraging smile. "I love the story about how you two met," he said. "Why don't you tell that?"

Blake frowned. "Everybody's heard that story."

"Tonight's a night for remembering," Zack said. "Lily's role in building Falconer Shreve was as significant as any of ours. Besides, it's a great tale. Dee, you always said it would make a perfect Julia Roberts movie."

Delia had clearly softened and seemed pleased to be drawn into the conversation. "That's because the story starts out with a loutish man and a smart woman."

Blake laughed and raised his hand in a halt sign. "Hey, no editorial comments. Maybe I should just tell the story. It was back in the early days when our office was on Broad Street. We were above a company that made dentures. The scent of false teeth was always in the air."

"But the fake teeth smell had to battle it out with the smells of the decomposing take-out food that we'd start eating and forget about." Zack's glance took in all his partners. "Did any of us ever actually empty a waste basket?"

Delia shook her head. "Not me," she said.

Kevin and Blake exchanged a quick look. "Nope."

"That explains it," Zack said. "And the office always smelled like stale beer."

"Spilled drinks from our Friday happy hours," Kevin said sagely. "It was a helluva mess."

"Agreed," Blake said. "Anyway, one Friday afternoon, when I was already well on my way to getting pleasantly drunk, I looked across the office and standing by the door was a woman with legs that wouldn't quit and waist-length shining black hair. By that point, everybody in the room was sweaty and stumbling. The woman was so cool, so still, so much her own person, that I knew I had to be with her. I walked across the room, stroked that incredible hair, and said, 'I can make all your dreams come true.' She shook me off and said, 'I can make all your dreams come true too. For a price.' And she handed me her resumé.

"It turned out her price was being our office manager. I offered her the job. I made a pass. She told me 'no thanks' and asked for an office key. I gave her the key. Monday morning when I came to work, the office was transformed – clean, organized, professional. Even the denture smell was gone. And that was the beginning. We were on our way to becoming a big-time firm and Lily was part of every decision we made. She selected the firm's logo. Both times we moved offices, Lily chose the space she felt best reflected our image. She sat in on personnel meetings and changed the Canada Day party from a BYOB beer and burgers bash for buddies to a slick event that was the hottest ticket of the summer."

"Lily played a huge part in making us what we are today," Delia said. "For that and for so much else, we are in her debt."

Blake reached across the table and took Dee's hand. When he spoke, his voice was hoarse with emotion. "Thanks," he said. "You and Lily really understood each other, didn't you?"

Dee nodded. "We did, and I miss her."

Candlelight is kind to aging faces, and as I looked around the table it seemed that the founding partners looked younger and less careworn than they had when we sat down. Blake especially seemed more hopeful than he had been since Lily died. Listening as others remembered with fond admiration the woman he loved had soothed Blake. A sense of satisfaction and relief flooded me. We had done the right thing.

Blake's grey eyes rested on me for a second and then, as if he'd read my thoughts, he said, "I don't know whether our gathering tonight has brought Lily close. I hope it has. Knowing that you all respected her would have meant a great deal to my wife.

"The day after Gracie was hurt, Jo and I had lunch at the hospital. I've always been guarded about discussing my marriage to Lily. Everyone knows we had problems – problems that, in the end, I guess were insurmountable, but until the end we gave each other moments of such incredible joy that I felt like the luckiest man on earth, and I believe that in those moments, Lily felt lucky too." His grin was shamefaced. "So, Lily, if you're listening, I want to say it was worth it. Everything. We put each other through hell, but I want you to know that it was worth it. You were worth it. And I would do it all again just to bury my face in your hair and smell that grassy scent one more time."

It was a moment of such intimacy that we all knew the evening was over. Embracing and murmuring words of affection and support to each other, we said goodnight.

The drive from our house to the Wainbergs took five minutes. It had been an emotional evening, and Zack, Taylor, and I were silent, absorbed by our own thoughts as we drove home.

Muted screams and the smells of popcorn and scorched pumpkin meat met us when we came through the door to the kitchen. Since we were going to be at the Wainbergs, Angus and Patsy had volunteered for Halloween duty, and they had spent the evening doling out candy to Halloweeners and watching horror movies. The door to the family room was open and when I peeked in I saw a very young Jamie Lee Curtis on the TV screen. Her face was frozen and her mouth was agape in horror. Had Jamie Lee known that the Halloween franchise would thrive, and that her character, Laurie Strode, would be terrorized by the psychotic Michael Myers for the next thirty years, her mouth might have gaped even wider. Angus and Patsy came out of the family room hand in hand. Patsy's makeup was mussed, and they both looked shamefaced but happy.

"Thanks for taking care of everything," I said. "Did we get a lot of kids?"

"There's not much candy left," Angus said. "But Patsy has a thing for peanut butter cups, so the fact they're all gone might not mean much."

"You two go back to your movie," I said. "It's been a long day, and Zack and I are both bushed."

"So am I," Taylor said. "But I think I'll scope out the left-over candy and see if there's anything I like."

I was pleased but not surprised when Taylor gave us a quick hug before she headed to the kitchen. Zack's face creased with pleasure. "Our daughter always makes me feel better," he said. "All the kids do. We have a great family, Jo."

When a coughing jag punctuated his fond remarks, I said. "Why don't you take a shower? The steam might help that cough."

"I love you," he croaked.

"I love you too," I said. "And I'm glad tonight's over."

I topped up the humidifier, filled a carafe with water, and put it on Zack's night table alongside the bottle of ASA and a box of man-sized tissues. Then I opened the dresser drawer where I kept nightwear. The black silk nightgown with the lilies that Zack loved was still ready for action but Zack was not, so I took out the Charlie Brown flannelette pyjamas that Madeleine and Lena had given me for my birthday. Once again, fate had moved the football just as I was about to kick.

CHAPTER

14

Zack was feverish the next morning. I hated waking him, but I was counting on the ASA to bring down the fever and he needed to stay hydrated. When I drew him closer, he murmured, "Am I about to get lucky?"

"No, you're about to get Aspirin and a sponge bath," I said. "But as soon as you're better, I'm slipping into the black silk nightie with the lilies and sliding in next to you."

"Bring on the aspirin," he said.

Before I took the dogs on our run, I stuck my head in Taylor's room. Surprisingly, she was already awake, sitting up, propped by pillows, reading *Odes to Common Things*, the collection of Pablo Neruda's poetry I'd given her for her fourteenth birthday. Taylor believed that socks, like air, belonged to everyone. My politics were far left, but when it came to socks, I wasn't a socialist. That year for Christmas, Taylor had copied out Neruda's "Ode to My Socks," decorated the margins around the poem with whimsical drawings of socks, and had the piece handsomely framed. It had been one of the best gifts I'd ever received.

"Is there another drawing in my future?" I said.

Taylor's smile was impish. "Who knows when it might be your lucky day. But right now I'm interested in 'Ode to the Cat.' Isobel texted me. Her mother has finally caved on her 'no pets policy,' so Noah, Isobel, and I are going to take Jacob to the SPCA this afternoon to let him choose a kitten. I thought I'd copy out the poem and draw some funny cats around the margins for him."

"Jacob will love that," I said. "The dogs and I are about to head out. Could you go in and check on your dad in a few minutes?"

Taylor's dark eyes were anxious. "Is his cold worse?"

"It's no better," I said. "He shouldn't have gone out last night, but I'm glad he did – I'm glad we all did. Did you notice how relaxed everyone seemed when we were leaving?"

"I noticed," Taylor said. "I also noticed that Gracie's dad was smiling, really smiling at the end of the night. Talking about Gracie's mum seemed to help him."

"And I think that when Isobel played the music Abby loved, she got through to her mother." Taylor put her arms around her knees and squeezed them close. "Now, *that* was a miracle," she said.

"It's certainly right up there," I said. "Speaking of, I don't think we'll go to church today. Your dad needs a day to rest up."

Taylor's forehead crinkled. "You hate missing church," she said.

"I do," I said. "And today's All Saint's Day – the day when we pray for the ones who went before."

"I remember you explaining that to me when I was little," Taylor said. "You told me you always prayed for my mother."

"I pray for your mother every day, Taylor. Sally made me

feel loved when not many others did, and she gave us you. I never stop being grateful."

November 1 was mild and overcast. On past All Saints' Days, the dogs and I often had the creek path to ourselves, but the good weather had brought the runners out in force. When a skein of Canada geese flew over, I noticed that they were flying north. Winter was coming, but even the Canada geese were befogged by the weather.

When I came back from my run, Taylor had her jacket on. "I called the Bonnevilles," she said. "I'm hitching a ride to church with them."

"You're going to church by yourself?"

Taylor smiled. "I'm almost seventeen, Mum. And you've known the Bonnevilles forever. I think I'm safe with them."

"I know you are," I said. "Taylor, say a prayer for us."

"I always do," she said.

Zack was sleeping again; his face was flushed and his sheets were soaked with sweat. I picked up my phone and called Zack's physician and long-time poker partner Henry Chan.

Before Zack and I married, he made an appointment for us both with Henry. Zack wanted me to understand what being married to a man in a wheelchair would mean medically. Henry was frank, and I filled several pages of my notebook with information that I had consulted many times, but there was one sentence I never needed to revisit because the words had embedded themselves in my consciousness. "There are no small illnesses for a paraplegic."

It was Sunday, but Henry came over immediately. He was frowning when he came into the kitchen after examining Zack.

"Is there a problem?" I said, my voice thin with worry.

"Not yet, but let's be pre-emptive. The last time Zack had this we let it get away from us. You must have noticed the pressure ulcers on his back."

My heart dropped. "No. Zack's plane was late yesterday. We had dinner with his partners, and afterwards he had a shower and went straight to bed. He was in Toronto at meetings all week and I'm sure he was in his wheelchair pretty much all the time he was up."

Henry wrote out a prescription and handed it to me. "Every four hours for this one," he said. "And let's be on the safe side." He wrote two more prescriptions. "These should do the trick. You know the drill: bedrest, plenty of liquids, keep the humidifier humming and the chicken soup simmering. And, Jo, get a look at those pressure ulcers ASAP. You need a baseline so you can watch for changes. In the meantime, put soft pillows or pieces of soft foam between the parts of Zack's body that press against each other or the mattress."

Henry picked up his coat. "Call me at home if anything concerns you, and see that Zack gets a real rest this week. Travel's always difficult for him, and he's working too hard. He's trying to do two high-stress jobs well and that's one high-stress job too many."

"I know. There've been management problems at Falconer Shreve, but they're adding some new partners – the announcement will be made tomorrow. The founding partners and the new recruits are getting together this morning for a photo session."

"They'll have to postpone. Zack's not going anywhere today. Doctor's orders." Henry read my face. "Nothing to worry about, Jo. He just needs to stay put till we get that fever down."

My mood was far from light, but I tried a joke. "Gilda Radner was right," I said. "'It's always something.'"

———

It was 10:30 in the morning when Kevin arrived. He was wearing a closely tailored business suit, dove grey with a matching shirt, and a silk tie that was a swirl of all the colours of sunrise.

"This is a nice surprise," I said. "You look very handsome. And I love the tie."

"After today, the tie is yours," Kevin said. "You can have the suit too. Where I'm going I won't need Harry Rosen."

"Are you really leaving today?"

"Yeah. I was going to make the big announcement last night, but there was so much emotion in that room. It seemed prudent just to stand back and let everyone find their way. Anyway, I figured I'd see Blake and Dee at the photo session this morning. But I needed to talk to Zack and you, and I didn't want to leave without saying goodbye to Taylor."

"Taylor's at church and Zack is sleeping. Kev, he won't be at the photo shoot. Henry Chan has sentenced Zack to bedrest till he gets that fever down."

"But Zack will be okay."

"Yeah, of course. It's just the flu, and I'm on the job. Why don't you and I sit down and have some coffee and kick back. When we're finished, you can say goodbye to Zack."

"Thanks, but I'm coffee'ed out, so let's just kick back."

We sat at the kitchen table. "I want to talk with you about Taylor's birthday," Kevin said. "I was planning to stick around till the 11th, so I could be there when she got her gift, but I've already waited too long to make the break."

"I understand," I said. "Taylor will too."

"She always does," Kevin said. "Taylor's a terrific young woman. I know she'll like my present, but I thought I should check with you." He picked up his messenger bag and took out a vintage leather journal.

"It's beautiful," I said. "But why do you have to check with me?"

"Because this is a guest book, and it comes with a cottage – my cottage, to be exact." Kevin was watching my face carefully. "Jo, before you say anything, I've given this a lot of thought. Except for my partners and their families, I've never been close to many people. That's not going to change. As Popeye says, 'I Yam What I Yam and Dat's All What I Yam.'"

"What you are is pretty terrific," I said.

"I feel the same way about you and Taylor. I know my parents would want the cottage to stay in the family. Taylor's like family to me. I've always planned to leave the place to her, but I've decided there's no point in waiting. I want to clear my path. I don't need to own things any more, and it's wrong to hang on to something I no longer need or want."

"Kevin, this is incredibly generous, but Taylor's just turning seventeen."

"And she's graduating from high school this year. Next year she'll be in university. When I was in university, I had some of the best times of my life with Zack, Dee, Blake, and Chris at Lawyers' Bay. If Taylor has a place of her own, she'll be able to bring friends up to the lake. She'll be independent, but she'll be close enough to you and Zack so that he'll still be able to harrumph if he feels Taylor and Declan need to cool it." Kevin grinned. "Well, say something. Are you okay with this?"

"Of course."

"Good. Now, I should get downtown. I'm meeting Dee before Simon Weber arrives to take our pictures. Since Zack's not going to be there I should probably say goodbye to him now."

Zack was still sleeping. I stayed in the hall and watched as Kevin went in, bent, and kissed Zack on the forehead. When Kevin left our room, he put his arm around my shoulder. "I'm going to miss you, Jo."

"I'm going to miss you too," I said. "But it's time."

"Yeah. It's time."

He started for the door. "Don't forget your messenger bag," I said.

Kevin laughed. "I don't need it any more. Taylor's birthday card, the keys to the cottage, and all the legal papers are in there. No need to wrap it. Just give Taylor the whole thing."

"Environmentally responsible," I said.

"It's time for that too," he said.

As soon as Taylor returned from church, I left for the drugstore at River Heights to pick up prescriptions, and then I cruised Safeway for ginger-lemon tea, crackers, and fruits that Zack might enjoy. When I got home and pulled into our driveway, my plans were simple. Zack and I would spend the afternoon drinking tea and watching the Packers/Broncos game with the sound turned low, so he could drift off when the Broncos didn't need his full attention. Seeing him in the front hall in his wheelchair and dressed for the office did not fit my script. "So where are you going?" I said.

"Downtown to Falconer Shreve," he said. "You must have heard us talking about it last night. Simon Weber's coming to the office to take pictures of the founding partners with the new guys. We need photos for the official announcement."

I waited till his latest coughing fit subsided. "Not reason enough," I said. "Henry was clear on this point. You're not going anywhere today. When you and I went with Delia to Port Hope to work out the custody of Abby's baby, we let your condition get ahead of us. I'm not going to take that risk again."

Zack wheeled towards the door. "I'll get Simon to take the pictures of us with the new partners first, then I'll come straight home."

"Zack, this isn't negotiable. Simon Weber's a friend. He'll figure out a way to make you part of the picture."

"The way Emmett made himself part of the picture of us at the lake?" Zack said, but he was too weary for vitriol. By the time I had him settled in fresh pyjamas and bolstered with foam and pillows in all the necessary places, he was asleep. Pantera and Esme flattened out on either side of the bed. I turned on the gas fireplace and stretched out with an Elizabeth Strout novel on the chaise longue beside the French doors to the patio. The TV stayed off. That afternoon, the Broncos were going to have to win without us.

At one, Noah, Isobel, and Jacob arrived to pick up Taylor. They came in to say hello, and as Jacob described the kind of kitten he was hoping to find, the delight on Noah and Isobel's faces filled me with hope. Their family, like the Falconers, had turned a corner. And Kevin Hynd now felt free to find his answers without shouldering a burden of guilt about Falconer Shreve and the troubles of his closest friends. I made myself a fresh pot of tea and returned to my place by the window with Elizabeth Strout. Finally, the universe was unfolding as it should.

I closed my eyes – "just resting them," as my grandmother would have said – but it wasn't long until I dozed off. A loud, insistent hammering at the front door awakened me. I looked over at Zack. He was still sleeping, but as the pounding continued, he stirred. Still half-asleep, but angry, I ran to the door. When I opened it, I was confronted by a sea of blue. There were police officers everywhere. The one facing me put her hand on my chest and pushed me hard so that I was no longer on the threshold but completely inside. As I stood in the entrance hall, more officers came through the door. Without explanation, they blew past me, spread out, and began searching the house. I felt their urgency and I began to shake.

"What's going on?" I said.

The young constable who'd shoved me inside said, "There's been a shooting."

"On our street?" I said.

She shook her head. "No. Downtown – in your husband's law office.

"Was anybody hurt?"

She didn't answer. I grabbed her arm. "I asked you a question," I said. "You and your colleagues just forced your way into my house. I deserve to know what's going on."

The officer lowered her eyes. "I can't give out that information."

Just then Police Chief Debbie Haczkewicz came through the open front door. The scene had taken on the fragmented quality of a waking dream. "Debbie, what are you doing here?" The words came out of my mouth but I didn't sound like me. I sounded like a bewildered child.

Debbie took my arm. "Jo, I don't have time to break this news gently. Delia Wainberg, Blake Falconer, and Kevin Hynd have been shot."

"What?" I heard her words, but at first I couldn't grasp their meaning. When I did, I started to shake. "Are they going to be all right?"

"No," Debbie said. "They died at the scene. Where is Zack?" My knees buckled. Debbie led me to the bench in the hallway. "Put your head down and take some deep breaths," she said.

Meek as a child, I followed her instructions. I couldn't stop shaking, but I was able to speak coherently. "Zack's down the hall in our bedroom. He wanted to go to the office, but he's sick and I made him stay home. Debbie, I don't understand."

"I know you're reeling, but for your family's sake, you have to focus on what I'm about to say. We think the shooter had a grudge against the founding partners of Falconer Shreve. Zack wasn't there, so the shooter wasn't able to finish the job."

"And you think whoever did this is out there looking for Zack?"

"We have to consider that possibility. Is Taylor here?"

"No, she went to the Humane Society with Noah Wainberg and his daughter and grandson."

"Call her and tell her to stay there." Debbie ran her hands over her eyes. "The Wainbergs won't know yet about the shooting. Don't explain anything to Taylor. Just tell her to stay where she is until an officer comes. We'll take it from there."

"They shouldn't be in a public place when they learn that Delia's dead."

Debbie's voice was gentle. "Joanne, what happened is unbearable. The place where Delia Wainberg's family hears the news won't change that. Please just trust me."

Three officers came in. They were all tall and powerfully built. Debbie glanced at them briefly. "Zack's not going to sleep through this. Jo, you're going to have to tell him what's happening."

"I will," I said.

"You should probably call Taylor first," Debbie said.

"Of course. Debbie, I'm having trouble hanging on to my thoughts."

"You're in the middle of a tsunami," Debbie said. "Just grab whatever you can."

I called Taylor and told her that her dad needed more rest. I said that she should stay put at the animal shelter, that the Wainbergs should remain with her, and that someone was on their way to the shelter to explain. Taylor had questions, but I simply told her that for now she needed to do as I said. I told her we loved her and broke the connection.

Zack had pushed himself up in bed. His back was against

the headboard. I was on automatic pilot, but remembering the pressure ulcers I picked up a pillow and slid it behind him. He was flushed and his eyes glittered with fever. "What the hell's going on?"

I sat on the bed and put my arms around him, then I tightened my embrace. "Zack, something terrible has happened." As I said the words that severed the life he had known from the life he would live from now on, I could feel the energy seep from my husband's body.

I pulled away so I could see his face. "Lie down," I said. Then I lay on the bed beside him and began stroking his back. "I love you so much," I said. "I don't know what to do." He drew me closer but he said nothing.

A police officer entered our bedroom. She locked the French doors, peered through the windows, and then, apparently satisfied that she'd missed nothing, pulled the drapes. She repeated the sequence at every window in the room and she was unhurried.

"Could you give us a moment alone, please?" I said.

The officer kept on with her task. It was as if Zack and I didn't exist.

"Please," I said. "We've had just had horrific news . . ."

"We know that," she said. "But there's a lot of ground to cover. Those creek banks alone . . ."

"Do you really think the person who killed them is near our home?"

"The three victims were named partners of a law firm," she said. "Your husband is the only named partner still alive."

Zack's eyes were dead with disbelief. "Jesus Christ, I can't believe any of this is happening." A thought struck him. "Where's Taylor?"

"She's going to be safe," I said. "She's with Noah, Isobel, and Jacob. They went to the Humane Society to choose a kitten for Jacob. Debbie's sent an officer over there."

"Is there anybody here who can tell us what happened?"

Zack's pyjama top was soaked through again. "Debbie's here," I said. "We should change your pyjamas first."

"Jo. It doesn't matter."

"I don't know what else to do," I said, and I realized I was crying.

After the officer left us alone, I ran a cool damp facecloth over Zack's body, helped him into fresh pyjamas, and arranged the pillows so he could sit up. Debbie was still in the living room, and I went to her. "Zack wants to see you," I said.

Debbie came into the bedroom, pulled a chair over, and took Zack's hand. "I'd give anything not to be breaking this news to you, Zack."

Zack nodded. "Might as well get it over with."

"All right." Debbie pulled out a paper notebook. "This is what we know so far," she said. "Feel free to ask questions, but I may not have answers. We've just started the investigation and the information is spotty. At 2:15, Delia Wainberg's executive assistant, Lorne Callow, went to the Falconer Shreve offices on the twentieth floor of the Peyben Building. Callow had found a wristwatch Ms. Wainberg believed she'd lost, and she asked him to bring it to her. As you know, the elevator to the twentieth floor opens directly onto the reception area of the executive offices. Callow saw nothing amiss until he started towards Ms. Wainberg's office. Kevin Hynd and Blake Falconer were both lying face down in the hall that led from their respective offices to hers. Callow felt for pulses. Both men were dead. Delia Wainberg was sitting at her desk. She'd been shot in the chest three times. Callow felt for a pulse, but there was none. He used the phone in Ms. Wainberg's office to call us."

"And just like that, they're gone," Zack said, and his voice was dead with disbelief.

"No witnesses?" I said.

"A grey Sunday afternoon on the twentieth floor of a downtown office?" Debbie said. "The security guy who sits behind the big desk in the lobby downstairs is old school. He makes everybody he sees enter the building sign in, note the time they arrive and who they're seeing, and sign out, noting the time they leave. Counting Lorne Callow, Simon Weber, who wrote the word 'photographer' in parentheses after his name, and the man who delivered coffee and Danish from the coffee shop next door, fourteen people signed in. Except for Lorne Callow, they all arrived between 12:50 and 12:55. All of them were headed for the executive offices of Falconer Shreve. Nine signed out. The coffee delivery person left at 1:10." Debbie consulted her notebook and recited a list. "Margot Hunter, Katina Posaluko-Chapman, Ben-Aaron Dushek, Sandra Mikalonis, Maisie Crawford, Aashish Parwani, Raymond Stonechild, and Simon Weber left together at two o'clock."

"So it appears Dee, Blake, and Kevin were there alone," Zack said.

"There must be security tapes," I said.

Debbie nodded. "And we'll look at every second of them. We'll interview everyone who was recorded to be in the building, and, as a matter of procedure, we've tested Callow's hands for gunshot residue." Zack was gazing fixedly into space. Debbie gave me a quick worried look, leaned closer to Zack, and raised her voice. "Zack, why were your partners at the office on a Sunday afternoon?"

Zack turned to her as if he'd forgotten she was there. "We're announcing six equity partners tomorrow, and the office had arranged for Simon Weber to take photographs." He looked puzzled. "I don't get this. If Simon had already taken the pictures, why didn't Delia and Blake and Kevin leave with the others?"

"I don't know," she said. "We'll do what we can to find out." For all the years she had known him, Zack had been the man in charge; now he had the thousand-mile stare of a victim. But Debbie was accustomed to dealing with victims. She moved so close to Zack that their faces were almost touching. "I know you're going through hell, but if we're going to find the person who murdered your partners, we'll need help. That starts with you. Do you have any idea who did this?" Debbie's tone was severe but it did the trick.

The blankness left Zack's face. He was himself again, focused and furious. "Find Emmett Keating," he said.

Debbie took out a pen and began writing. "We've been investigating his disappearance for almost a week. Do you think Emmett Keating is capable of murder?"

Zack nodded. "There were indications that he might have gone over the edge."

"And the indications were . . ."

"Photographs," Zack said. "Specifically, a photograph that was taken of Delia, Kevin, Blake, Chris, and me the summer after we opened our law office."

I took the photo from Zack's dresser and handed it to Debbie. She looked at it carefully for a few moments and then shook her head. "It's always so hard to believe . . ."

Debbie didn't need to complete the sentence. Zack and I knew how it ended.

She handed the photo back to Zack. "It's beautiful. You were beautiful – all of you."

"Emmett Keating made a copy of that and doctored himself into it," Zack said.

"Did Keating send you the photograph?"

"No, we came upon it after he went missing." Zack shifted his body and grimaced. "It's probably still in his apartment," he said.

"It's not," Debbie said. "In the past week, we've gone over that apartment with a fine-tooth comb. Zack, the police should have been made aware of that photograph."

"We have a digital copy of it," Zack said. "I'll send it to you."

I took a breath. "There's more," I said. "Last Monday, each of the founding partners received a copy of the original photograph – without Keating in it – hand-delivered to their home mailbox. Someone had smeared feces on the partners' faces."

"And you believe Keating is responsible."

"It's hard to imagine," I said. "Emmett Keating is obsessive about his personal cleanliness, but on Saturday morning the video of Annie Weber ejecting him from the dinner for Zack was sent to everyone who works at Falconer Shreve, and to a few lawyers outside the firm."

"I'll need all the names," Debbie said. "Who took the video?"

"You saw the crowd that night," I said. "Most of us were taking pictures with our phones at one point or another."

Debbie was incensed. "And none of you thought to alert the police to any of this?"

"Zack was in Toronto," I said. "And the others wanted to keep the situation with Emmett Keating an internal matter. He'd been treated badly and they were hoping to undo the damage."

"And to cover up anything that would incriminate Falconer Shreve," Debbie said sharply. "Too late now. But the video is a lead worth following and we will." Debbie turned back to Zack. "I can't even imagine what you're going through right now, but I have to ask one last question. Did you perceive the photo with the excrement on it as a threat?"

"Jo told me about it, but I didn't give it much thought," Zack said, and he was so hoarse he could barely speak. "I was 2,700 kilometres from here, and I was in meetings all day and business dinners most nights."

I'd had enough. "Debbie, you have to back off. Delia assumed Emmett was responsible for the photos. She wasn't frightened, but she was distressed that anyone would do that to the partners of Falconer Shreve."

Debbie raised an eyebrow. "It was a *photograph*," she said, and from her tone it was clear that Delia's reaction baffled her as much as it had baffled me. Debbie flipped the page in her notebook and tried another tack. "Can either of you think of anyone else who might have been responsible for what happened today?"

Zack's expression was bleak. "Four lawyers, each of whom has been practising law for over twenty-five years? There are probably a thousand people in this city who at one point wished one or all of us was dead." The reality of what he said hit Zack hard. He started coughing again and this time his cough had a croupy edge.

Debbie didn't need to be prodded. She stood. "Zack, I'm sorry. I know you're sick, but we have to find out who did this and every second counts."

I followed her out to the hall. There were police everywhere. "Debbie, you may also want to speak with a man named Esau Pilger. He lives on the Standing Buffalo reserve and he also had a copy of that picture," I said.

Debbie paused to jot down the name. "How did Esau Pilger come to have a photograph of Zack and his friends?"

"I don't know," I said. "I don't know if he would do a thing like that . . ." My head began to spin as the reality of the deaths once again set in. "Debbie, I don't know if we can handle this."

"You can, and you will." She reached out and touched my arm. "You have my private number," she said. "Use it, and, Jo, keep me posted on Zack's health."

"I will."

———

Henry Chan listened without comment as I told him everything that had happened in the last hour. When I'd finished, he said, "I'll be right over."

"I don't think the police will let you in, Henry. They believe the person who did this may be waiting to finish the job by killing Zack."

"I can't let that happen," Henry said. "Zack's the only guy I can consistently beat at poker. Tell the cops this is a medical emergency, and if they don't let me through, I'll be taking names."

CHAPTER

15

In the first terrible moments after I learned that Blake, Delia, and Kevin were dead, my mind swam. Whenever I tried to focus, my thoughts, like minnows, finned out in a dozen directions. Debbie said that I was in the middle of a tsunami and all I could do was hang on. I tried, but I had responsibilities, and as their number grew, my brain stubbornly refused to function. Fearing that I'd let something essential float away, I became a compulsive note-taker. Each of my tasks had a list: Zack's care; Taylor's schedule; Delia's funeral; Blake's funeral; Kevin's funeral; questions about Falconer Shreve for Margot and Brock, who immediately and magnanimously agreed to manage the firm; questions for Norine about City Hall; calls to Gracie, Noah, and Isobel to check in. The lists helped, but I was still swimming for the surface.

One night, unable to sleep, I'd gone online, keyed in the word *tsunami,* and hit Search. I learned that tsunamis were like sloping mountains of water filled with debris, and it was impossible to predict either how many surges there would be or how much time would elapse between waves after they hit – the perfect metaphor for grief. Early the following morning, I had called the funeral home and made arrangements for Kevin's cremation. As I picked up his funeral list and put a check mark beside "cremation," I was heartsick, but ticking off tasks was proof that I hadn't drowned, so I carried on.

All morning the rain had been steady. When the officer who had been answering our door for the last five days called out to tell me that Debbie Haczkewicz had arrived with news, I went to the living-room window to watch for her. The gloom outside matched my mood. The only bright spots on the street were the yellow Gore-Tex rain jackets of the police officers guarding us. The speed of Debbie's dash between her car and our open front door was impressive. I took her coat. "I see the desk job hasn't slowed you down," I said.

Her smile was wry. "After fifty, you have to keep proving yourself."

"Tell me about it," I said.

Zack's nurse, Kym with a Y, was coming out of our bedroom when Debbie and I started down the hall. On the afternoon of the murders, Henry Chan had come to our house, assessed Zack's condition and mine and called Nightingale, a private nursing company. Kym had cared for my husband the previous time he'd been seriously ill, and he fit in well with our household. Zack was a big man, and Kym was a bodybuilder who had no problem giving Zack the help he needed to move his body. Kym was also a dog-loving Broncos fan with a gentle, oddball sense of humour that lifted our spirits.

He greeted us both. "Zack's expecting you, Chief Haczkewicz. He's all slicked up and out of bed, Jo. If you need me, holler."

Zack's robe and the linen on his bed were fresh, and he was bathed, shaven, and in his chair. I'd always believed that when people said someone had aged overnight, they were speaking figuratively, but since his partners died, my husband had grown visibly older. The lines that bracketed his mouth like parentheses had deepened; the shadows beneath his eyes had grown darker; and the vitality that made him dominate every room he walked into had been sapped.

In the five days since the murders, facts had emerged. Lorne Callow had been reluctant to reveal details about Delia Wainberg's private life, but the police can be persuasive and Lorne had seen the wisdom of being helpful. When she had left the family home earlier in the week, Delia had asked Callow to pick up her things and take them to the Hotel Saskatchewan. After the gathering at the Wainberg house on Halloween, Delia hadn't returned to her suite at the hotel. When she'd dressed for the meeting with the new equity partners Sunday morning, she realized she didn't have her watch with her, but she was running late. It wasn't expensive but it had sentimental value, and she'd called Lorne, asking him to stop by the hotel, check the suite, and bring the watch to her at the office. Callow's phone had been turned off when she called, but when he turned it back on a few hours later, he saw the messages from Delia.

He went straight to the hotel, found the watch, took it to the executive offices of Falconer Shreve, and walked into a nightmare. In addition to the horror of finding the bloodied bodies of three people he liked and respected, Lorne discovered that the murderer had smashed a ceramic sculpture that was Delia's most treasured possession. To celebrate the founding partners' twenty-five years together, Delia had commissioned Joe Fafard to create a ceramic of the five of them on the day they graduated from the College of Law. Fafard worked from photographs, and he'd managed to capture their sureness and their youthful impatience to get on with their lives. They were wearing their academic robes:

the day had been windy, and the robes of the young gradu-
ates swirled. The wind was at their backs. From the day the
artist delivered it, the ceramic had enjoyed pride of place on
the teak credenza in Delia's office. Now it was rubble.

The field of suspects, never large, had narrowed to one
man. The search for Emmett Keating intensified, and now
Debbie had news.

She went over to Zack. "How are you feeling?" she said.

"Like homemade shit," he said.

"It must be going around," Debbie said. "That's how I feel
too. But down to business." She pulled a chair over so she
was facing Zack. "This morning, acting on an anonymous
tip, the RCMP found Emmett Keating's body in a cabin on
Long Lake. He was slumped over the kitchen table apparently dead of a single shot through the temple. A Glock 22
was on the floor beside him. Ballistics will compare the bul-
lets, but we're pursuing the possibility that Keating killed
himself with the same semi-automatic pistol that killed
Delia Wainberg, Blake Falconer, and Kevin Hynd. A letter
confessing to the murders was on the table. The letter
appears to have been typed on Keating's laptop and printed
on the printer at the cabin. There was no signature."

"Oh God," I said. "How long had he been there?"

"The definitive answer will take time," Debbie said. "But
the officers who found the body said it had been there awhile."

"Who did the cabin belong to?" Zack said.

Debbie took a deep breath and exhaled before she
answered. "Darryl Colby."

Zack leaned forward. "What the hell?"

"That was pretty much Mr. Colby's response," Debbie
said. "At first he was flabbergasted. He said Keating must
have broken in. But when we told him Keating had keys to
the cabin, Colby came up with a theory we're checking out.
Apparently, before Keating came to Falconer Shreve, he

worked for Darryl Colby." Debbie leaned towards Zack. "Did you know that?"

"Not until very recently," Zack said, "but, yes, I knew."

"Colby said he'd let his employees use the cabin occasionally. He couldn't remember if Keating had used it, but it was certainly possible that he had and that Keating simply hadn't returned the key, or had a copy made. When he killed your partners, Keating might have panicked, remembered the cabin, and fled there." Grey with exhaustion, Debbie rubbed her eyes. "Look, there are still a lot of I's to dot and T's to cross in this investigation, but I think we can safely consider this case solved."

The silence hung heavily in the air. Finally, Zack said, "There's an Italian proverb: 'At the end of the game, the king and the pawn go back in the same box.'" Zack had a beautiful mouth, full-lipped and sensual, but anger had twisted his lips into a snarl. "No matter who we are or what we accomplish, we all end up in the grave," he said. "So, Emmett Keating has finally joined The Winners' Circle."

"He realized his dream," Debbie said.

"And we all paid the price." Zack was pale and his breathing was laboured. He shifted his weight in his chair and grimaced. "Deb, I should be there when you tell the Wainbergs and Gracie about Keating. Would you excuse us while Joanne helps me get ready?"

Henry Chan's warning about Zack's blood pressure was never far from my mind. "You're staying put," I said. "I know Deb's news is a body slam, but I'm not about to let you become Emmett's fourth victim. Next Wednesday is Taylor's seventeenth birthday. She's counting on you being here. So are all the other people who love you. I'll go with Debbie when she talks to the Wainbergs and Gracie." I bent and gave him a serious kiss. "Let me do this, please."

———

The squad cars that had lined the street in front of our house since November 1 had already disappeared. It seemed we were no longer in danger. Debbie and I drove to the Wainbergs separately. Debbie was on police business, and I wanted to be free to stay if I was needed. The shootings had brought a temporary reconfiguration in the Falconer Shreve families. Despite our around-the-clock police protection, Zack and I had been concerned about Taylor, not just about her safety but also about her inability to lead anything resembling her everyday life. The north wall of Taylor's studio was a three-metre-high window that faced our street's back alley, and the police were quick to declare it off limits.

Taylor's art had always been her refuge. The studio she'd used on Halifax Street was still empty, and Margot's building had a reliable security system, so I'd asked Margot if Taylor could stay with her until our situation changed. The arrangement meant I was able to pick up Taylor after school and be beside her until I delivered her to Margot's front door. The police wanted all of us to stay close to home, and for Taylor that meant a life confined to school and Margot's condo. Zack and Taylor texted and skyped. It wasn't a great solution, but it was the best we could manage.

The Wainberg household, too, had reconfigured. In the hours after Delia's death, Noah, the man to whom we all turned to solve our problems, fell apart. Isobel, dealing with the death of her mother with whom she'd been reconciled for less than twelve hours, was numb; Ryan, Jacob's part-time caregiver, had booked the week off to study for his mid-terms. He offered to stay on, but Noah insisted that Ryan stick with his original plan.

Rose Lavallee had driven in from Standing Buffalo as soon as she heard of Blake's death. Gracie, dazed with grief, couldn't face the prospect of spending the night of her father's death in a house filled with reminders of his absence.

That night she and Rose slept at the Wainbergs. When Rose broached the subject of returning to the house on Leopold Crescent, Gracie refused to consider the possibility, and Rose suggested a solution that she felt would work for both families. Until Gracie was ready to return home, she and Rose would stay at the Falconers, and Rose would care for Jacob.

It was close to noon when Debbie and I arrived at the Wainbergs. When Gracie answered the door, I was shocked at the physical toll her father's death had taken on her. Her normally rosy face was so pale her freckles looked painted on, like a doll's, and when I reached out to embrace her, she clung to me. As was frequently the case in those terrible days, words failed me, so I just held Gracie, stroking her hair and hoping that the words that would connect us to the old familiar life would come. When the unmistakable fragrance of Rose's hamburger stew drifted from the kitchen, I had an opening. "Rose is making lunch?" I said.

"Jacob loves her hamburger stew," Gracie said. Her gaze took in both Debbie and me. "There's plenty if you'd like to join us."

"Thank you," Debbie said. "But I'm here on police business. I need to talk to you and the Wainbergs."

Gracie held out her hand to me. "Jo, you'll stay, won't you?"

"As long as you want," I said.

"I'll get Noah and Izzie." Gracie gestured to the living room. "Please make yourselves comfortable."

On a fine day, the sun pouring in through the vast expanses of glass in the Wainbergs' open-concept main floor was glorious, but that afternoon the sheets of rain streaming across the glass threw the room into a watery half-light. Debbie and I sat side by side on a couch facing the windows. "A dark day for dark news," she said in a voice so muted it seemed she was speaking to herself. As Noah, Isobel, and Gracie joined us in the living room, I was struck by their air of bewilderment. They were all strong and capable people, but none of us was prepared for the roles we were playing.

Noah accepted the news about Emmett Keating's written confession to the murders and his suicide with poignant resignation. "Well, that's it," he said, and he stood and held his hand out to Debbie. "Thanks for coming."

"You don't have any questions?"

Noah shook his head. "None that you could answer."

"I'm so very sorry," she said. "We'll be releasing the bodies tomorrow. You can begin arrangements when you're ready." Debbie turned to Isobel and Gracie. "Do either of you have questions?"

Isobel shook her head, and Gracie whispered, "No."

"Please call if I can help in any way," Debbie said.

During the next hour, Jacob was our salvation. As soon as Debbie left, he came running out to meet me. From the moment Zack laid eyes on Jacob, he'd been struck by the little boy's resemblance to Isobel and Delia. Like his aunt and his grandmother, Jacob had an explosion of curly black hair, an alabaster complexion, and brilliantly blue eyes. That morning he was wearing red corduroy overalls and carrying his new kitten, a tiny brown male.

Jacob cocked his head when he saw me. "Can you guess this cat's name?"

"I'll try, but I think I'll need a hint."

Jacob nodded solemnly. "Think of things that are brown."

"Fudge," I said. "Mud. Brown socks. Wood. Leaves in the fall. Cocoa."

Jacob's small face managed to express both pity and exasperation. "Toast," he said. "Toast is brown. My cat's name is Toast."

I reached over and stroked between the kitten's ears. "Hi, Toast."

We were all smiling when we went to the kitchen for lunch. Rose had set a place for me at the table. We were quiet as we ate. When he'd finished his soup, Jacob looked up at me. "Delia died," he said. "Did you know that?"

"Yes," I said. "I knew."

"That's why everybody's sad," he said.

"I'm sad too."

Jacob scooped up Toast and placed him on my knee. "You can hold Toast for a while," he said.

After we'd cleaned up the kitchen, Rose, Jacob, and Toast went upstairs for stories and a nap. Gracie smiled as she watched them. "The Three Amigos," she said. "Rose, Jacob, and Toast. They get us through the day." She returned her focus to me. "Esau Pilger hasn't come back to the reserve yet," she said. "It's been almost a week. I'm glad Inspector Haczkewicz came by. At least now we know that Esau wasn't involved in . . ."

"Did you think he might have been?" I said.

Gracie shrugged. "I try not to think about it at all," she said. "I know that sounds childish."

I put my arms around her. "Not childish. Just human."

Gracie drew me closer. "I miss being hugged by my dad," she said.

"I haven't been a very good friend to you in the past few days."

"You've had a lot to deal with too," she said. "How's Zack doing?"

"About the same," I said. "The nurse we had last time has signed on for the duration. Kym can pick up on the smallest change in Zack's condition without ever seeming to hover – an art I have yet to master."

"We're all glad you're there, Jo," Noah said. "We couldn't take losing Zack too." His words hit us all with the force of a blow. For a beat we stood together, frozen with the awareness that these moments of feeling the magnitude of what we had lost would assault us for the rest of our lives. The doorbell rang, breaking the spell, and the four of us moved into the hall.

When Noah opened the door, Lorne Callow was standing on the doorstep shaking the rain off his umbrella. He was dressed for the weather. Rubber overshoes shielded his leather oxfords, and a tailored navy blue trench coat protected him. "I hope I'm not intruding," he said. He closed his umbrella, stepped into the hall, and shut the door behind him. After greeting us all, he turned to Noah. "I know you were planning to sort through Delia's personal papers today," he said, "and I wondered if you needed a hand."

Noah swallowed hard. "Thanks, but something's come up. I think I need more time before I tackle Dee's private correspondence."

"I understand," Lorne said. "You have my number. Call if you need me."

"I will. Lorne, ever since this nightmare started, you've been going the extra mile. I may not always show it, but I appreciate the effort."

"I do what I can," Lorne said. He turned to me. "Ready to brave the elements, Joanne?"

"No use putting it off," I said. Lorne opened the door, stepped outside, and put up his umbrella. Noah bent and kissed my cheek. "Thanks for coming, Jo. Having you with us today helped."

As Lorne and I walked past the bears that Noah had created as his family's totems, a wave of sadness hit me. Noah was as strong and fearless as the bear he had carved to represent himself, but he hadn't been able to protect the wife he loved so deeply. Remembering the warmth that had existed between Lorne Callow and me on the sunny day when he helped me carry out our marigolds, I touched his arm. "It's good to see you," I said. "Today's been especially difficult for everybody."

Lorne was quick to pick up on my comment. "Did something happen?"

I didn't deliberate before deciding to tell Lorne Callow about Emmett Keating's confession and suicide. It would be public knowledge soon enough. His reaction was pragmatic. "At least now it's over," he said, and then, having deposited me at my car, he turned on his heel and strode smartly towards his Honda.

The weight of sorrow that had washed over me when I walked by the bear carvings stayed with me. Lorne Callow believed that Emmett Keating's suicide and confession ended our ordeal. I wasn't that optimistic, and as I drove home my stomach was in knots. The absence of police vehicles in front of our house did nothing to dispel my anxiety.

Kym met me at the door. "You just missed the Webers," he said.

"Was Zack awake to see them?"

"Better than that. For twenty minutes, he sat in his wheelchair fully engaged in conversation with them. And Zack's not the only one who's springing back to life. Pantera's been moping around since I got here. He knew Zack was sick, but when the Webers came, Pantera plastered himself against the side of the chair in case Zack felt the need to scratch his head." Kym chuckled. "Looks like your husband and his dog are getting their mojo back."

Zack was sitting up in bed with his back supported by the pillows piled against the headboard. He was wearing his reading glasses and working on his laptop. The air in our room still held faint traces of the fresh-flowery scent of Anaïs Anaïs.

"Annie Weber's been here," I said. "I can smell her perfume."

Zack smiled. "Can't get much past you," he said.

I sat in the chair already in place beside him. "Kym tells me you and the Webers had a good visit."

"A good visit and a necessary one," Zack said. "After you and Debbie left, Kym gave me something to knock me out, but before it hit, I called Warren to tell him about Keating's confession and his suicide. I figured since Warren had been there for the fireworks after the dinner and had tried to extend an olive branch the next day, he deserved to know the latest. He listened, thanked me for the call, and told me to take care of myself. I dozed off. When I woke up, Kym came in and told me that Annie and Warren were at the house, and they had something they wanted to discuss with me. They promised not to stay long, so Kym said it was my call."

"And the Webers stayed twenty minutes," I said.

Zack rubbed his hand over his eyes, a sure sign that he was tired. "It was important. After Warren and I talked on the phone, he and Annie went over the timeline for the night of the dinner and the next morning. Jo, they think something doesn't add up about Emmett Keating's suicide, and they want more information."

"Have the Webers shared their concerns with Debbie?"

"They have, and so have I. The police will finish their investigation, but Warren and Annie aren't convinced they're going to look for the kind of answers that they want. Warren's going to call in Harries & Associates."

"His private investigators," I said. "What's Warren's interest in this?

"Annie wants to set the record straight. She had no problem frogmarching Emmett out the door when he was humiliating Delia at the party, but she does have a problem with someone using a video of her strong-arming Emmett to set in motion a series of events that ended in the death of four people. The Webers want to find out who made that video and why they sent it out." I could see that Zack's energy was flagging. I put his laptop on the night table, rearranged the pillows, and helped him into a horizontal position.

"Thanks," he said. He managed to get out a half sentence about Harries & Associates' fine personnel and impressive resources before he fell asleep. I smoothed his sheets, kissed him on the forehead, and glanced at the clock. Ten minutes until I had to leave to pick up Taylor at school.

I could hear Kym whistling in the kitchen. It was the kind of innocent domestic moment that I now thirsted for, and I joined him. Glass bowls of sliced summer squash, bell peppers, and asparagus still glistened with water on the counter and Kym was slicing zucchini.

"You know you don't have to do that," I said.

"I know, but Zack's ready to start eating real food again, and I was hoping pasta primavera might tempt him."

"It tempts me," I said. "And Zack likes pasta. So does our daughter, and now that the threat is gone, I'll be bringing her home."

Kym frowned. "About that. Would it be possible for Taylor to stay with your friends for another night?"

"Of course," I said. "Zack will be disappointed, but if you think it's for the best . . ."

"I do. If his daughter's here, Zack will push himself to be super-dad, and none of us wants a relapse. Tomorrow's Friday. Why don't you bring Taylor home tomorrow afternoon, and give yourselves a relaxing weekend."

"But you *are* going to stay around, aren't you?" I said.

"I am. You could easily handle Zack's medical needs now, but you've been dealing with a lot. I'll stay till you decide it's time for me to go."

"That's music to my ears," I said. "Thanks." I picked up my phone. "Time to call Margot and fill her in."

As soon as she heard my voice, Margot was on full alert. "Everything okay with the big man?"

"Moving in the right direction," I said. "But he still has a way to go. Just now we were talking and he fell asleep in mid-sentence."

"Your sentence or his?"

"His," I said.

Margot chuckled. "That's a first."

"Right. Margot, there've been some developments."

When I finished giving her the news about Emmett Keating, Margot whistled softly. "Well I guess that's not a surprise," she said. "Jo, would it be possible for Brock and me to get together with Zack today? We need to talk about Falconer Shreve."

"It's going to have to wait," I said. "Zack's doing better, but Kym's concerned that if he pushes it, there'll be a relapse. I was hoping to bring Taylor home with me this afternoon, but Kym vetoed it. Would you mind if she stayed with you another night?"

"Of course not. We love having her around, but could you come in for a few minutes when you bring Taylor by?"

"I'll be there in half an hour."

Kym had finished slicing zucchini and he'd covered the bowls of vegetables with cling-wrap. "I can almost taste the pasta primavera," I said.

Kym narrowed his eyes at me. "Are you all right? You look a little bent."

"I am a little bent," I said. "I don't think this misery is ever going to end."

Kym gave me a crooked smile. "Everything ends, Jo. You know that."

CHAPTER

16

By the time I pulled up in front of Taylor's school, the rain had stopped. All my children had gone to Luther College High School, so the scene was a familiar one, and as Taylor, wearing her two-toned yellow and grey slicker, came out of the building and began walking towards my car, I slipped into the dream haze that had overtaken me often in the past five days. During these times, my mind slid into the old comfortable ruts and I was once again the woman with the incredibly fortunate life. When my daughter came nearer and I saw her face, the sharp edge of reality sliced my dream.

Taylor was fighting tears. As soon as she got in the car, she turned to me. "Did Dad have a heart attack?"

My chest tightened. "He has the flu, Taylor. You know that. Whatever made you think he had a heart attack?"

"Spenser Ridout told me he and his family were praying for Dad. Spenser's mum's a lawyer and she'd heard that Dad had had a heart attack – a bad one – and they didn't know whether he was going to live."

When I heard the fear in our daughter's voice, I knew that words, no matter how reassuring, would be inadequate.

Taylor had to see Zack for herself. "Your dad isn't dying," I said. "Now, here's the latest. Margot and Brock want to talk to me about Falconer Shreve business. While we're chatting you're going to pack up your things and play with the kids. When we're through talking, you and I are going to hug the little ones, thank Margot, and drive home. Kym's making us pasta primavera and the four of us are going to have dinner together."

Taylor's dark eyes were filled with hope and doubt. "But the police will still be there," she said.

"No, they're gone. The person who killed Delia, Blake, and Kevin committed suicide. He left a written confession."

"Who was it?"

"A lawyer at Falconer Shreve," I said. "His name was Emmett Keating. He felt the firm had treated him badly."

"So he killed three people."

"I know it doesn't make any sense."

Taylor was wary. "And the police are sure it's over?"

"Yes. Debbie Haczkewicz came over late this morning to tell us about Emmett Keating. By the time she left, there wasn't an officer or a police car in sight. Our house looks the way it always has."

"Normal," Taylor said, but her voice was small and she still looked uncertain. "I wonder what 'normal' will be from now on."

"That will be up to us," I said.

"Gracie, Isobel, and I have been texting constantly, and we talk every day. I always ask how they're doing, and they always say 'fine,' but you've seen them. How are they really?"

"They're devastated," I said. "But having Rose there is helping and, of course, it's impossible not to feel better when Jacob's in the room. I met his new kitten today."

Taylor's lips curved towards a smile. "Toast," she said. "Izzie told me Jacob chose the name because Toast is brown." As quickly as it came, my daughter's smile vanished. "I haven't seen any of them since it happened. Maybe now the three of us can be together again."

"No reason why not," I said. I touched her cheek. "Taylor, I won't lie to you. I have no idea how we're going to move forward. All I know is that tonight we'll have dinner together and you'll sleep in your own bed, and your dad and I will be just down the hall."

"We're the lucky ones," Taylor said. "A week ago, the Wainbergs, the Falconers, Kevin – all of us – we were all lucky." She turned away and pressed her forehead against the coolness of the car window. For a time, she was very still, seemingly absorbed in watching the rain. When she spoke, her voice was full of yearning. "Why didn't we realize it, Jo?" she said. "Why didn't we know how lucky we were?"

Margot, a committed non-cook, had often threatened to have the appliances ripped out of her kitchen and replaced with a jungle gym for her kids, but when she and I lived across the hall from each other we always gravitated towards her kitchen to talk. That day, as soon as Brock joined us, I passed along the rumour about Zack's health that had terrified Taylor. Margot and Brock exchanged a glance. "One more reason to rein in this situation," Brock said.

Brock was always well dressed, but as the director of a recreation and training centre and councillor for an inner-city ward, he most often chose outfits that were business casual. That afternoon, he wore a charcoal three-piece suit, a crisp white shirt, a cranberry-and-grey striped silk tie, and hard-polished black dress shoes.

"Margot says you want to talk about the firm," I said. "I take it from the three-piece suit that you've been at Falconer Shreve today."

Brock nodded. "I have," he said. "Margot and I decided

that out of respect for the late partners, we should stay closed on Monday, but we were both there when Falconer Shreve opened Tuesday morning, and we've both been at the office for the past two days. Jo, the situation is not good."

Margot nodded. "Not only are people grieving, they're frightened," she said. "They don't know who's in charge. Brock had a long talk with Delia's EA, Lorne Callow, yesterday. Understandably, he was concerned about his job, but his concern goes beyond himself."

"I'm not surprised," I said. "The night of the dinner, the doorman at the Scarth Club was prepared to call a taxi after the incident with Emmett, but Lorne was worried about what Emmett would do if he was on his own, so he drove him to his apartment. Lorne came by our place the next day. When I thanked him for smoothing the ragged edges in a terrible situation, he said, 'There are times when we really are our brother's keeper.'"

"The firm needs to foster that kind of presence," Brock said. "Lorne and I also had a conversation about office morale."

"How bad is it?" I said.

Brock shook his head. "Terrible. The immediate problem is leadership. People don't know who's in charge and they're worried about where the firm's heading. The story about Zack having a serious heart attack is making the rounds. We can refute that rumour, but there's no refuting the fact that the firm's only remaining senior partner has a full-time job as mayor of Regina."

"And he's torn," I said. "Zack's feelings about Falconer Shreve run deep, but when he was sworn in he made a commitment to this city."

Margot leaned towards me. "Jo, Zack just lost his three best friends. And unless we come up with a solution fast, he's going to lose the firm that he's given his life to."

"I can't believe Falconer Shreve is that vulnerable," I said.

"Other law firms certainly think it is," Margo said. "I've had inquiries – discreet but pointed – about Falconer Shreve's future."

"It hasn't even been a week since Dee, Blake, and Kevin died," I said.

"'The race is to the swift,'" Margot said tightly. "And the legal profession is not noted for its empathy."

"Margot and I are planning a meeting of the new equity partners tomorrow morning," Blake said. "In addition to everything else, our clients are panicking. All the late partners had heavy caseloads, and like most lawyers, Dee and Blake carried a great deal of information about their files in their head. Kevin had already passed the baton to Tina, but she was planning to get in touch with him if something critical arose. There are junior lawyers at Falconer Shreve who worked closely with Delia, Blake, and Kevin in the past, but it's tough for them to take charge of files when they can't access the information they need."

"And you're short one of your new equity partners," I said. "Maisie's still on maternity leave."

Margot and Brock both hesitated. Margot's nod to him was almost imperceptible, but Brock picked up the cue.

"Since Monday morning Maisie's been putting in longer hours than anyone," Brock said. "She's working from home, but she's planning to be back in the office from tomorrow on."

"Charlie and Colin were born less than six weeks ago," I said.

Margot's voice was gentle but firm. "I know they're very young to be away from Maisie, but we're talking about the survival of the firm here. Your daughter-in-law understands that."

I remembered the flush of joy that suffused Maisie's face when she nursed her sons. This would not have been an easy choice for her. That said, Maisie made her choice, and it was time I made mine. Politics had taught me the importance of collective action. "I understand the need for a partners' meeting," I said. "There are legal problems that have to be worked out quickly and confidentially, but don't shut out the associates and support staff. Everyone at the firm needs to feel they have a role to play in giving Falconer Shreve a secure future."

"Agreed," Margot said. "And they have to know that they still have a leader. Jo, we need Zack at that meeting. Do you think if we schedule it for late afternoon, say around four tomorrow afternoon, he could make an appearance? Knock together a short, inspirational speech for him. Please. Then all he has to do is show up."

I'd written scores of speeches for Zack, but suddenly that routine task seemed overwhelming. "I'm not going to risk Zack's health," I said.

"If Falconer Shreve goes under, Zack will never recover," Margot said. "You know that as well as I do. We have to get out the message that, despite its tragic loss, the firm will maintain the level of excellence its clients have come to expect. Jo, the truth is that founding partners die all the time, but their law firms live on. In the next few days we have to make decisions that will convince our clients and the legal community that Falconer Shreve will not only survive, it will be stronger than ever." Margot reached across the table and took my hand. "We can do this, Jo. The hard part will be forcing ourselves to get out of bed every morning and take that first step."

As Margot, Brock, and I discussed how to handle the next afternoon's meeting, information new to me about the past few days emerged. Amid all the details, one thing was clear: Lorne Callow was a godsend. He had been with Falconer Shreve for five years, and for three of those years, Delia had been managing partner. As her executive assistant, Callow had become knowledgeable about the firm's lawyers, the associates and the paralegals with whom the lawyers worked most closely, and the clerical staff who handled the firm's day-to-day business.

Now there would have to be reassignments, and that meant juggling employees who were comfortably ensconced in their positions and matching their areas of expertise and temperaments with those of associates and partners – not a simple task – and the firm's head of HR, Raema Silzer, would be on medical leave for another eight weeks. Lorne Callow was committed to doing whatever he could to help the firm survive, and he would be in charge of any reappointments within the firm.

Delia and Blake's positions had to be filled quickly but wisely. Brock and Margot had approached Marion Beyea – known to all as "Bey" – a retired barrister from Margot's old firm, Ireland Leontowich, to consult and make discreet inquiries about experienced lawyers who might be interested in joining Falconer Shreve. Zack knew and respected Bey, so Margot was confident he would have faith in her judgment.

Brock, Margot, and I had agreed that the announcement of Lorne Callow's and Bey Beyea's respective roles in the restructuring had to be carefully explained; that Katina must be given the support she needed to run the Calgary office; and, finally, that Zack, Brock, and Bey would be in change of filling the vacancies left by the loss of Delia and Blake. The three of us differed on only one point. Margot and Brock believed that only Zack had the authority to convince his Falconer Shreve colleagues that the future of the firm was secure. Out of concern for Zack's health, I disagreed, but Brock won the argument by stating the obvious. Zack was now the lone face of Falconer Shreve, and he was the only partner left who could say what needed to be said.

We were still at Margot's kitchen table, pondering that uncomfortable truth, when Taylor, Lexi, still wearing her *Wild Things* suit, and Kai came in. It had been twenty-three days since Margot had congratulated me for suggesting she buy Lexi a second identical costume so the first one could be smuggled into the washing machine. A lifetime. Lexi's suit was now much the worse for wear as, of course, we all were.

Kai was drooling. His two bottom front teeth and his two top front teeth had already appeared; now another lower incisor had popped through. He held out his arms to me and I took him from Taylor. When I breathed in the scent of the castile soap Margot used to wash her son's hair, it seemed for a moment that all was right with the world, but the moment soon passed. We said our goodbyes. Brock helped us carry Taylor's art supplies down to our car, and Taylor and I drove into our uncertain future.

I'd called Zack to tell him we were on our way, and when we arrived he was in his chair at the front door, freshly shaven and dressed in a blue-and-white striped sports shirt and jeans. Zack and Taylor had always shared a deep and uncomplicated love, and my heart skipped when I saw their joy at being reunited after a five-day separation. When Zack wheeled into the living room, Taylor was beside him. They needed time alone together, so I went into the kitchen to check on dinner.

Kym was brushing garlic butter on a baguette. "Are you bucking for sainthood?" I said.

Kym's laugh was low and infectious. "Saint Kym," he said. "I like the sound of that."

"Then keep brushing on that butter," I said. "How's Zack doing?"

"Physically, he's definitely doing better. But wellness is a mixed blessing. When you're as sick as Zack was, the body

sometimes gives you a pass on reality. Now that Zack's
better, the truth is sawing away at him. He's going through
hell, Jo. You were right to bring Taylor home."

"Thanks. I'm doing a lot of second-guessing these days."

"Don't. You're smart and you love him. Trust yourself."

"Okay. Here's a decision I could use some help with." I
laid out the situation with Falconer Shreve and explained
why Margot and Brock felt it was imperative that Zack
attend the meeting. "Do you think he should go?"

"No, but there's nothing you or I could say that would
dissuade him, so let's just get him to the meeting and home
as fast as possible."

Inching further along on his journey to sainthood, Kym
had arranged to meet a friend for a quick bite downtown so
that Zack, Taylor, and I would have privacy. Zack and
Taylor had just taken their places in the dining room when
the landline rang. I answered in the kitchen. The voice was
muffled. It sounded male, but I wasn't sure. "They thought
they got away with murder," the voice said. "They didn't,
and they won't." Not surprisingly, the number was blocked
on caller ID.

My first husband had been attorney general of the province; Zack had been a criminal lawyer for over twenty-five
years and mayor for two. I had lost count of the number of
times I picked up the phone and heard an anonymous voice
threatening, accusing, uttering obscenities, or just breathing
hard. This was nothing new, and my husband and my daughter deserved a peaceful dinner. I made a mental note to
finally arrange with the phone company for an unlisted
number, and then I reached for the box of matches on the
top of the refrigerator where I had kept it, and its thirty-five
years of predecessors, since Mieka was a toddler. It was time
to embrace the new normal. I joined Taylor and Zack in the
dining room and lit the candles.

For the first few minutes, the three of us limited our table talk to expressions of pleasure at the crisp greens in the salad, the savoury bite of the garlic bread, and the all-round excellence of the pasta. When we'd exhausted the subject, Taylor placed her utensils carefully on her plate. "I want to talk about Kevin," she said.

"Okay," Zack said. "Let's talk about Kevin." The words were casually uttered, but I could feel the hurt behind them. As Kym predicted, the effort of being the father Taylor had always known was costing Zack, but the smile he gave our daughter was warm. "So where do we start?"

"With something nice I just remembered," Taylor said. She faced Zack. "Did Jo ever tell you the story about the boy who made fun of my hair when I was a flower girl?"

Zack shook his head. "I'm all ears."

Taylor pulled her chair closer to the table. "When Jo's friend Jill was getting married, she asked me to be her flower girl. I was eight and I saw a picture in a bridal magazine of a girl with the most beautiful ringlets. As soon as I saw that picture, I knew I had to have that girl's hair."

"I wish I could have seen you with ringlets," Zack said.

"They were pretty spectacular," I said. "The woman who was doing the hair for the wedding spray-gelled, dry-rolled, and did who knows what else to give Taylor a head full of Medusa curls." I smiled at our daughter. "You really did look lovely."

"Danny Jacobs didn't think so," Taylor said darkly. "Danny was in my class at school, Dad. He thought he was funny, but he was really just mean. Anyway, Jo and I had gone to the mall to buy Jill a garter to wear at her wedding. We were crossing through the food court on our way back to the parkade when Danny saw me. He was at Orange Julius and he jumped up on his chair and yelled, 'Hey, Taylor, you know what you look like with that crazy

hair? One of those Chia Pets – you know – like on TV –
'Ch-Ch-Ch Chia.'"

Zack winced. "I hate the idea of anyone hurting you."

Taylor patted his hand. "I'm over it now, but at the time,
I thought it was tragic. When we got home, Jo put me in
the shower so she could wash the goop out, and then she
put my hair in a French braid and we went to the wedding." Engrossed in the memory, Taylor's face was glowing. "As soon as we got to the reception, I looked for Kevin.
It was when he had his pastry shop and he'd made Jill's
wedding cake."

"Kev and Jill were both Deadheads," I said. "The cake
was a tribute to Jerry Garcia and Company."

"And it was totally amazing," Taylor said. "Anyway, as
soon as I saw Kevin, I told him about Danny Jacobs. Kev's
always been on my side, and I was sure he'd know how to
pay Danny back."

"So what did he come up with?" Zack said.

Taylor was pensive. "Something very Kevin. He said, 'It's
the holidays, and I have a lot of big orders to fill. Why don't
you phone Danny tomorrow and ask him if he'd like to
come to the bakery and learn how to make marzipan pigs?'"

Zack swallowed hard. "That is very Kevin," he said.

"Well, I didn't get it at all," Taylor said. "So I asked Kev
how inviting Danny to do something fun was going to make
Danny feel bad."

Zack's voice was near breaking. "And Kevin said, 'It's not
about making Danny feel bad. It's about planting a seed.'"

Taylor's eyes widened. "That's exactly what he said. He
said, 'If the seed takes root, Danny will grow. If it doesn't,
Danny will have to wait for the next seed.'"

"So did Danny accept your invitation?"

"No. He just laughed and sang the Ch-Ch-Ch-Chia song,"
Taylor said. "I'd forgotten all about what happened until

our grade eight farewell ceremony. Our teacher asked us to write down something we wish we'd said to a classmate. We didn't have to sign the note, just put it in an envelope with the classmate's name on it. In my envelope there was a note that said, 'I wish I'd said yes when you asked me to make those candy pigs.'"

"You never told me that part of the story," I said.

"I never told anybody but Kevin, and he was really pleased. He said, 'Karma has a way of surprising us. I'll bet it surprised Danny Jacobs.' And then he laughed – a real laugh – the kind of big, walloping laugh he had when he still had his pastry shop."

"I remember that laugh," I said.

"He loved that place," Taylor said. "I never understood why he sold it."

Zack cleared his throat and both Taylor and I looked towards him. When he spoke, his voice was strained. "He sold it because I asked him to, Taylor. I told Kevin the firm needed him and it was time he grew up."

Silence fell over the table. Zack picked up his fork and then stared at it as if he had no idea of what it was doing in his hand. Taylor didn't hesitate. She went to her father and bent to kiss the top of his head. "You didn't know," she said.

Zack lay his fork on the plate. "You're right," he said. "I didn't know, but I should have." He sighed heavily. "I've had enough for one day. I'd better hit the sack."

When Zack turned his wheelchair towards the door, Taylor moved in front of him. "Dad, if Kevin were here, he'd tell you not to blame yourself for something you couldn't see at the time. He'd also tell you to forgive yourself for being human." She embraced her father, then leaned across and squeezed my shoulder. "I'll get the dishes," she said.

I helped Zack into bed and then crawled in beside him.

"You don't have to waste your time trying to convince me that I'm not a total prick," he said.

"Well, for the record, you're not a total prick," I said. "But even if you were, I took those vows. There was a lot in there about for better or for worse and in sickness and in health. But what I really remember is what you whispered after the dean said we were husband and wife. You said, 'This is forever. A deal's a deal.' Convincing you you're not a total prick is just part of the deal."

It might have been wishful thinking on my part, but Zack seemed to sleep more soundly that night than he had since the Sunday of the murders. I wasn't so lucky. In the middle of the night, remembering the muffled voice on the telephone threatening revenge for an unpunished murder, I awoke with a start. But I'd lived through a week of unimaginable horrors; an anonymous call held no terrors for me, and I moved closer to Zack and drifted off.

The next morning, Zack said he felt stronger. I told him about the four o'clock meeting, its purpose, Margot and Brock's plans for the firm's future, and their belief that Zack had to be the one to drive home the message that Falconer Shreve would continue to be a vital force in the legal community.

When I'd finished, Zack said, "Guess it's time for me to step up to the plate."

"Are you sure you're up to this?"

Zack shrugged. "Doesn't matter," he said. "There's nobody left on the bench."

CHAPTER

17

There were one hundred and fifty employees in the Regina Falconer Shreve office, and arrangements had been made to live-stream the meeting into the Calgary office. The meeting was being held on the fourteenth floor of the Peyben Building, the space dedicated to the firm's clerical work. The office furnishings of the meeting room had been cleared away, replaced by rows of chairs facing the front of the room where portraits of Delia, Blake, and Kevin had been placed on the teak credenza from Delia's office. Zack wanted all the equity partners to march in together to suggest solidarity and continuity, so Lorne Callow had made certain there was an aisle between the rows of chairs.

By four o'clock, every chair was filled. The following Wednesday would be Remembrance Day, and, for me, there was a special resonance to the fact that everyone in the room wore a poppy. The flowers that grew in Flanders Field were a tender reminder that we all make this journey together. The new equity partners had assembled at the back of the room, and at the stroke of four, they marched two by two up the aisle. All were dressed in black suits and white shirts, and each carried three white orchids. The room was silent as they stopped in front of the credenza, placed an orchid in front of each photograph, and then moved into place at the side of the credenza. Zack was the last to come up the aisle. He pushed his chair with vigour and he held his head high. He, too, carried an orchid for each of his partners and after the three orchids had been placed, he wheeled close to the audience and began his comments.

He spoke without notes in a voice that was still hoarse but rang with conviction as he assured the staff of Falconer Shreve that the firm would carry on and explained the plans that would take the business into the future. When he finished his remarks, he offered to field questions, but no one had any. The firm's leader had said everything that needed to be said. After it was clear there would be no questions, Zack thanked everyone for coming, turned his chair around, wheeled closer to the credenza to spend a few moments in silent communion with the portraits of the three people who had shared his life, and then, dry-eyed, he wheeled back down the aisle.

Lorne Callow then stood and announced that the firm would be closed Wednesday for Remembrance Day, Thursday afternoon for Delia's funeral, and Friday afternoon for Blake's. Kevin's funeral was private and would be held at Lawyers' Bay. The equity partners walked back down the aisle and the meeting was over. Of the five original partners only Zack remained, but there had been no discussion about changing the firm's name. The continued existence of Falconer Shreve Altieri Wainberg and Hynd was proof that while human life is transient, a law partnership is enduring.

Zack had asked me to sit on the aisle in the front row so he could see me while he spoke. As the last of the partners filed out, Lorne Callow motioned to those of us in the front to follow them. Being one of the first to pass down the aisle

I was able to gauge the reaction of the firm's employees. Margot and Brock had been determined to keep the emotional temperature of the meeting cool. There would be time enough for grief at the funerals, but the goal of this meeting was to reassure and strengthen the will of everyone who worked at Falconer Shreve, and while many of the faces I saw were tear-stained, people were composed.

Anticipating that people would be eager to speak with Zack one on one and knowing that he was not yet ready for prime time, I'd asked Noah to take us downtown and get Zack out of the building as quickly as possible after the meeting adjourned. I was already counting the minutes till I could slide into the back seat with him and let Noah drive us home when I spotted Gracie and Isobel in the back row. As soon as they saw me, they were on their feet.

"What Zack said was perfect," Isobel said. "He seems fine. Is he really better?"

"Definitely moving in the right direction," I said. "It will mean a lot to him that you two were here."

"Where else would we be?" Isobel said. "We wanted to represent our parents. Falconer Shreve was the most important thing in my mother's life. Knowing that it was going to continue would have meant everything to her."

"My dad would have wanted this too," Gracie said, then checked her watch and turned to Isobel. "We'd better get home. We promised Jacob we'd take him to the park before supper. Thanks for being here today, Jo, and please thank Zack. It must have been so hard for him to be up in front of everyone today."

I hugged Gracie and Isobel before we parted ways. "Say 'hi' to Rose and Jacob and Toast for me."

Though I was looking forward to getting home, Lorne Callow's handling of the event had been smooth and I felt I should thank him for everything he'd been doing for

Falconer Shreve since the terrible event. A number of people
eager to talk Lorne had already gathered around him, so I
decided to take a recess in the hall until most of the crowd
had returned to their offices. Standing alone near the bank
of elevators, I was fair game, and when a bell chimed, the
elevator doors opened, and Darryl Colby in his cloak of
musk stepped onto the fourteenth floor of Falconer Shreve.

I was too wrung out for games. "What are you doing
here?" I said.

"I'm looking for Zack," he said.

"He already left."

"Did he go back to City Hall? This is important."

I could feel my gorge rise. "Darryl, Zack didn't go back to
City Hall. He went home. He's sick and he's suffering. If
you're here to pick the bones, you're wasting your time.
Zack has already been picked clean."

Another elevator sounded and this time Noah emerged.
He was aware of the antipathy that existed between Darryl
and Zack, but he apparently had as little appetite for confrontation as I had. He spoke directly to me. "Zack's already
in the car, Joanne. We have to leave."

He took my arm and pressed a call button. Darryl Colby
kept his habitual, unpleasantly close stance. He took out a
business card and handed it to me. "Have Zack call me," he
said. "It's important."

Zack wheeled towards our bedroom for a nap as soon as we
were inside our front door. He was tired, but he knew the
meeting had gone well. The firm's direction had been set,
and if it stayed the course, Falconer Shreve would continue
to grow and flourish. Zack awoke for dinner with Taylor and
me and was bathed, back in bed, and asleep by seven-thirty.

I was drained too, but Darryl Colby's appearance at
Falconer Shreve had unsettled me. In my bones, I knew

something was wrong, but I lacked the clarity of mind to think the situation through. Normally, Zack was my sounding board. I had come to rely on his responses when I raised a question and floated possible answers, but he needed peace and rest, not dark and muddled suspicions. I showered, then, remembering the old dictum that "lavender is especially good for all griefs and pains of the head and brains," I rubbed on lavender oil, slipped into my coolest cotton pyjamas, and hoped for a respite. It wasn't to be. Just as I turned out the light on my night table, my phone rang. Not wanting to awaken Zack, I took it out to the hall.

Gracie got straight to the point. "Rose just got off the phone with Betty," she said. "There's been a fire at Standing Buffalo. Esau Pilger's house burned down."

"Was Esau inside?"

"No. But he was on the reserve. Betty says he got back to Standing Buffalo yesterday. Apparently, the morning after Rose called him to see if he'd used bad medicine on my family, Esau drove up to Wahpeton."

"The reserve up north, near Prince Albert."

"Right," Gracie said. "The people of Wahpeton are Dakota Sioux like we are at Standing Buffalo. Esau told Betty that at Wahpeton he went to a sweat and spent time with a traditional healer. He says he came back yesterday and cleaned out his house. He built a big fire outside to burn up the trash, and the wind changed. By the time the fire truck got there, his house had burned to the ground."

"But Esau is all right," I said.

"Yes, and his cats and dogs are fine too. So no worries there, Jo, the dog whisperer."

"You know me too well," I said. "Gracie, does it sound to you as if Esau is planning to make a new start?"

"The indications are certainly there," she said. "The first thing he did when he got back to the reserve was go to

Betty's house. Betty told Rose it took her a moment to recognize him. Esau was clean, his hair was neatly braided, and
he was wearing fresh clothes. He said he wanted to see me."

"Did he say why?"

"According to Betty, Esau said he wants to tell me he's
sorry for everything."

I felt a chill. "A blanket apology," I said. My mind raced.
I didn't want to upset Gracie, but a half-formed thought had
been gnawing at me. I hesitated, and then said, "Gracie, you
don't think the police got it wrong about Emmett Keating,
do you?"

Gracie sounded surprised. "I don't believe that Esau had
anything to do with what happened to my dad and Delia and
Kevin, if that's what you mean. And, Jo, Emmett Keating
confessed."

An image of Esau sitting at the table, sharpening his knife,
in the midst of the detritus of his wasted life as I called 911
for the granddaughter of the woman he loved flashed through
my mind. "You're right," I said, but my body was taut with
worry. "Of course, you're right."

That night sleep did not come easily for me. When, finally,
I did fall asleep, I dreamed I was facing the iron pickets of
the entry gate at Lawyers' Bay, the one that kept the cottages secure. It was a bitter day, bitingly cold, windy and
snowy, but I could see the cottages. Ours was the only one
with the lights on. I knew Zack was inside waiting for me,
but the gate was locked. The digital code that I had to punch
in order to enter was as familiar to me as my own name but,
numbed by cold, my fingers were too clumsy to hit the correct numbers, and the gate remained stubbornly locked. I
called out for help, but no matter how often or how loudly I
called, no one came. I grabbed the iron pickets of the gate
and tried to shake it open. When one of my palms started to

bleed, I gave up and turned to walk away. I took a step but then stopped to look back at the cottages one last time. I saw that ours had burst into flames. Frozen, I watched as it burned to the ground. With that terrible suddenness that comes at the critical juncture of a nightmare, I awoke. My usual pattern after awakening from a bad dream was to slow my breathing until my heart beat normally, move closer to Zack, and, as I tried to decipher the dream's meaning, gradually drift back into sleep.

Carl Jung's theory that a dream is a message that can be understood only if you turn it over and over again in your mind had often led me to some surprising insights about my life. That night, I didn't need to turn the cube to uncover what the dream was telling me: my husband was in danger, and I had to find a way to save him.

CHAPTER

18

The next morning, for the first time since the tragedy on All Saints' Day, I felt as if my brain was functioning. I was certain that my dream of the fire had been a warning. I had no plan, but I knew I had to take action. I had always been fond of a line in a book about medieval knights that my children had loved. Before a knight mounted his steed and set off, sword in hand, he would cry, "I'll take the adventure God sends me." Though I was without steed or sword, I was prepared to use whatever came my way.

In one of those meaningful coincidences that suggest there's a pattern to our lives, Noah Wainberg called just after breakfast to ask if we could get together that morning to talk about the service for Delia. Zack was planning to work a half day at City Hall, so as soon as I dropped him off, I went to the Wainbergs. I had seen Noah the day before, but when he answered the door I was taken aback. He had always moved with the ease of a man confident in the power of his body. That day he moved cautiously, like someone recovering from a serious illness.

After he'd hung my jacket on the coat rack, he led me

into the kitchen, where Jacob and Rose were making cookies. Rose was putting small spoonfuls of dough into Jacob's palm so he could use his hands to roll the dough into balls. Over the years, I had made cookies with many children, but Jacob brought a unique and profound seriousness to the task. Standing beside me, Noah saw the similarity that had struck me. "Look at the way Jacob sets his mouth," he said. "That boy is so much like Dee."

"And Isobel," I said. I approached the cookie-makers. "What happens to the dough after you roll it into balls, Jacob?"

"We put the balls on the cookie sheet and put the cookie sheet in the oven. And then – voila – we have cookies!"

I laughed. "Voila?"

Jacob nodded solemnly. "Granddad says you have to say 'voila' or the cookies don't turn out. That's why Rose and I say 'voila.'" He looked up at Rose. "Don't we?" he said.

"We do," Rose said. "And it works every time."

"I'm looking forward to tasting one of those voila cookies," I said.

"Jacob will make sure you get one when we're through with the planning," Noah said. "Meanwhile, Jo, Isobel's in the dining room with her laptop."

When she heard her father and me come in, Isobel half-stood. "Jo, we're so grateful you're helping with this. Dad and I aren't making much progress." She indicated the chairs on either side of her. "Sit close to me so we can all see the screen," she said. "We've decided on Thursday at two and we were able to rent the university theatre, so the venue's decided. That's as far as we've gotten."

"We have made a few decisions," Noah said. "The ceremony's going to be secular." His mind seemed to drift.

I pressed on. "Beyond that, do you have any ideas about the kind of service you want?"

Noah's laugh, normally warm and robust, was a harsh bark. "I don't want a service at all," he said. "I want Dee to be alive. I want her to walk into this room, and I want to spend the rest of my life with her."

Isobel kept her eyes on the laptop screen. "That's not going to happen," she said. "Dad, if you don't want a service, we don't have to have one."

"We're not having it for me, Izzie. Your mother was a remarkable woman. People need the chance to reflect on her life. She was a brilliant lawyer, one of the most prominent in the province, with an extraordinary record in front of the Supreme Court."

"So I've heard," Isobel said tightly. She continued to stare at the screen for a few moments before she raised her eyes to meet her father's. "Dad, do you think Delia changed at the end? She stood with us while we listened to the Ravel quartet. Was she just following a momentary impulse or did she suddenly see her life differently?"

Noah seemed defeated. "I don't know," he said. "I think your mother would have tried to be different, but she was fifty-two years old. It might not have been possible for her to change."

Just as the silence in the room became unbearable, a small bright voice in the kitchen called out, "Voila!"

All of us smiled. "Time to carry on," I said.

We made our choices quickly. Zack would deliver the eulogy. A string quartet would play Debussy and Ravel. Isobel had always been a reader and she volunteered to choose the readings. Delia was being cremated, so her ashes would be placed in a carved teak box Noah had made for her when they married. The funeral would begin with Margot, Zack, and the new Falconer Shreve equity partners processing up the centre aisle of the university theatre and taking their seats with the family in the front row. The service would end when they all left. Lorne Callow had volunteered to work out the details of the reception.

The first part of our meeting was over. Noah, Isobel, and I joined Jacob and Rose in the kitchen to snack on warm cookies and cold milk. Comfort food on a day when we sorely needed comfort.

Isobel had decided it was time for her to go back to classes, and after she left for the university, Noah and I returned to the dining room. We had always been comfortable enough with each other to stay silent if we had nothing to say, and it took me a while to decide how to broach the subject that had been not far from my mind all morning. As I told him about my nightmare, Noah listened intently.

"I haven't been able to shake it off," I said. "That dream embodies a possibility I find almost impossible to face."

"The possibility that this isn't over," Noah said. "I can't shake that thought either. I've tried to convince myself that Emmett Keating's confession and suicide really was the end, but I can't."

"Neither can I," I said. "And here's another loose end to pull on. There was a phone call on our landline the day the police discovered Keating's body. The voice was muffled, so I'm not certain whether the caller was male or female. Whoever it was said, 'They thought they got away with murder. They didn't and they won't.'"

The muscles in Noah's face tensed. "Did you report the call to the police?"

"No. Since . . ." I stumbled and started again. "Since the day everything happened, Taylor had been staying with Margot. The night the phone call came was Taylor's first night back with Zack and me. We were all fragile, and I thought the three of us needed a quiet family dinner. I honestly didn't give the call much thought. Noah, I've been involved in electoral politics for much of my adult life.

Crank calls come with the territory. None of them has ever been a real threat."

"But this caller mentioned not letting someone get away with murder," Noah said quietly. "Which means the call *might* amount to something. Joanne, Delia never knew the specifics about the information Keating had on Chris. She told the partners she assumed it was about the defalcation but, in private, she confided in me that she was worried Keating had found out about the circumstances of Murray Jeffreys's death."

As Noah's words trailed off, I felt a coldness grow in the pit of my stomach. It was a story I had not thought of often since I had learned of it a few years ago, but I had never forgotten what Zack had told me about that ugly passage in the otherwise golden story of the young lawyers' early years.

It began when Noah, along with Delia, Zack, Blake, Kevin, and Chris, crashed a Christmas party thrown by Murray Jeffreys & Associates. Over the years, Jeffreys had earned a reputation for being a successful but unscrupulous lawyer. The party had been out of hand and, except for Chris, the young friends were drinking heavily.

At some point in the evening Murray Jeffreys came onto Delia. When she rebuffed him, he turned mean. Chris saw the threat and shepherded their group out of the building into a back alley. Jeffreys followed them. When he lunged at Delia, Noah began throwing punches, and the older man went down. Noah was certain none of his punches had connected, but when Chris knelt beside Jeffreys, there was no pulse. Chris made a quick decision. Recognizing that his friends were too intoxicated to deal with the authorities, he sent them away. When the police arrived, he told the officers that Jeffreys was already down when he found him. Later, the autopsy concluded that the cause of death was a massive heart attack.

"That case was closed the year they were all articling," I said. "If Delia thought Keating might be blackmailing her about Jeffreys's death, why didn't she say something the night of the dinner?"

"She was caught off guard," Noah said. "Dee believed she'd handled the situation with Keating. Suddenly, he was standing in front of her making accusations, and Margot was demanding answers. Delia made her case with the first thing that came to her mind: the defalcation."

"Even if Emmett Keating did know something about Jeffreys's death, from what Zack told me Chris was the only one of you who did anything wrong, and in the end, what he did didn't make a difference. The coroner ruled Jeffreys died of a heart attack. Delia knew that," I said. "She could easily have called Keating's bluff and told him to do his worst." Not until I uttered the words did I realize how ill chosen they were.

Noah stood, shaking his head. "That's what Keating did, Jo. That's exactly what he did."

When Zack came home after his half day at City Hall, it was clear that half days would be in order until we'd made it through the funerals. I decided not to burden him with speculations about the nature of Emmett's blackmail. He was tired but in good spirits. LivingSkies, one of the Toronto production companies Zack had courted during his week in Toronto, had secured funding for a CGI project about a young girl who searches for her grandmother among the polar bears and northern lights of Churchill. The company was moving its offices to Regina at the beginning of the New Year. Movie jobs were clean and they paid well. Between LivingSkies and Caritas, which would occupy its former offices on the old campus of the university, Zack was hopeful the city's film industry had been born again.

That afternoon, Norine stopped by with paperwork for Zack to catch up on. He'd had a rest after lunch and he mowed right through the paperwork and asked Norine to bring more on her way home in the evening. He was doing a credible imitation of a man who was back in the saddle, but the sorrow never left his eyes. We had dinner with Taylor and were in bed early again that night.

Within moments of Zack's resting his head on the pillow, he fell into a deep sleep, but I lay awake. That morning, I had been ready to take on whatever came my way, feeling sure that the day would yield answers to niggling thoughts and uncertainties. Now, all I had was more speculation, and any answers there might be, it seemed, were snuffed out when Emmett Keating took his own life.

Tuesday morning, after a fitful night's sleep, I was weary and on edge, but it was the day before Remembrance Day, and the service to commemorate those who had died in war was being held that morning at my granddaughters' school. I had promised to be there. Madeleine was reciting a poem and Lena was carrying up the paper wreath her class had made. Both girls were in the choir and were singing "In Flanders' Fields." Zack had planned to attend the ceremony, but he'd already missed too much work, and on Wednesday he would be presenting a wreath on behalf of the city at the cenotaph in Victoria Park. He needed the time in the office to catch up on more paperwork before his first public appearance since he'd fallen ill.

When Gracie Falconer called that morning to ask if I had any time to meet her, I told her I was free all day except for the 10:30 service at the girls' school. Gracie said she'd made arrangements to go through her father's safety deposit box as soon as their bank opened, but she'd be through by ten, and as a graduate of Pius X she'd welcome the chance to go to the Remembrance Day service with me.

The ceremony was being held in the gymnasium. Gracie had been withdrawn when she picked me up, but the moment she walked into the gym, she was her old self. She gazed at the walls filled with banners for teams that had won championships. Gracie had been on the Pius Patriots for four years, and in every one of those years, the Patriots won the girls' basketball city championship. When the school principal, Mo St. Amand, spotted Gracie, he came over and embraced her. "I'm so very sorry about your father," he said. "He was a good man. I don't think he ever missed one of your games."

"He didn't," Gracie said. "He was a terrific dad."

Mo turned to me. "It's good to see you too, Joanne. Madeleine and Lena are excited about their part in the program. All the children are. It's important for them to remember the ones who went before."

"It's important for all of us," Gracie said. She drew Mo's attention to a teacher standing at the door to the gym who was gesturing to him. "You're being summoned," she said. "Thanks for your condolences."

As the classes filed in, each child wearing a poppy, Gracie was intent. "I think I remember every second I spent at this school. Not much has changed. More kids. New portables. Some new teachers, but it still feels like home here. I'm glad I came, Jo."

"So am I," I said.

Gracie leaned closer and looked at me closely. "Are you okay, Jo? You look a little pale."

I was inwardly debating the wisdom of telling Gracie about the questions that had been nagging me since Noah and I had talked the day before when my eldest child arrived. Mieka never missed her daughters' events, but owning and managing UpSlideDown and April's Place kept her busy, and that day, as always, she arrived breathless, with only seconds to spare before the program began. She slid into the chair next to mine. Mieka relished her role as Taylor's big sister and as honorary big sister to Taylor's friends. When she asked if we could trade places so that she could sit next to Gracie, Gracie's face lit up. The two of them sat close as the program moved along, and both had their cameras out when the girls performed. We managed to stay dry-eyed until the choir sang "In Flanders' Fields," and then Mieka had to pass the tissues. After we'd praised the ladies for their respective performances, and congratulated Mo St. Amand on another moving Remembrance Day service, the three of us walked together to the parking lot.

Mieka had to get back to UpSlideDown, but Gracie and I were without a destination. As soon as we'd snapped on our seat belts, Gracie said, "Are you feeling up to coming out to Standing Buffalo? I said I'd go see Esau today. I could use your support, but if you're under the weather . . ."

I did not want Gracie to go back to see Esau alone. I reached into my purse, took out my blush, rubbed it along my cheekbones, and then presented my face to Gracie. "Voila," I said. "Instant robust good health. Let's hit the road."

CHAPTER

19

After our previous encounter, I felt anxious about visiting Esau, but it was a beautiful day for a drive. Winter was definitely in the air, but the sun shone brightly. The road into Standing Buffalo was clear, and Gracie navigated the hairpin turns with ease. As we approached Esau's driveway, Gracie slowed to a stop. We could smell the smoke from the fire. On the hilltop where the house once stood was a pile of rubble. Esau was sitting in front of the ruins on a folding chair, his dogs beside him. As soon as he saw us, he called out. "I'll come down."

Gracie shook her head. "No. I'll come to you."

"Are you sure?" I said.

"Might as well give my new DonJoy brace a workout," she said. We hadn't travelled far when Esau and his dogs met us. Surprisingly, he offered Gracie his arm, which she accepted tentatively. I gave the dogs a liver treat, and then the four dogs and the three of us climbed the rest of the incline together. An orange safety-barrier fence had been installed around what was left of Esau's house. Nothing had escaped the flames. The walls were gone and beams of wood, scorched and charred from flames, lay on the ground. Broken glass littered the area around the foundation.

Esau led Gracie to the folding chair on which he'd been perched when we arrived. The two framed photographs that had been on his wall were propped against a Saskatoonberry bush along with a smoke-damaged tin coffee canister that sat next to them. He pointed to the chair. "This is for you," he said.

"*Philamaya*," Gracie said.

"*A he ya eh*," Esau said. He eyed me. "The girl said 'thank you' in our language and I said 'you're welcome.' We'll talk your language now."

The dogs began sniffing me. I pulled out my baggie of liver treats and scattered some more on the ground. Periodically, minute particles of burnt wood drifted from the debris into the air, but when we looked across the valley it seemed we could see forever.

"This view is amazing," I said.

"The old ones knew that," Gracie said. "Farming this land was backbreaking, but they worked hard. At the end of the day, their reward was sitting out here, looking at the valley." She seemed relaxed with Esau. "Rose and Betty's parents had the land next to yours, didn't they?"

I had been apprehensive, but witnessing the changes in the old man began to put me at ease as well. An expression of peace had replaced the rage that had gnarled his features. It was as if his anger, like his house, had mostly burned away. There was still an edge in his rusty voice, but there was kindness too. "Them girls liked to sleep outside so they could watch the stars," he said.

Gracie smiled at him. "Rose and Betty still talk about those summers. Did you sleep outside too?"

Esau nodded. "Saw the same stars they did," he said, and then he looked away.

The dogs had gathered around my feet. I shook the last of the treats into my hand and held it out. The dogs licked my hand clean.

"Them dogs like you," Esau said.

"I like them," I said. "Since I left boarding school, I've always had a dog."

Esau's brow furrowed. "How come they put you in one of them schools?"

It took me a minute to realize that he'd misunderstood my words. "The place I went to wasn't a residential school," I said.

"But you couldn't have a dog," he said.

"No."

"And you couldn't go home."

"No, I couldn't go home," I said.

"So it was the same," he said. "They took you away from your people."

"Not the same," I said. "And my family wanted me to be there."

Esau narrowed his eyes. "Your people didn't want you with them?" he said.

"They thought it was best," I said.

He peered at me. Though his manner was gentler than it had been at our last meeting, Esau's attention remained an unnerving force. "But it wasn't best, was it?"

My throat closed. "I don't know," I said. "It was just the way it was."

"A sad thing," Esau said. He turned towards Gracie, "I heard about your father and the others," he said. "That was another sad thing."

"It was," Gracie said quietly. "Esau, I'm sorry Rose upset you when she asked if you had used bad medicine on my family. It was because I thought you might have, and she wanted to protect me."

Esau stared at Gracie before he replied. "The day after you got hurt, I looked until I found that rock," he said. "When I found it I threw it in that pile down the road. Then I went away to think about what I done that night you came. I'm sorry you got hurt, Lily's girl."

"My name is Gracie."

"I seen you jingle dance at the powwow," he said. "You feel the drums inside you."

Gracie nodded.

"I knew it," he said. "Can you still dance?"

"Nine months to the Standing Buffalo Powwow," Gracie said. "I'll be able to dance by then."

"Good."

One of Esau's dogs wandered over and gazed up at him. Esau reached down and gave the dog an unhurried rub. After the dog curled up contentedly by his feet, Esau spoke again. "When my house caught fire, I got out the stuff that mattered – my animals and those there." Esau pointed to the photographs and the charred canister. "I love the girl that was your grandmother, Gracie. I was too scared to tell her, so she married another man. I should a told her. That's the thing I should a done." He handed Gracie the framed photograph of her father and his friends that first summer they were together. "Take this," he said. "It belongs to Rose. I took it from her house. I guess she knew, but she never said. She'll be happy I gave it back." He tapped the picture Gracie was holding with his forefinger. "That there is the thing I shouldn't a done. I used up half my life hating those ones. That's the thing you shouldn't do. Don't use up your life hating the ones that hurt you."

"I won't," Gracie said. She hesitated. "Esau, what's in the coffee canister?"

He looked surprised. "That? That's my money. People around here have trouble with banks. Nobody ever had trouble with a coffee can."

"So I should keep my money in a coffee can?" Gracie said teasingly.

Esau grinned. "I'd advise it," he said.

"That's good enough for me," Gracie said, and she reached out and touched his arm.

As he walked us down the hill to Gracie's car, Esau's face showed traces of joy.

Neither of us spoke until Gracie turned onto the highway.

"Are you all right?" I said.

"I will be," Gracie said. "Jo, I *was* hating Emmett Keating."

"And now?"

Gracie's grey-blue eyes were determined. "And now," she said, "I'm going to stop doing what Esau told me I shouldn't do."

Just past Fort Qu'Appelle my phone rang. It was Warren Weber. "Just calling to pass along the latest from Harries & Associates," he said.

"Gracie Falconer's with me," I said. "I'm sure she'll be interested. Shall I put us on speakerphone?"

"If she agrees."

As soon as I'd mentioned including her in the conversation, Gracie had nodded her assent. I pressed the button for speaker mode and said, "Now, Warren, what's the news?"

"Well, the investigators from Harries haven't learned much we didn't already know, but in their opinion it might be worthwhile to look more closely at Emmett Keating's relationship with Darryl Colby. We know that Emmett Keating worked for Colby. Given that Keating committed suicide in Colby's cabin, and that guests witnessed the two men sitting together at the fund-raiser dinner and having a heated discussion minutes before Keating exploded at Delia Wainberg, the investigators have decided to dig deeper."

"Good," I said. "Because there may be something there. The night of the dinner, I thanked Darryl for supporting the evening by buying a ticket. He said his ticket had been a gift from a friend. I saw Colby and Keating together at dinner that night, and the reports the guests gave the Harries investigators were accurate. There was something serious going on between them. It would be interesting to know who bought Colby his ticket."

"Patsy Choi will have a record," Warren said. "I'll check with her and get back to you."

Gracie's spine had stiffened. "Do you think Darryl Colby had something to do with what happened? My dad mentioned him in passing a few times. He didn't like him."

"The feeling was mutual," I said. "And Darryl's enmity wasn't just directed against your dad. Darryl loathed them all – Chris, Delia, Kevin, and especially Zack. Gracie, I don't know what to think any more. I met Emmett Keating the night of the fund-raiser. I saw him twice that evening: once before dinner, when he believed the firm was about to offer him an equity partnership, and afterwards when he felt Delia had betrayed him."

"So what did you make of him?"

"I'm not sure. I've played those scenes in my mind a dozen times. Emmett Keating was certainly eccentric, and he was obsessed with The Winners' Circle, but I just can't see him murdering the people who he had dreamed of having as colleagues. Why would he kill the people whose approval he wanted most?"

Gracie sighed. "Jo, it happens. A nerdy high-school kid is desperate to join the cool kids. He talks about them constantly; his social media accounts are filled with pictures of them; he follows them around. Finally, the situation hits the tipping point. The cool kids reject the nerd. He's shattered, so he kills them."

"But those are extreme cases."

Gracie gave me a quick glance. "From what I've learned – especially that weird business of Emmett Keating photoshopping himself into their picture – when it came to the partners of Falconer Shreve, Emmett was operating on a pretty unusual level."

"You're right, of course," I said. "Emmett was the classic super-smart kid who wanted to be part of the in-crowd. But even given that, there are facts that can't be dismissed." Gracie swerved to avoid the remains of a tire shredded on the highway. "Darryl Colby had ties to Murray Jeffreys," I said, almost to myself. "He worked for him many years ago." Gracie glanced at me questioningly and then reverted her eyes to the road. My pulse quickened as a theory began to take shape in my mind. "Noah thinks Keating's blackmail might have been about something other than the defalcation," I said.

Gracie listened stonily as I told her about the night Murray Jeffreys died, and as I rolled out the theory that Darryl Colby might have used Emmett Keating to punish Delia and the others for Jeffreys's death. When I'd finished, she said, "So you think Darryl Colby was behind this?"

"I don't know," I said. "But I think the police should be aware of the possibility."

I was reaching for my phone when it rang. My caller was Warren Weber and I put him on speakerphone immediately.

"Emmett Keating did not purchase Darryl Colby's ticket," Warren said. "And Darryl did not purchase a ticket for himself. I suggested a few possibilities; Patsy checked them out, and she didn't come up with anything definitive. A number of businesses bought multiple tickets, and Lorne Callow was the only guest who purchased two tickets and came solo."

"So no smoking gun," I said. "Anyway, thanks for clearing that up, Warren."

"You're welcome. Gracie, Annie and I will see you on Friday at the funeral. Your father was a fine man, and he will be missed."

"He will," Gracie said.

Without discussion, Gracie and I dropped the idea of calling the police. There didn't seem to be much point. At best, my conjecture was based on circumstantial evidence, and the case was closed. When we reached the city limits, Gracie turned to me. "Do you mind if I run into the drugstore and get some Aspirin? I never get headaches, but today I have what Rose calls a 'humdinger.'"

"I never get headaches either," I said. "But I just might borrow an aspirin from you. There's been a lot to process in the past few hours."

When we pulled into the strip mall, Gracie grabbed her backpack and began rummaging for her wallet. "I'm losing it," she said. "I totally forgot about this." She pulled out a worn and weathered leather passport case and handed it to me. "This was in my dad's safety deposit box at the bank. It belonged to Chris Altieri. I don't know how it ended up with my dad, but I thought maybe Zack would want it."

"He will," I said. "These days, Zack treasures mementos."

"I kind of figured that," Gracie said. "Do you want to come in with me?"

"Thanks, I'm fine." I said. I watched Gracie cross the parking lot. She was usually a strider, but the knee brace was hobbling her, and she was taking her time. When she disappeared through the front doors, I looked down at the wallet and felt a pang. Chris would have been carrying his passport in it when he came home from Japan. When I opened the wallet, I saw that his passport had indeed been stamped the week before he died. The edge of a photograph peeked out of the opening of the wallet's inner pocket. I put my finger inside to nudge it out. The photo was of Gracie and Isobel. Both girls were grinning and both grins revealed missing teeth, so they would have been around six. A newspaper clipping had been tucked behind the photo.

The clipping was an obituary. I didn't recognize the face of the man in the obituary, but I certainly recognized his name. It was Murray Jeffreys. I skimmed the text to see if he'd been married or had a family. There was no mention of a spouse or children. He was survived only by "'his beloved brother, Lorne Callow.'"

Suddenly Lorne Callow's biblical reference to being our brother's keeper flashed through my mind. I was reeling, but it didn't take me long to make a decision. I was certain now that what I'd dismissed as a prank call had been a warning for Zack, and that Callow, Keating, and Colby were cohorts in a plan to eliminate every member of The Winners' Circle. I was on the phone with the police when Gracie got back to the car. After I hung up with them, I told her what I'd found in Chris's passport case and then I tried calling Zack. I knew he was at home, but when there was no answer on either our landline or his phone, my heart began pounding.

Traffic in the city was light, and Gracie was a skilful driver, but when we turned onto our street and I saw a shiny black Lincoln in our driveway, I was sure my worst fears had been realized, and we were too late. Darryl Colby drove a black Lincoln. He'd come to finish the job that Emmett had started.

I ran towards the house. Gracie wasn't far behind. Our front door was unlocked. The house was silent, and I stopped to catch my breath. The first shot was fired after I stepped into the front hall. It sounded as if it came from our bedroom, and I began running. The bedroom door was open, but when I reached the threshold, I stopped. For a moment, I couldn't make sense of the scene.

There was a man on the floor but it wasn't Zack. It was Darryl Colby. Lorne Callow stood a little more than a metre inside the room, his back to the doorway. He wasn't aware of my presence, but Zack was facing me. As he spoke to my husband, Lorne's baritone was pragmatic but pleasant. "You're the last of The Winners' Circle still standing, Zack, so I guess you didn't win in the end. Of course in your case, 'standing' is just a figure of speech, and I would enjoy knocking you out of that wheelchair and watching you crawl, but time is of the essence. If I play it right – and I will – I'll be a hero of the story. I came in, heard the shot, found you dead, struggled with Darryl for the gun, and killed the man who killed you."

When I heard Lorne Callow's words, my fight-or-flight reflex kicked in. I rushed him from behind and knocked him flat. As Callow pitched forward, the gun fell out of his hand and clattered across the floor. He scrambled for it, but Zack was fast.

I had never seen my husband hold a gun, but when he picked up the Glock and pointed it at Callow, he appeared to know what he was doing. Callow clearly believed he did. Seconds later, when the police arrived, Callow was standing with his hands above his head, watching Zack with loathing.

Gracie had called for an ambulance, and the paramedics arrived not long after the police. When they examined Darryl, his vital signs were good. He had been lucky. I listened as Zack explained to the police that Darryl had come to warn him about Callow. Later we would learn the full story, but all I cared about then was that Zack was alive. He told the police that Darryl Colby had been shot as he pushed Zack out of harm's way.

When the police and the paramedics finally left, I told Zack what I had learned about Lorne Callow's relationship with Murray Jeffreys.

Zack heard me out and then shook his head in disbelief. "All that grief for a thirty-year-old grudge over one stupid, drunken evening."

"Remember what Lorne Callow said when I thanked him for taking Emmett home the night of your dinner?" I said.

Zack nodded. "He said 'There are times when we really are our brother's keeper.' I guess for Lorne, that moment came after thirty years."

For a time, Zack and I sat together in our family room watching the pine siskins at the birdfeeder and trying to somehow absorb the shock, the horror, and the desolation of the past ten days. "We're never going to be able to make sense of this, are we?" Zack said finally, and his face was etched with a grief and a sorrow so profound that my whole body ached for him.

"You know what I can't get past?" he said. "The tragic irony of everything that's happened because of a stupid joke I made when Blake, Delia, Chris, Kevin, and I finished our first year at the College of Law. For us, learning the law was as natural as breathing. It was easy and it was fun, but our profs were blown away at having five students of our 'calibre' in the same class. Individually, we'd always seen ourselves as losers. When I referred to us as 'The Winners' Circle,' I was being a smart-ass. I was pointing out that if five losers like us were considered winners because we were able to master some very simple concepts, the system was totally screwed."

"And no one understood the joke."

"No one, except for the five of us. I guess it doesn't matter now. The game's over, and all the pieces have been put back in the same box."

CHAPTER

20

Our family has a birthday tradition. The birthday person awakens to presents on the breakfast table and gets to eat junk cereal, oeufs en gelée, or whatever else strikes his or her fancy. The next morning was Taylor's birthday. The police cars and the ambulance had left by the time Taylor returned from school, but Zack and I gave her the broad strokes of what had happened. Once she knew we were safe, Taylor seemed to relax, but the horror of those moments was still fresh in Zack's mind and mine as we got ready for bed.

When Zack came in from his shower, I told him I was about to arrange the gifts on Taylor's birthday table. "I have presents from both of us," I said, "but you usually get Taylor something on your own. Did you have a chance to find something this year?"

Zack turned his chair towards his closet. "I do have something," he said. "I'd forgotten about it, but it's in here." He came back with a gift-wrapped parcel that he handed to me. "This is a Matt & Nat Blinkin black crossbody bag," Zack said.

"With everything that's been going on, you remembered

that the crossbody bag was exactly what Taylor wanted," I said. "You continue to amaze me."

"That's always good to hear," Zack said. "But Taylor deserves the kudos. She's the one who sent me the little reminder about the crossbody bag that kept popping up on my phone."

"All's well that ends well," I said. "And I am going take this perfect gift and the other lesser gifts and put them on Taylor's place at the table."

"Are you going to put Kevin's gift out too?"

"What do you think?"

"I think Kevin would want Taylor to know he was thinking of her on her birthday."

In the kitchen, I placed the gifts from the dogs and from Taylor's cats and from Zack and me at her place at the table, and then I opened Kevin's messenger bag. I took out the keys to the cottage and the leather guest book, but before I placed them on Taylor's plate, I opened the guest book to see if Kevin had written anything.

He had. On the title page Kevin had drawn an elaborately goofy birthday cake decorated with images of the things Taylor treasured: a cat; a seashell; an inuksuk like the ones she, Gracie, and Isobel had built on the shore of Lawyers' Bay; a book of poems; and a marzipan pig. Towards the bottom of the page, Kevin had copied out a passage that Taylor and I both loved from C.S. Lewis's *The Last Battle*.

All their life in this world and all their adventures in Narnia had only been the cover and the title page: now at last they were beginning Chapter One of the Great Story which no one on earth has read: which goes on forever: in which every chapter is better than the one before.

I read the quotation through three times, then I closed the guest book, put it back on Taylor's plate, and sat down and cried until I had no tears left. Finally, I put the messenger bag on Taylor's chair, turned out the lights and, knowing that Chapter One was still ahead, I went to bed.

———

Our grandsons, Colin Crawford Kilbourn and Charlie Crawford Kilbourn, were baptized on November 29, the first day of Advent. The temperatures had continued to be above freezing, but it seemed the sun had deserted us, and the succession of grey days did nothing to lessen the pain of mourning. Zack had been back at City Hall for two weeks. He was putting in full days and dealing with Falconer Shreve in the evenings. When I asked him to slow down, he bristled, so I'd stopped asking, but we both knew he was no longer the man who could put in sixteen-hour days, play poker till one in the morning, catch a couple of hours of sleep, shower, change, and be back in the office by six the next day. We also both knew that he was working to avoid dwelling on what he had lost, but neither of us knew how to stop the downward spiral.

After the service we were all driving out to Lawyers' Bay for lunch. This would be the first time the Falconer Shreve families had been at the lake since Thanksgiving, and I was hoping that the baptism, the peace of the lake, and the presence of a cottage full of family, friends, and kids would get us all through.

St. Paul's Cathedral was built in downtown Regina in 1895, and that makes it one of the oldest structures in our prairie city. The building is not grand, but it is welcoming, and I walked through the doors and breathed in the mingled scents of fresh-cut evergreen boughs and melting candle wax I was overwhelmed by memories of other Advents and other Christmases. The baptismal font of St. Paul's is at the back of the cathedral, and by the time we arrived, our family and friends had already gathered in the pews that would be closest to the action. They were not alone. Twin two-month-old boys with springy copper curls were a magnet, and Peter, Maisie, and their sons were surrounded by well-wishers. Mieka was the godmother of both babies, and Angus was Colin's godfather, but Peter had asked his childhood friend Charlie Dowhanuik to be godfather of the boy who was named after him.

Charlie D., as he was known professionally, was a magnet too. For ten years he had been the heavy-hitter on-air personality for the Toronto-based CVOX ("All Talk All the Time"), a privately owned radio network. The title of his call-in show, *The World According to Charlie D.*, said it all. The music reflected Charlie's eclectic tastes; his riffs on subjects ranging from erotomania to the art of cool were funny and smart; and when it came to discerning exactly what his callers needed to hear, he had perfect pitch. Every night a half-million people tuned in to *The World According to Charlie D.* Charlie's six-figure salary plus stock options reflected how crucial he was to CVOX's success. He was famous, revered, and well paid, but in mid-November, when his contract came up for renewal, Charlie had explained that it was time for him to explore options. He left Toronto and came back to Regina.

I had known Charlie literally since the day he was born, and I had always loved him. The reasons he returned to Saskatchewan were a mystery to many, but not to me. During a trial involving Charlie's father, Zack had offered Charlie support and friendship. Charlie was returning the favour, and I was grateful. Zack and I had always shared everything, but we had both been rocked by grief and we were trying to spare each other. There were moments when both of us needed to cry and to mourn. I had Mieka to talk to, but three of Zack's lifelong confidants were gone. Charlie D. had an extraordinary ability to recognize and respond to the needs of others. That ability had brought him great success as a call-in host; now he was bringing his gift to Zack, and I was grateful beyond measure.

When he spotted us entering the church, Charlie D. leapt effortlessly over the back of the pew where he'd been sitting, embraced me, hugged Taylor, and shook hands with Zack. Zack gave Charlie the once-over. "Looking good," he said. "Yesterday, when you dragged me to the gym to shoot hoops, you were wearing a T-shirt that says, 'I leave bite marks.'"

Charlie D. shrugged. "It didn't seem quite right for a baptism."

"Good call," I said. "And Zack's right. You make a very handsome godfather."

Indeed he did. Charlie D. had inherited his mother's classic features: her sleepy hazel eyes and sensitive mouth. He was reed slim, and his three-piece dove-grey suit was closely tailored; the Windsor knot of his navy-and-grey striped silk tie was perfect; his dark hair was freshly barbered; and his black leather lace-ups shone.

We settled into the pew: Angus, Charlie D., Mieka, Madeleine, Lena, Taylor, me, and, next to me in his wheelchair, Zack. As soon as Zack and I were ready, Maisie and Peter brought the boys to us. The Ayershire christening dresses Charlie and Colin wore were family heirlooms. Maisie and her twin, Lee, had worn the same delicate ivory gowns when they were baptized. The gowns were exquisite, but Maisie and Peter's sons had neither the build nor the temperament for flowing dresses. Charlie and Colin had Peter's green eyes and full lips, but they had inherited Maisie's broad shoulders and athletic lankiness. The tiny pearl buttons on the boys' gowns were already straining.

As the choir sang the first thrilling notes of the plain-song "Oh Come, Oh Come, Emmanuel," the boys squirmed. When I leaned close and whispered, "Hang tight. Grand-dad and I will get you out of those dresses in two hours max," Zack chuckled, and for a fleeting moment his face lost its haunted look.

Madeleine and Lena were wearing hunter-green turtle-necks, Black Watch tartan kilts, and dark-green tights. Both girls had tied their hair in a high ponytail. They were on the cusp of the next stage of girlhood, but the memory of their young parents watching anxiously as the bishop baptized first Madeleine and then, eighteen months later, Lena was vivid. Wondering if Mieka, too, was remembering the past, I glanced towards her. She was whispering in Charlie D.'s ear and they were both trying not to laugh. Clearly, their minds were focused on the pleasures of the present.

As the dean announced that the candidates for Holy Baptism would be presented, I handed Colin to Mieka and Zack held Charlie out for Charlie D. to claim, then the twins' parents and godparents formed a quarter circle to the left of the font, and the rest of us gathered close by. The baptism was underway. The dean of the cathedral had a young family and even the most obstreperous child grew calm in his arms, but when Charlie D. handed his namesake to the dean, and the dean poured the shell of baptismal water on Charlie's head, the baby howled furiously. He continued to howl through the prayers, the lighting of the baptismal candle, and the walk up the aisle towards the altar where the dean introduced the newly baptized to the congregation. Charlie didn't settle down until he was once again in Charlie D.'s arms. Colin, on the other hand, was quiet and con-templative, looking around thoughtfully throughout the ceremony, a model baptismal child. By the time we returned to our places in the pews, Charlie D. was holding a blissfully sleeping baby and wearing a Cheshire cat smile.

The boys' hockey team at Standing Buffalo needed new hockey equipment, and Rose, Betty, and four other ladies from Standing Buffalo were raising money by catering. When we arrived for lunch at Lawyers' Bay, the buffet was laid out on the long partners' table in the sunroom. The food was plentiful and, with two exceptions, predictable: baked ham, potato salad, baked beans, coleslaw, deviled eggs, homemade bannock, fry bread, and crusty rolls.

Betty had just completed a course in vegetable and fruit art in Fort Qu'Appelle, and in addition to some vegetable floral arrangements that were stunning, she had carved a pair of watermelon sea turtles for Colin and a ferocious-looking watermelon shark for Charlie. Not to be outdone, Rose had made each boy a cookie tree with branches hung with sugar cookies in the shapes of T-shirts and running shoes, each cookie iced in blue with the boys' initials in white.

It was a relaxed and happy lunch. Betty and the other ladies from Standing Buffalo lined up behind the table to help serve and accept compliments. The women all wore spotless white aprons and hairnets, and they were particularly solicitous of Brock, who had grown up in North Central Regina in a family broken by drugs, alcohol, poverty, and hopelessness. They made certain Brock and Margot's children had a sample of everything. Brock noticed and was clearly touched.

After a heated discussion, Lexi had agreed to wear civilian clothes to the baptism, but she had now changed back into her Max suit. When Brock passed us carrying his own loaded plate and a smaller loaded plate for Lexi, he said, "I'm glad our kids are growing up with this. I hope you both know that although Margot and I are working for Falconer Shreve, we're still deeply committed to making sure kids in North Central have family parties too."

"We know," Zack said. "Jo and I are working on that too."

Brock grinned. "Good. Take care of yourself, Zack. People are counting on you."

After we'd eaten, we regrouped in the family room, and Maisie and Peter opened Colin and Charlie's baptismal gifts as the little kids played and the adults oohed and aahed over the presents. Angus and Patsy's gifts drew the most attention. They gave the boys what Patsy explained were traditional Chinese gifts for a new baby – six red envelopes of money, each marked with a separate wish: Happy Life, Good Fortune, Wisdom, Peace, Longevity, and Classic Luck. They also gave the boys a combination soother and soft plush tiger called a "WubbaNub." Angus said that in Chinese mythology the tiger is believed to protect babies and keep them from harm. When Charlie began attacking his WubbaNub with ferocious enthusiasm, Margot asked if there was an animal that protected WubbaNubs against little fingers.

Simon Weber lived year-round at the Weber cottage across the lake from Lawyers' Bay, and he'd joined his father and Annie at the cathedral and come back with them for lunch. Simon was a lawyer, but his mental health had always been precarious. Living at the lake allowed him to continue seeing his therapist at Valleyview, a private psychiatric facility near Fort Qu'Appelle, and to work full-time at his passion: photography. Simon was photographing the baptism and lunch as his gift to the Crawford Kilbourn family, and I had already put in my order for duplicate prints.

Zack and I had always been fond of Warren and Annie, but since Lorne Callow's arrest and confession to the murders we had been drawn closer together by the need to learn everything we could about the man who, for thirty years, had been obsessed with my husband and his law partners. Warren and Annie's connection to the tragedies had been peripheral, but both Webers had a strong moral sense and when Annie learned that it was Lorne who had taken and distributed the video he shot of her frogmarching Emmett out of the Scarth Club, she had been troubled. Whatever troubled Annie troubled Warren. When the facts emerged and we understood as much as we could ever understand of Lorne Callow's story, the Webers' burden was lifted.

That afternoon as Annie and Warren sat with Peter, Maisie, and Margot looking at the photos of the baptism Annie had taken on her tablet, their easy laughter drifted across the room, and I felt the truth of the Latin motto of the school I had attended for thirteen years: *Vincit Omnia Veritas – Truth Conquers All.*

Murray Jeffreys had, in fact, been Lorne Callow's half-brother. After Murray Jeffreys's father died, his mother married Dwight Callow. Lorne was a late-life baby, and he idolized his much older brother. He was sixteen years old when Murray died. Desperate to talk to anyone who had known his brother, Lorne went to Murray Jeffreys's law office.

Darryl Colby had been Jeffreys's junior partner. He loathed the attention given to the accomplishments of the lawyers of Falconer Shreve from the moment they graduated from the College of Law. From Darryl's perspective, the behaviour of the golden five and their friend on the night of the Christmas party had not been blameless. Jeffreys had been drunk at the party, but so had a lot of people, and that included all the members of The Winners' Circle, except choirboy Chris Altieri. Jeffreys's comments about Delia Margolies had been crude, but in Colby's opinion, Delia had it coming. Rumour had it that she put out for anybody who could help her get ahead. Colby believed that when Jeffreys left the party to run after her, he was only trying to get what other guys had helped themselves to.

Darryl Colby knew Jeffreys's blood pressure and cholesterol levels were high and that he was an out-of-shape smoker who drank too much. He read and reread the coroner's conclusion that Murray Jeffreys had died of acute myocardial infarction, but he wasn't convinced that The Winners' Circle had been innocent of wrongdoing that night. In Murray's grieving brother, Colby found the perfect receptacle for his own suspicions. The two became close, and when Lorne graduated with a diploma in office administration from a three-year program, Colby steered him towards a position in a law office. Over the years the two men, fired by their shared conviction that The Winners' Circle had gotten away with murder, stayed close.

Lorne Callow had proven to be a smart, discreet, and hard-working employee, and when an opportunity to join the staff at Falconer Shreve presented itself, he pounced. Suddenly he was in a position to do real damage. The night Callow learned he'd been hired as Delia Wainberg's executive assistant, he invited Darryl Colby out to celebrate. But it was on that night of triumph that the first cracks appeared in the men's relationship. Darryl was a successful lawyer, and he was content to limit his revenge to fighting attempts at out-of-court settlements proposed by Falconer Shreve lawyers and mercilessly attacking them in the courtroom. Colby had been surprised by Callow's decision to work for Falconer Shreve, though he had not believed that Callow's dreams of vengeance went beyond those of meddling with Falconer Shreve's business. He was wrong. Lorne Callow wanted more. He wanted blood. The student had outstripped the teacher.

When Falconer Shreve hired Emmett Keating, Callow saw his chance, and the sequence of events that would ultimately lead to four deaths, including Emmett's own, was set in motion. From the beginning, Lorne Callow played Iago to Emmett Keating's all too credulous Othello. Over the years, Callow stoked Keating's dream of an equity partnership at Falconer Shreve and fuelled his paranoia with insinuations that the partners were contemptuous of him. Meanwhile, Lorne Callow bided his time waiting for the information that would smooth his pathway to revenge. It was when he saw Delia's terse note rejecting Emmett Keating on the list of potential new equity partners that Callow made his move. While Delia was in a meeting, he stole the list off her desk and copied and distributed it.

Distraught when he saw Delia's comment, Emmett went to his friend. Callow reassured Emmett that the decision did not have to be final. He told Emmett he was in possession of information about Christopher Altieri that would force Delia to back down. Ironically, Emmett never knew what the information was. He simply trusted his friend Callow and believed it existed. At the fund-raiser dinner for Zack, Callow intimated to Keating that Delia had reneged on her agreement to promote him. Then he sat back and watched as Emmett made a public spectacle of himself. When Keating confronted Delia at the dinner, he had been bluffing.

Callow had been standing in the shadows as Emmett verbally assaulted Delia, and when Annie Weber frogmarched Emmett out of the Scarth Club, Lorne moved into place to capture the moment on his camera. He made and distributed the video and convinced the deeply humiliated Emmett Keating that he should not jump at Warren Weber's job offer but should instead retreat to a quiet place where he could consider his options. Callow escorted Emmett to Darryl Colby's cabin the afternoon that Warren made his job offer.

On the morning of November 1, he drove back to the cabin, shot Keating, and wrote the confession note. The stage was set, and Lorne Callow had been preparing himself to play his part for thirty years. Except for the fact that Zack wasn't at Falconer Shreve on the morning Callow exacted his revenge, the final act went off exactly as he had planned.

However, there was a loose end. During the years he worked for Darryl Colby, Emmett Keating had made no secret of his desire to someday work for Falconer Shreve. Colby thought he was a fool and told him so, but he valued Keating's work ethic and was willing to put up with his eccentricities. Like most experienced trial lawyers, Darryl Colby prided himself on his ability to read character, and he was convinced that whatever else he was, Keating was neither a killer nor a likely candidate for suicide. The fact that Keating had chosen Colby's cabin as the place to end his life also nagged at him.

Darryl Colby shared his concerns with Lorne Callow, and though Callow dismissed them, Colby's uneasiness was not assuaged. Believing that, at the very least, Lorne Callow had been complicit in the murders, Colby had gone to Falconer Shreve the day of the firm meeting to warn Zack that he might be in danger. When Zack failed to get in touch with him, Darryl decided to approach Zack at home. Lorne had been keeping an eye on his old mentor, and when the black Lincoln pulled up in front our house, Lorne was right behind it. Gracie and I had arrived just in time.

Lorne Callow's actions would shadow our lives forever, but that afternoon as Zack wheeled over and held out his arms to take Charlie so that Maisie and Peter could enjoy their guests without the distraction of an active little boy I felt a stirring of optimism. When I joined them, I scooped up Colin. "Brock and Noah are outside playing with the kids,"

I said. "Zack, let's take the little guys over to the window so they can watch."

Madeleine and Lena had been invited to a friend's birthday party, so Mieka and Charlie D. had taken them back to the city after lunch, but the other children were out in force. The day was nippy enough for jackets and mitts, and Brock had pulled Kai's Roughriders toque over his ears. Snug on his father's chest in his Baby Bjorn, Kai's expression was merry as his dad and sister threw a football around with Noah, Jacob, Angus, and Patsy. Charlie and Colin were eager spectators. They had no idea what the game was, but they were enjoying the colour and the movement, and when Pantera, Esme, and Peter and Maisie's dog, Rowdy, joined the game, the twins cooed their delight.

I could see Zack's nerves unknotting. "Having fun," I said.

"Getting there," he said and then his brow furrowed. "Where's Taylor?"

She and Gracie and Isobel are over at the Hynds'. Taylor thought the old grey cottage needed to have some people in it – especially today."

"Because that's where we're burying Kevin's ashes," Zack said.

"Right. The plan is that after everyone else leaves, the five of us will say a few words and then bury the ashes in the spot near the front door where Kevin's mother planted that bleeding heart the first summer she and Kevin's father were here. Taylor chose the location. She's taken care of everything. Noah came out earlier in the week to get the earth ready."

Zack shook his head in amazement. "Thanksgiving weekend, Taylor called me to come into her room to remove a spider on her windowsill, and now she's handling this."

"Taylor and Kevin were always close," I said. "This isn't

easy for her, but she's doing it." I sniffed the air. "Zack, unless I'm mistaken we have a more immediate problem. One or both of our grandsons needs a diaper change."

Zack lifted Charlie cautiously and inhaled. "It's Charlie," he said.

"Looks like you're on deck," I said.

"I've never changed a diaper in my life."

"Everybody has to start somewhere," I said. "And babies are forgiving."

After all the guests at the baptism had signed the new guest book and the last car had pulled out and headed for the highway, Taylor took my hand. "It's time," she said.

Zack led the way to the Hynd cottage in his wheelchair, and Zack, Noah, and I waited by the bleeding heart while Taylor went into the cottage to get the ashes. She came back with a brilliantly coloured, exotically patterned drawstring bag. "I found this online," she said. "It's Tibetan, and Kevin used to say he always felt at peace in Tibet."

"Kevin would want us to keep it simple, so that's what we're doing," Isobel said. She and Gracie were doing their best to keep their tone briskly objective, but they were struggling. Isobel bit her lip and looked at Zack, Noah, and me. "Is there anything you'd like to say before we put the ashes in the earth?"

Noah, close to breaking, shook his head. Zack was struggling too. "Joanne has something that we both thought was right," he said.

I took out the postcard of the Jokhang Temple that I'd used as a bookmark for years. As I told Kevin the morning we'd had breakfast in our kitchen, I'd memorized what he'd written, but that afternoon, I wanted to see his handwriting, so I read the words as I spoke them out loud. "The Tibetans used to believe their country was connected to heaven by a rope. Today the clouds are low and the mountains seem to scrape the sky. Heaven feels close."

I handed the postcard to our daughter. She opened the drawstrings of the silk bag, slipped the card in, then dropped to her knees, placed the silk bag in the earth, and patted it gently. Gracie, Isobel, and Noah joined her and scooped earth over the bright silk until the colours disappeared under the earth. Zack rolled his chair close, bent, picked up a handful of soil, and scattered it. He wheeled back and I dropped to my knees and smoothed the earth on the grave. "Be at peace and be held in love forever," I said.

Noah whispered "Peace," and then Taylor held out her hand to me, and I stood.

"Further up and further in . . ." she said. "I guess you all know what comes next. It's what Jewel the Unicorn says in *The Last Battle*: 'I have come home at last! This is my real country. I belong here. This is the land I have been looking for all my life, though I never knew it till now. . . . Come further up, come further in.'" Taylor rubbed her hands on her jeans, looked at the fresh-turned dirt, and then gave a little wave and said, "Be at peace, Kevin, and be held in love forever."

Noah, Isobel, and Gracie said their farewells to Kevin and to us, and then Noah and the three young women headed to Gracie's car for the drive back to the city.

For too long Zack stared at Kevin's grave, motionless. I placed my hands on his shoulders. "How would you feel about taking the dogs for a last run on the beach?"

He tried a smile. "Sure, why not?"

As always when we got to the beach, Pantera and Esme loped off in search of adventure. Most years by the twenty-ninth of November, frost, snow, and polar temperatures would have transformed Lawyers' Bay into a world painted in the icy silvers, greys, and blacks of the winter palette, but this was not most years. The lake, the beach, and the trees looked just as they had when our families were together at our cottages for the last time on Thanksgiving weekend. Everything was the same, but nothing would ever be the same again.

When Zack didn't give his all-terrain wheelchair the usual exploratory push to check the firmness of the sand, I bent and tested the sand with my fingertip. "The beach seems navigable if you're in the mood to navigate," I said.

Zack didn't move. "Would it be all right if we just stayed here for a while?"

"Of course," I said.

For an uncomfortably long time, we watched the choppy waters in silence. The depth of Zack's despair tore at my heart. Finally, I pointed towards the yellow vinyl boat bumper that Noah had attached to the anchor line of the raft.

"It's still there," I said. "Next May long weekend, you and I will give Noah a hand taking the canvas off the raft, and Noah and whoever's around will carry the raft down to the water, and summer will begin again. Maddy and Lena will jump off the end of the dock and swim till Mieka tells them to come in because their lips are turning blue, and the girls will say their lips are not blue, and you and I will sit on the beach with a stack of towels and wrap the girls up when they finally admit defeat and come out of the water."

Zack still hadn't moved. I wasn't certain he'd even heard me, but I pushed on. "You and I have to be there with the towels, Zack. And we have to be there to keep Charlie and Colin and Jacob and Lexi and Kai from eating sand or going too far into the water. And we have to be there to tell Gracie and Isobel and Taylor that when summer's over, they can go away to university and we'll be all right.

"And, Zack, we *are* going to be all right. It will take time, but you heard what Brock said at lunch. People are counting

on you. There's still so much to be done in this city. The day
you were sworn in as mayor, you took an oath. You have to
honour it. And there were other oaths – the ones we took in
front of the altar of the cathedral. After the dean pronounced
us husband and wife you said, 'This is forever, Joanne. A
deal's a deal.' I'm holding you to that, Zack."

After what seemed like forever, Zack turned, looked up at
me, and said the words he'd said a hundred times when we
knew we had to leave Lawyers' Bay and get back to our daily
lives. "Time to piss on the fire, call in the dogs, and go
home?" he said.

When he held out his arms, I felt a bloom of hope. "Yes,"
I said. "It's time to go home."

ACKNOWLEDGEMENTS

Thanks to:

Kendra Ward, my editor, for her friendship, her sensitivity, and her unerring intelligence;

Ashley Dunn, for her warmth and professionalism;

Heather Sangster and Kelly Joseph, for the essential final polishing of the manuscript;

Jared Bland, for bringing passion and commitment to M&S, a publishing house that has always put authors and readers first;

Najma Kazmi, MD, for knowing the value of a gentle touch;

Wayne Chau, BSP, for being smart, funny, and understanding;

Hildy Bowen, Brett Bell, Max Bowen, Carrie Bowen, Nathaniel Bowen, and Jennifer Taylor, for being the family I always dreamed of having;

Kai Langen, Madeleine Bowen-Diaz, Lena Bowen-Diaz, Chesney Langen Bell, Ben Bowen-Bell, Peyton Bowen, and Lexi Bowen, for being the sunshine of our lives;

Ted, my love of forty-eight years, who continues to make every day a joy;

Esme, who is faithfully by my side whether I want her there or not.

The text from *The Last Battle* by C. S. Lewis excerpted on page 239 can be found in *The Chronicles of Narnia*, Omnibus Edition (New York: HarperCollins Publishers, 1956) on page 767.

The text from *The Last Battle* by C. S. Lewis excerpted on page 252 can be found in *The Chronicles of Narnia*, Omnibus Edition (New York: HarperCollins Publishers, 1956) on page 760.

Discover more books in the
Joanne Kilbourn Mystery Series

www.gailbowen.com
www.penguinrandomhouse.ca

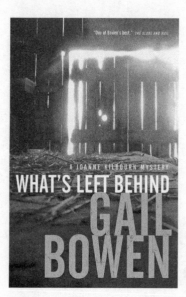

"All is revealed in breathtaking fashion . . ."
—*Toronto Star*

NATIONAL BESTSELLER
GAIL BOWEN

"Confirms Bowen's growing reputation
as 'the queen of Canadian crime fiction.'"
WINNIPEG FREE PRESS

A Joanne Kilbourn Mystery

THE
GIFTED

NATIONAL BESTSELLER
GAIL BOWEN

"Bowen writes beautifully in catching the tone and the minutiae of [Joanne's]
almost flawless familial existence. . . . Keeps readers turning the pages."
TORONTO STAR

A Joanne Kilbourn Mystery

KALEIDO-
SCOPE

"Stellar . . . one of Bowen's best." GLOBE AND MAIL

GAIL BOWEN

A Joanne Kilbourn Mystery

THE
NESTING
DOLLS

NATIONAL BESTSELLER

GAIL BOWEN

"Elegant. . . . Slips along with grace and style."
TORONTO STAR

A Joanne Kilbourn Mystery

THE
BRUTAL
HEART

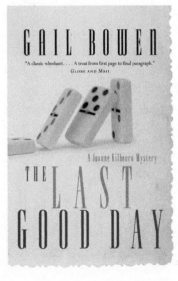

"[Bowen] shines best when Joanne is in
the thick of the small dramas . . ."
—*National Post*

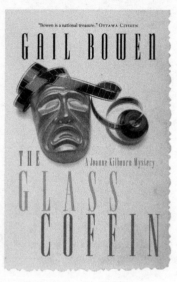

"Characters whose commitment to tough ideals makes them worth caring about . . ."
—*Kirkus Reviews*

"A seamless blend of honest emotion and artistry." CHICAGO TRIBUNE

GAIL BOWEN

A Joanne Kilbourn Mystery

VERDICT IN BLOOD

WINNER OF THE ARTHUR ELLIS AWARD FOR BEST CRIME NOVEL

GAIL BOWEN

"A terrific story with a slick twist at the end." GLOBE AND MAIL

A Joanne Kilbourn Mystery

A COLDER KIND OF DEATH

GAIL BOWEN

"Kilbourn is a wonderfully complex character . . . you cheer for her." WINNIPEG FREE PRESS

A Joanne Kilbourn Mystery

A KILLING SPRING

"An author in full command of her métier."
—*Calgary Herald*

"Bowen's books are grand mysteries." HALIFAX CHRONICLE-HERALD

GAIL BOWEN

THE
A Joanne Kilbourn Mystery
WANDERING
SOUL
MURDERS

GAIL BOWEN

"A tense, masterfully written
character study; then the killing begins . . ."
PUBLISHERS WEEKLY

A Joanne Kilbourn Mystery
MURDER
AT THE
MENDEL

"Compelling . . . inventive and diabolical." MONTREAL GAZETTE

GAIL BOWEN

A Joanne Kilbourn Mystery
DEADLY
APPEARANCES